A Wrongful Death

KATE WILHELM

A Wrongful Death

MIRA®

MIRA

ISBN-13: 978-0-7783-2491-1
ISBN-10: 0-7783-2491-5

A WRONGFUL DEATH

www.MIRABooks.com

Printed in U.S.A.

A
Wrongful
Death

1

The New York branch of the Farrell Publishing Group had six offices, a small reception room and enough books and manuscripts to fill a space triple the size it occupied. Much of the overflow was in Elizabeth Kurtz's tiny office. Boxes were stacked on boxes and the filing cabinets were so packed that they were seldom opened, since it was almost impossible to remove a folder to examine its contents. On shelves and on the floor were stacks of dictionaries, science reference books and pamphlets. A bulletin board held so many overlapping notes and memos that some of them had yellowed and curled at the edges. The small sign on her door read: Elizabeth Kurtz Assistant Editor. That door had not been closed all the way in the three years that she had used the office on Mondays and Thursdays. The door would start to close, then stick, leaving a three- or four-inch gap. It had bothered her in the beginning, but she never thought of it any longer, and paid little attention to any activity in the hall beyond it.

That October day she was frowning at a sentence she was trying to unravel, something to do with paleontology, she assumed, since that was the subject of the manuscript.

The door was pushed open and Terry Kurtz entered and tried to close the door behind him. When it stuck, he gave it a vicious push, to no avail.

"What are you doing in here? Get out! Whatever you're selling, I'm not buying," Elizabeth snapped, half rising from her chair.

"I have a proposition for you," he said, and tried again to close the door. He cursed and kicked it when it stuck.

"I'm calling security," she said, reaching for the phone. He rushed around the desk and grabbed her wrist, wrenching her hand back.

"Just shut up and listen," he said in a low voice, keeping an eye on the door, holding her wrist in a numbing grip. "I just came from the hospital. They're going to operate on Dad in the morning, emergency open-heart surgery, and they don't think he'll make it. He told me something. Mom left us alone for a couple of minutes and he told me. Taunted me with it."

Elizabeth felt no more sense of loss or grief than Terry was showing. She tried to pull away from his grasp, and he tightened his hold and leaned in closer, whispering now. "When he found out you were pregnant, he assigned a share of the company to us, in both our names. He was going to hand it over when Jason was a year old and I was thirty-five, a present to celebrate my birthday, our marriage and a grandchild, but you spoiled it when you got on your high horse and kicked me out. He put the assignment away somewhere. It's still valid, except Mom will get her hands on whatever that document is and she'll shred it faster than she'll order his cremation. I've got his keys, and I intend to find it first. You have to help me."

"I don't have to do anything," she cried. "Get out of here and leave me alone!"

Voices in the hall outside her door rose as the speakers drew nearer. Terry released her wrist and straightened up, and she jumped from her chair and stepped behind it. Neither spoke until the voices faded, then were gone.

"If you touch me again, I'll have you arrested for assault!" she said.

"That assignment means a hefty income for the rest of your life and Jason's if you sell it back tomorrow. And when the company sale goes through that amount will triple, quadruple! No more dingy office where the door won't even close. You have to think what it will mean for our son."

"Our son!" she said furiously. "As if you care a damn about my son. How many times have you even seen him? Three! Goddamn you, three times in five years!"

But it still hurt, like a phantom pain from an amputated limb, she sometimes thought. A year of magic, the princess and her incredibly handsome prince, playing, making love, seeing the world like two wide-eyed children with fairy dust in their eyes. Then her pregnancy. He had walked out when she was just under five months pregnant, and he had not returned until Jason was six months old. She had met his return with divorce papers.

He was still the incredibly handsome prince, with curly dark hair, eyes so dark blue they appeared black until the light hit his face in a particular way and they gleamed with an electric blue light. Muscular and lean, athletic, with the perfect features of a male model, he had won his princess without a struggle, but while he still lived in fairyland, she had put illusions behind her and regarded him now with loathing.

"You can sell your share tomorrow, easily a million dollars. Hold it for six months, and that figure rises astronomically. Two million, three, God knows how high it'll go."

He was whispering again. "I have his keys to the office files, and to his home files. Mom will stay at the hospital for now, but if she finds out that I lifted his keys, she'll head for wherever that document is. The office, or the condo. And we have to get that paper before she gets to it. She knows where it is, and she'll get it, believe me. You can take the condo, and I'll hit the office files. We'll find it first."

She knew he was right about his mother. Sarah Kurtz felt about Elizabeth the same way Elizabeth felt about Terry. She shook her head. "I can't get inside the condo or the office, so forget it. Go search by yourself."

"I'll take you to the condo. I can get in, and I can take you in with me and leave you there while I go over to the corporate office. But, Goddamn it, we have to do it now! Before she realizes I took the keys."

In a cab minutes later, sitting as far from him as the seat allowed, Elizabeth asked, "What sale are you talking about?"

"I don't know," he said, almost sullenly. "They don't tell me anything. I just know it's in the works, a Swiss conglomerate. They're doing the preliminary investigation, whatever that means."

She did know they told him nothing about the business. The playboy son had never wanted a thing to do with the business of prosthetics that had made his family wealthy. Then his hasty marriage to a half-breed Spanish dancer, was how Sarah Kurtz had put it when she found out. He had deserted Elizabeth, but Sarah had her own spin on that as well. Elizabeth had snared him, enticed a rich, innocent American boy, got herself pregnant and kicked him out to bring in her real lover, another woman. Elizabeth's lawyer, a savvy, hard-faced woman, had hired a detective to track Terry down on the Riviera, then photograph him frolicking on a nude beach with a movie starlet. The divorce had been a piece of cake, she had told Elizabeth. There was a very good settlement, and Sarah Kurtz would never forgive Elizabeth for threatening to besmirch the family's spotless reputation. Attorneys had handled the whole affair and, as far as Elizabeth knew, not a word had ever been printed about the matter.

In the cab, Elizabeth, gazing out the side window, seeing little of the passing scene, knew she was going along with this as much to strike back at Sarah as for the money itself. Not for how they had treated her, but for the way they treated Jason. No one in the family had ever seen Jason except Terry, who had visited his son twice after the divorce and wouldn't recognize him unless he was wearing a nametag.

Elizabeth had been in the condo several times before, the last visit had been for dinner, when she had told the family that she was pregnant. Joe Kurtz had been delighted. She remembered that scene, as she looked about the luxurious suite, decorator-perfect and lifeless, like an illustration from a glitzy magazine. "Now, he'll settle down," Joe had said that day. "You've turned our boy into a man, a family man, by God!"

Fat chance, she said under her breath, following Terry to Joe's home office. There was a kidney-shaped desk with a black mirror-smooth surface, two file cabinets, black-leather-covered chairs and a tub with a palm tree. She left her briefcase by the door and took off her sweater.

"Here's the key," Terry said, handing it to her. "It will open them both. If you find it, call my cell. I'll give you a call if I find it." He handed her a card with his number, and she told him her own. He hurried out, and she opened the first file cabinet.

At three-thirty she had finished one cabinet, and was midway through a drawer in the second one, when she pulled out a file labeled: Knowlton. After a glance, she replaced it and reached for the next file, then paused as a faint memory stirred. Knowlton. Something. She took it out again and looked more closely at the contents. She saw drawings of prosthetics, joints, arms, legs, things she didn't recognize. Slowly she walked to the big desk and sat down, gazing at the drawings. She caught her breath as the memory took shape. Knowlton had sued the company, accused them of stealing or something. The file was thick, and her fingers fumbled as she picked up and put down papers after scanning them hastily.

"Oh, my God!" she said.

Moving fast, she closed the file folder and ran back to the cabinet to close the drawer, then hurried across the office to where she had put down her briefcase with the manuscript she was to edit. She stuffed the file folder inside, put on her sweater, snatched up her purse and left the beautiful apartment.

Her cell phone rang as she stood on the street and hailed a cab. She ignored her phone. Outside her bank minutes later, she made a call of her own.

"Leonora, something urgent has come up. You have to collect Jason and take him home, then pack a suitcase for him, and one for me. We have to go somewhere. I'll explain when I get there." Leonora wanted to know what was wrong, and impatiently Elizabeth cut her off and said, "Just do it. I'll tell you when I get there. Do it now."

At the bank she made out a withdrawal slip for ten thousand dollars from her savings account. When the teller looked puzzled, she said, as lightly as she could manage, "A friend is selling her car, but she has to have cash. It's a sweet deal." No hassle, she thought. Just don't give me a hassle. The teller asked her to wait a few minutes, and while she waited, she made plans.

She would need a computer, a laptop. Pay for it with a credit card, but no more credit card purchases after that; they could find her through them. No cell phone, possibly they could trace her through it. But she needed the computer and, later, possibly a printer. She had a lot of research to do. She'd sell her car, buy something less noticeable and use cash for everything…

Leonora had done exactly as Elizabeth had told her. She had collected Jason from kindergarten and packed a suitcase for him, and was still packing for Elizabeth when she arrived home. It was a spacious apartment, shared by Elizabeth and Terry for several months, until his departure, and then retained by Elizabeth. Her attorney had insisted that she should be awarded enough not to have to make any drastic reductions in her living arrangements. Leonora, her friend from childhood, had moved in to help out during the pregnancy and stayed on afterward.

Leonora's mother had left her abusive husband when her daughter was twelve and Elizabeth's mother had taken the child into her own household and the two girls had become sisters in most ways. Elizabeth's father, a State Department employee at the UN for years, had died in a boating accident when she was eleven. Her mother had remained in the States to see her daughter safely enrolled at Johns Hopkins, where she had been an honors student, and then had gone back home to her native Spain. The two girls had shared a bedroom, worn each other's clothes, then had drawn apart when Leonora married early and Elizabeth had gone to university. They had drawn together again when Leonora had come to realize she had married a man very like her own father. After two stillbirths and several beatings, she had left him, and had maintained a close friendship with Elizabeth ever since.

That day her face was drawn with worry as Elizabeth said, "I have to get Jason out of here and have a little time to think about something I came across. I'll call you in a few days and tell you what it's all about, but not now. I want you to go get my car. I'll finish packing up. A pillow case, that's what I need, for some toys." She rushed through the apartment, looked in on Jason watching television. He waved and said, "Hi, Mama Two." There was a mischievous gleam in his eyes those days when he called whichever one was with him first Mama One, and the other Mama Two. Until recently they both had simply been Mama. Elizabeth ran to the bedroom, with Leonora at her heels, and began tossing things into her own suitcase, rushing back and forth from her closet or dresser to the bed and the open case. "After we're out of here, you'd better go somewhere and stay a few days, maybe even a week. They'll want to ask you questions, and it's best if they can't find you. I'll call your cell phone."

"For heaven's sake, Elizabeth! What's going on? Are you in trouble? Who will ask questions?"

"Just go get the car!" Her voice was shrill. She swallowed hard. "I can't stop to talk about it now. Just get the car. Please! Terry and his mother. They can't find me here!"

Leonora's face hardened, and she nodded. "On my way."

At six-thirty Sarah Kurtz entered her condo where Terry was sprawled on a white sofa with a tall drink in his hand. He raised the glass as a greeting. "How's he doing?"

"He's sedated. They said he'll sleep all night and for me to come on home. The surgery is scheduled for seven in the morning." She looked tired. Every year for the past ten or fifteen, she had put on a few pounds, never much at a time but never lost again either, and the accumulation had become close to obesity. Her hair was as blond as ever, and would continue to be that color no matter how many more years she had to enjoy. Normally her complexion was good, her cheeks a nice pink, but that day her face looked splotched with red patches.

"What are you doing here?" she asked, taking off her jacket.

"Waiting for you. Miss Dad's keys yet?"

"What are you talking about? What keys?"

"To his filing cabinets here and those at the office. I took them today. And you didn't even notice. I'm surprised."

She had been moving toward the bar across the room, but stopped to look at him. "What are you up to?"

"I found the share assignment," he said lazily. "Thought it would save you a little trouble if I did it myself. Elizabeth helped me look. Thought you'd like to know that we can still cooperate if necessary."

"You let that woman look at his files?"

"Not at the office. While she looked here, I found it at the office. See, cooperation."

Sarah Kurtz's face became noticeably more mottled as she stared at her son. Wordlessly she turned and hurried to the home office. Terry got up and followed her. The key was still in the lock. Sarah yanked open the file drawer and riffled through the folders.

"I told you, I found it, down at the office. She didn't find anything."

Abruptly Sarah swung around, and her hand flashed out in a sharp slap across his face. "You bloody, blithering idiot! Go get her and bring her back here! Now!"

"She won't come. I told her I had the assignment. No reason for her to come back." He rubbed his cheek and stepped out of his mother's reach.

"Bring Jason! She'll come! Go get her now!"

2

The first time Barbara Holloway entered the office of Dr. Marjorie Sanger, she had been restless and wary, and spent minutes prowling about the office, examining books on shelves, a series of miniature paintings in a frame, a globe. She had not expected to see the doctor. Being given the time because there had been a cancellation had taken her by surprise, but driving from Eugene to San Francisco she had promised herself to make the call, to seek help in untying the tangle of messy knots she had made of her life. Her own attempts to unravel the knots only succeeded in drawing them tighter.

"Are you going to tell me why you're here?" the psychologist had asked after a few minutes.

"I'm trying to decide where to begin," Barbara said. "It's difficult." In her mind she was trying to decide not where to begin, but *if* she would begin, or say it was all a mistake, excuse herself and leave.

"Yes, it often is. But let me start you. You're a professional woman facing a crisis of some sort. You've never consulted a therapist in the past and you rarely talk about personal difficulties."

Barbara paused her restless wandering and looked hard at her.

"No, I didn't look you up. Hardly time for that, was there? But you're guarding your reputation. You asked my receptionist for the charge in order to bring enough cash. No insurance record or credit card. No paper trail. Outsiders often seize any opportunity to paint us all as unstable, don't they?"

She was a wizened little woman, hardly more than five feet tall, and she couldn't have weighed more than a hundred pounds. Her hair was gray and frizzy, natural, Barbara assumed, since no one would get a perm like that and live with it. Indeterminate age, fifty-five, seventy?

The doctor smiled. "People who are garrulous have no trouble at all in starting to talk. Often about inconsequential matters, but they can no more resist talking than they can stop breathing. Many others seek out a neutral figure, one who knows nothing about them, another form of guarding the self, and quite often they find they don't know if they want to talk at all. And it's a crisis for you, or you wouldn't be here. See? Simple."

She laughed, and Barbara sat down opposite her desk.

On her next visit the doctor had said, "Every professional person faces the crisis of faith, crisis of belief, of personal integrity, something, and each one of us has to decide. No one can do it for us. You understand that you're suddenly on the tipping point of a life, your own or someone else's, that what you decide will determine someone's fate. It isn't just a minor nuisance, but a life-altering fate, and how you tip the scale is irreversible. It's a heavy weight to bear."

The next time Barbara had come, she again moved restlessly about the office, unable to sit still.

"What happened, Barbara?" Dr. Sanger asked. "Something has changed for you, hasn't it?"

Tiredly, Barbara sank into a chair and nodded. "It seemed simple. He would accept that I'm not the right one for him and get on with things, and I would get over it. People do."

"And now?"

"He wants to marry me. I got an e-mail with a proposal." She jerked to her feet and went to the globe, gave it a spin. "I'll end up hurting him. It wouldn't work. Why can't he see that?" She returned to her chair.

"Perhaps he is looking at something you don't see."

"An ideal. He's looking at an ideal, and I'm looking at myself, the person I know I am."

"I asked you what you're afraid of. Have you arrived at an answer?"

Barbara nodded. "I'm afraid I'll hurt him desperately. I'm afraid it would come to that eventually."

Dr. Sanger said gently, "I think you can come up with a better answer than that. But consider this, Barbara. Consider if there are ever two people who are truly equal. Aren't there always daily accommodations that must be made by real people? If they become too unbalanced, tension rises, perhaps an irreconcilable difference, but how can one know in advance if such will be the case? And what may be seen by one as a major hurdle, to the other may appear to be almost insignificant. Again, accommodations are made. Or not."

"You aren't going to give me any advice at all, are you?"

"No, Barbara. Only you can decide your own fate. You won't be coming again, will you?"

Barbara shook her head. "I have to think about my own fate, make a few decisions. Thank you, Dr. Sanger." She stood up and put on her coat, walked to the door, where she was stopped by the psychologist's voice.

"Barbara, if ever I find myself in a terrible situation, accused of criminal activity, I'd want you to defend me."

Barbara turned around and regarded the other woman, then said, "Will you answer a question for me?"

Dr. Sanger nodded.

"Have you ever considered quitting, leaving it all and just quitting?"

For a moment Dr. Sanger didn't move, then she nodded again. "More than once," she said.

"Thank you," Barbara said in a near whisper and walked out.

She walked until city lights came on. Cars rushed by, a fire truck screamed through an intersection in front of her, boys on skateboards zoomed past, other pedestrians clustered at corners and she paid little or no attention to any of it. One hand held her purse strap, the other was in her pocket clutching the e-mail from Darren. She felt stupid for carrying it around, especially since the words had become imbedded in her brain, but she carried it in her pocket where she could feel it.

When her thighs began to burn, she knew it was time to

stop walking, to get something to eat and then return to her studio apartment. She would make notes of today's conversation with Dr. Sanger, exactly the way she always did after talking with a client or a witness. After that, she had to start from the beginning of her notes and give some thought to what she had said, what the doctor had said on various visits. But not in the city, she thought then. There was no need to remain in San Francisco. Someplace on the coast where she could watch a storm blow ashore and have peace and quiet enough to think through everything she and Dr. Sanger had discussed. And make a final decision about practicing law, and about Darren Halvord. Especially about Darren.

For weeks Joseph Kurtz had hovered between life and death, in a state neither one nor the other, in a deep coma following a stroke that occurred twenty-four hours after his surgery. That morning he had slipped into death.

Sarah Kurtz and her brother Lawrence Diedricks were in the living room of her condo and she half listened as Lawrence and her personal assistant Lon Clampton discussed arrangements for the next few days. The jet would be ready to leave in the morning, Clampton had said, whenever the family got there. He had arranged for removal of the body to the plane. The funeral would take place on Saturday, with only the family present, and a memorial service on the following Tuesday. Sarah's jaw was clenched with frustration and rage, and to her surprise even grief. They had been married for forty-three years, after all.

The voices droned on until she felt she might scream. Finally she broke in, "Clampton, what about that woman in Austin? Do they know yet?"

"Another false alarm," he said easily. Lon Clampton had been with her for more than twenty years, but he was not in her confidence and had no idea why she was so obsessed with finding Elizabeth Kurtz, only that she was, and that she was spending a fortune on private detectives. He didn't much care about why, not his job, but he was responsible for hiring the detective firm, and she took it out on him every time a false lead ended up at a blank wall.

Lon Clampton was a large man, broad shouldered and heavy without being fat. He worked out regularly and was proud of his well-developed body. He liked his job, even if Sarah Kurtz could be a bitch to work for at times. It was not demanding for the most part, and the pay was good enough to make up for a lot of her bitching. Arrange this party, see to the invitations, have the car ready, the plane ready to go, be on call presumably for twenty-four hours a day, but that was misleading. She rarely called in the evening and almost never on weekends. Now that Elizabeth Kurtz had come up again as a concern, he was ready to do whatever was required. More publicity, he could fix that. More rumors, he knew where to get them started. This time she had ordered absolute silence. Not a word to be leaked, not a hint they were looking for her. But finding her had proven to be a sticking point. Although the detectives really were some of the best, they had failed so far. And she blamed him more than she blamed them.

Sarah heaved herself up from a chair and cast him a venomous look. "If that crew of scumbags can't do the job, get some who can. I'm going to lie down."

At the door of the living room she paused to give her

brother an equally scathing look. "Tell Moira that plane will take off at eleven whether she's aboard or not."

"Now, Sarah, don't you worry about Moira. We'll be there. You go on and have a rest."

"Your wife has never been on time in her life," she said. "She'll be late for her own funeral. Eleven."

Lying down, she realized she was grinding her teeth and forced herself to stop. It was too much, she thought, just too damned much. Where could that bitch be holed up?

In the beginning they had reassured her. She can't hide with a little boy, she's an amateur, she doesn't know how to cover her tracks. Now, weeks later they were still chasing shadows. Only three people had known about that file—Sarah, Joe and Sarah's brother, Lawrence. And now that bitch had it. Joe should have burned it, she thought then. She should have let him burn it when he first proposed doing so. But she had known it was priceless and said to lock it up. We'll find a use for it. And they had, and would have found it even more valuable than she had dreamed years earlier. Or it could be a scalpel that could slice her dreams to shreds.

She'll get in touch, she told herself, as she had done repeatedly. We'll meet her demands now, and take care of her later, after the file is secure again. After things are settled.

She had been outraged and mortified when Terry called to say he would bring his bride over to meet the family, the first she had heard about a wedding. She had ordered Clampton to find out about the girl and her family, and the more she learned, the angrier she had become. A filthy Spanish girl, an equally filthy Spanish mother who had seduced another nice American boy. Elizabeth's father had come from a good

American family, probably as easy a pickup as Terry would have been. It didn't matter that her mother's family had money; they probably had stolen it. So they were highly regarded in Spain; anyone could buy a favorable press release. Sarah's outrage had only grown when she met Elizabeth. She had known she would be beautiful, of course. Terry always had an eye for a beautiful girl; she was just one of many. But she had snared him. It had mattered less that she was educated, a major in science, for God's sake! She didn't trust women who were driven, competitive. God alone knew what mixture of blood ran in that family, Spanish, Arabs, no doubt, blacks. Who knew?

She had to admit that Elizabeth was smart, showing off her intelligence, questioning Joe in a humiliating way, then dismissing him, probably laughing at him. And making up to Sarah's father, showing off her languages the way she did. Speaking French on his shortwave radio to some other foreigner who couldn't speak decent English. None of that mattered.

What did matter was that Sarah knew how to bring her down to the level where she belonged, helpless and pleading, abject and penitent. Once she got her hands on Jason, Elizabeth would understand what it meant to cross Sarah Kurtz.

Her head was throbbing painfully with a migraine coming on. Not now, she willed it. Not fucking now!

Elizabeth sat on a park bench with an open book, but she was not reading it. She had learned that if she pretended to be absorbed in a book no one stopped to chat and she always carried one when she took Jason to a park to play. He was swinging, calling for her to watch now and then, probably singing to himself, the way he did when he was content. He had stopped singing in the car. He was getting so tired of traveling, exactly as she was. So very tired. Now, in Las Vegas, she knew this had to stop. She had to go somewhere and stay, to let him settle down again, and to get some rest. She eyed a man warily, looked down at her book, then surreptitiously glanced at him again. She felt certain he was watching her, but she had felt that way so many times in the past weeks, she recognized it as a symptom of her fear, or paranoia, not necessarily a real threat. But what if he was?

Always the fear followed her reasoning.

She was very aware when the man stood up and took several steps in her direction, aware when he stopped, then turned and walked away. Only then did she really look at him, his hands thrust in his pockets, shoulders sagging. She drew in a breath of relief. Just another lonely guy looking for a friendly face. But she knew she had to make some kind of plan, do something besides drive endlessly with fear her constant companion.

She would finish scanning the material that night, she thought then, and tomorrow she would find a day-care center where she could leave Jason for an hour or two, take the original material and put it… Where? She couldn't use a bank safe-deposit box, not without an account. A locker. Train station? The airport, she decided. And when she was ready to pick it up again, it would be a simple matter to get it back. Then what?

Her mind was not functioning properly. She could think only in small increments of time. Time to find a motel. Time for lunch. Time to let Jason run and play for awhile. Time to drive on. Tomorrow hardly ever played a part in her planning, just the immediate needs to be taken care of.

That morning she had read in the newspaper that Joe Kurtz had died, and the family would have a private funeral in Portland, Oregon. She had been reading newspapers carefully whenever she could find one from a major city, looking for any mention of her and Jason. Although she doubted that Sarah would have called the police, it was a possibility, and she had looked. She had assumed Joe had already died, she realized, but apparently he had lingered for those past weeks. She looked at Jason swinging, and thought, *Your grandfather died and you'll never know a thing about it, or him.* With that thought, her hatred of Sarah flared again.

If she had known when she took the file what she now knew, would she have taken it? The question had come back repeatedly, and remained unanswered. Probably not, she thought. She had put Jason at risk, as well as herself. Probably not, no matter how much she hated Sarah. All thinking stopped then and she felt every muscle tense as a couple stopped strolling to gaze at Jason.

Move on! she willed. *Keep walking!*

It seemed a long time before they continued their walk. As soon as they passed, she got up and went to Jason. "Time to go," she said.

He shook his head. "No! I don't want to!"

"Tell you what I saw when we were coming over here," she said. "A toy store. How about that? Just waiting for us to come visit." She knew she was bribing him again and again with new toys, with promises to see something wonderful, or have more ice cream, whatever came to mind to avoid having a scene in public, drawing attention to them. Hating what she was doing, she took him to the toy store.

That night they built a LEGO castle, and she read to him. As soon as he was asleep she returned to her scanner to finish the original material, to get it all on her hard drive, print it out, back it up to disk. It promised to be a late night, but at last she was making a plan as she worked. Put it in a locker, check her road map. Buy some warm jackets, boots, rainproof outerwear. She knew where she would take her son, where they would be safe, where no strangers would stop and stare at her or her child, no one would follow them. A place where they could relax and she could decide what to do with the material she had stolen.

3

The little cove was no more than half a mile from one headland to the next, and it was very secluded. The south rock wall was possibly climbable for a dedicated mountaineer, or a goat, Barbara had decided, and the north wall was treacherous, a trap for the unwary. At low tide it was possible to walk between basalt skeletons of volcanoes, scramble over a few, ease between others carefully and find oneself a quarter of a mile from the coast village beyond with its own crescent beach. But when the tide came in, the rocks were aswirl with foaming water, and swift currents cut new channels, changing the landscape on a twice daily basis. Locals in the village knew all about the deceptive wall and newcomers learned quickly. At high tide the tiny beach vanished, waves washed against the surrounding cliffs, crashed and roared and the only way to return to the village was by hiking up a steep trail, finding the right place to reverse course and start back down to reach the other side of the stacks, a mile and a half of rough hiking through the rain forest.

Barbara liked her own private piece of beach, her own little ocean front, where no one bothered her, no one intruded. At least it had been like that for her until the last two days.

She had walked to the south cliff barrier that day, stopping at tide pools on her way to observe the many-colored starfish, crabs, a sand dollar one day, even a tiny pink octopus once, all minding their own business. She never bothered any of them, simply looked, then walked on.

It was time to head back now that the tide had turned and waves were tumbling in farther than only minutes before. It was like that; it seemed to come in faster than it went out. One of the mysteries of the sea.

A light rain had been falling all morning; it had become heavier as she walked, but she didn't mind the rain, swathed as she was in waterproof everything—slicker, boots, hood, even gloves. One hand, ungloved, was in her pocket, holding a folded sheet of paper.

She began to walk a bit faster, with the rain full in her face. Then the child appeared, slipping and sliding down the trail. She had seen him and a woman, presumably his mother, twice before, and the two women had nodded at each other without speaking. Barbara had left her private beach to them both times. Now the boy, having reached the sand, started to run toward the deceptive rocks, and she broke into a run also, caught up with him and seized his jacket collar, stopping his headlong flight.

"Hey, slow down! Where's your mother?" She looked

toward the trail he had come down, then back at the child. His face was streaked by tears or rain, impossible to tell which. His jacket was open, and he was hatless, and in socks without boots. He had run without hesitation through the shallows of a creek that tumbled to the sea here, with Barbara's trail on the north side of it, the one he had exited on the south.

He grabbed her hand and began to pull her toward the south trail. "Mama's hurt!"

"Hold it, kid," Barbara said, and picked him up. He was soaked, shaking hard and sucking in air in spasmodic gasps. She realized quickly that she couldn't climb the trail with him in her arms, and after a moment she stopped and said, "You'll have to ride on my back. You know, piggyback. Come on, let's shift you around." He wasn't very heavy, but she needed her hands to hold on to a tree or even a rock now and then. With him on her back, his arms nearly choking her as he clung, she climbed the trail. When it leveled out, she set him down and ran ahead. A woman was lying facedown in the dirt a dozen feet from a cabin where the door was standing open. The little boy had run nearly as fast as she had, and now stared and began to shake harder.

"Go inside and get warm," Barbara said. "I'll bring her in." She wasn't dead, she thought in relief as she knelt by the woman. A head wound had bled, was still bleeding. She was unconscious, but breathing. She was very cold, her lips looked blue. Although she had on a jacket with a hood, the hood had been knocked back and her hair was streaming water and blood. Moving quickly, Barbara took off her slicker and worked it around the woman's body as well as she could, then rolled her over so that it was under her, and she began to pull the slicker and woman toward the cabin, trying to keep her head from bumping on the ground. She was sweating by the time she reached the two steps up. She hesitated, but it couldn't be helped. She had to get her inside, no matter how bruised she became, and she could not lift and carry her. But she did have to get her out of the rain, warm her up and try to see how badly she was injured. She pulled her up the steps and inside.

The woman was beginning to moan and stir as Barbara moved her toward a low sofa. She managed to get her up on it and began to work on removing her boots. Strip her, she thought, wrap her in a blanket, get the kid dry, build up the fire, warm up the place, clean that head wound...

The little boy continued to stand nearby, big-eyed and shaking, and now it was clear that tears streaked his face. "Hey, kid, go get some dry clothes and bring them out here. Scoot!" He fled.

Minutes later, the woman was semiconscious, swaddled in blankets and the little boy crept in under the cover with her. He had put on dry jeans and a sweater. The woman's arms tightened around him, drawing him close.

"Look," Barbara said, "your phone doesn't work, and you need a doctor. That head injury probably needs some stitches. My name is Barbara Holloway, and I live in Eugene. I put wood on the fire so it will get warm in here. Now I have to go get some help. I'll be as fast as possible. Just stay still and rest until I get back. Can you hear me?"

The woman made an inarticulate sound without opening her eyes. At least she wasn't blue any longer, and the way she had reached for the child and now held him was reassuring. Barbara had tried to clean the head wound that continued to leak blood, and finally she simply pressed a washcloth on it. The woman's nose had been bleeding. Her face was swollen, scratched and dirty. Barbara had put a towel on her hair, both to soak up the water, and to help keep her warm. She regarded the woman and the boy for a moment, but there was little more she could do here.

"I have to leave," she said. "Can you understand what I'm saying? I'll be back as soon as I can. You just rest there and wait for me to bring help."

The woman raised her hand from the child's head, then let it rest again on him. He snuggled even closer.

Barbara pulled on her jacket and the slicker and left the cabin.

After a glance at the dirt road leading from the cabin, she shook her head. There was no way of knowing how many miles it might meander through the coast range, where it would come out to a real road finally. She didn't bother looking for a car, but turned to go back down the trail to a place where she could cross the small creek, go up the other side to her cabin, take her own car to the Norris house. He would know what to do.

Sam Norris was in his early seventies, wiry and so weathered that his face looked like bark. The day she had met him he had been wearing a wide-brimmed gaucho hat, complete with a chin strap, and he was wearing it when she found him hammering in one of the cabins near his house. When she told him a woman from a cabin across the creek had been injured and needed a doctor, he glanced at the forest between his cabins and the isolated one across the way. He nodded, and in what seemed slow motion, he walked across the narrow road to his own house, entered and returned with a metal box.

"First aid," he said, motioning toward a truck. "Get in, we'll go see to her. Cora will call the sheriff."

Neither spoke as he drove to the highway, about half a mile up a narrow winding road, then headed south. Barbara had spotted his cabins for rent by the week or month just six days earlier, after leaving San Francisco. Just what she needed, she had decided, and without further thought had turned in and rented a cabin for a week. And it would have been perfect if that other woman and her child had not appeared on the scene.

"Old man Diedricks' place," Norris said, breaking the silence. "Only cabin up this way."

He turned onto a road even narrower and twistier than the one to his house, unpaved, more like a forest service road than a real one. The trees crowded closer than they did on his road. The rain was coming down harder and his headlights were dim, his windshield fogged. He wiped it from time to time with his gloved hand, making it worse, leaving streaks. They came upon the cabin without warning, after a sharp turn in the road there it was.

There were no lights in the windows, no sign of life. Barbara was nearly holding her breath, fearful that the woman had died waiting for help. She jumped from the truck and ran to the front stoop, pushed the door open and entered. The room was empty, a soggy blanket on the floor by the sofa. Norris came right behind her and flicked on a light; he pushed past Barbara and went to the bedroom.

They were gone. The cabin felt empty, without a sound except for her boots and those of Sam Norris on the wood floor. He looked in the kitchen and she glanced inside the bathroom, then the one other room, but they were gone.

"Guess she wasn't hurt all that much," Norris said. He pulled out a cell phone and called his wife. "Tell Curtis we don't need a doc after all," he said and listened a minute, then said, "Right," and broke the connection without further conversation. "Deputy sheriff's on his way. I'll have a look outside." He nodded to Barbara and walked out.

Without touching a thing, she went through the rooms. The bedroom had a double bed, bedding in disarray, an open drawer on a chest of drawers, two miniature cars on the floor. The bloody washcloth was in the sink in the bathroom, a soiled towel on the edge of the bathtub. In the kitchen there were signs of a hasty exit, the refrigerator door not closed all the way, a half-empty carton of milk and a yogurt container inside, a skillet on the stove with a bit of egg sticking to it. The remaining room had a long table with several straight chairs and a floor lamp. Back in the living room she saw that the low couch was a futon, stained with blood and discolored where it was still wet. There was a wood-burning stove, overheating the cabin now, a wrought-iron wood holder with several split logs, two upholstered chairs and a television, a couple of end tables and another small table, with another straight chair. A wastebasket close to it held a used printer cartridge, and there was a computer cable on the floor, still plugged into an outlet.

Norris returned and leaned a split log against the wall near the door. He did not take off his hat, but he shrugged out of a poncho and draped it over a chair where it dripped water. She added her own slicker and jacket. It was wet and her back felt clammy.

"Old man Diedricks built this cabin fifty years ago," Norris said, standing near the stove, warming his hands. "I was a young fellow, just out of the army, and he hired me to help him, cut wood, keep the woods cleared back in case of fire. Going on ninety, I guess. Blind now. Hasn't been here in twelve, thirteen years, but he paid me to keep it ready for him so when he came, he would have wood to burn, have lights to turn on and I guess he never wanted for much more than that. He'd come to get some work done. Said he couldn't stand the commotion all the time up in Portland." He backed away from the stove and sat on one of the upholstered chairs. "Good man, Hank Diedricks. A good man. Won't be coming back, but they pay me to keep it ready, just like he said."

He became silent then and Barbara sat in the other chair as silent as Norris. He had not asked her a single question, and she was content not to initiate any explanation until the sheriff arrived. How much of that unconsciousness had been a sham? she wondered, remembering how the woman had held the boy, had drawn him in close to her. Why hadn't she spoken up? She had been like a dead weight all the way to the cabin, up the steps, none of that had been fake, but when Barbara had wrestled her onto the futon, she had been different. Dazed, certainly, but not the same kind of dead weight. And again, when Barbara pulled off her soaked jeans, she had lifted her hips, helping. Why hadn't she said something?

It was another half hour before she heard a car pull in and stop. Norris got up to open the door and admit two men.

"Curtis Connors, Dwayne Beacham," he said. "That's Ms. Holloway. She's renting one of my cabins."

They were both in their early fifties, one stout and swarthy, wearing a baseball cap, a fleece jacket and high boots; the other taller and thinner in a lined denim jacket and cowboy hat. They nodded to her and the stout one said, "What's going on here?"

She told them about the boy and finding the woman on the ground. When she finished, Connors asked, "Who was she?"

"No idea. I never met her. I saw them on the beach at a distance twice before today, but we didn't speak, didn't introduce ourselves."

Beacham left to look over the rooms. He returned holding the two toy cars. "Guess there was a kid here, all right," he said. "There's a bloody washcloth in the bathroom."

Connors asked more questions and clearly was not satisfied with her answers. "Why was the kid looking for you if you didn't know them?"

"He wasn't looking for me," Barbara said. "He didn't even see me until I caught up with him. I think he found his mother and was going to go to the village for help. He was terrified."

"He was going to swim over?" Connors said in a mean voice.

"The tide was coming in, but he probably doesn't know a thing about tides. He wouldn't have made it," she added. An image formed of that small figure being overtaken by a wave, swept to sea. In a lower voice she said, "And neither would his mother. She was freezing out there, soaked, unconscious. How long would she have lasted? It would have been a double homicide."

Connors looked disgusted. "No homicide. A cougar probably jumped her, scratched her up some."

"No cougar," Norris said, shaking his head. He went to the door and retrieved the split log he had brought in earlier and held it out to Connors, pointing to some long black hairs caught in the rough cut.

After a pause Connors said, "She's probably an illegal. Had a fight with her boyfriend and when you came he hid out until you left, then he hustled her and the kid into their car and took off."

This time Barbara was shaking her head. "She'd been out there too long, and someone must have taken a computer. Look." She pointed to the computer cable. "And there's a printer cartridge in the wastebasket. There wasn't a computer on that table when I got her inside. I tossed my slicker and my jacket down on that table. No computer. No printer."

Connors had a lot more questions after that, until finally she said, "I've told you everything I can. I didn't see a car. I didn't look for one. I wouldn't have driven out for help anyway because I had no idea where that road would take me. I didn't see a purse, and again, I wasn't looking for one. I was gone at least an hour, more likely an hour and a half, and what she did in that time, I have no idea. I intend to leave now."

Norris stood up. "I'll take her back to the cabin. Be at the house, you have anything else to ask." He was not asking permission to leave any more than she was. He pulled on his poncho, and she put on her jacket and slung the ruined rain slicker over her shoulders, and they left the two deputies in the cabin.

They were both as silent driving back as they had been coming in, until they neared his house. "Cougar!" he said in disgust. "You get in your car and drive on down and I'll follow along and have a look around. Won't nobody get in here tonight without I know it, Ms. Holloway, and won't nobody be coming in by the beach, not on a night like this. Tomorrow, you want to move in closer to the house, number two's empty and ready."

"Thanks," she said. "I'll think about it." But she knew what she would be doing the next day: moving on. Not quite ready to go home yet, no longer wanting the kind of solitude her isolated cabin here offered, it was time to move on.

4

The first time Barbara had come to Astoria, she had been ten, and thought this was the end of the world. With the broad Columbia River its northern boundary, and the limitless Pacific Ocean its western, the town had seemed caught in a time warp—quiet, with picture-book Victorian houses with widows' walks on bluffs, a fishing fleet at old piers or docks, no one in a rush. It might have been unchanged for a hundred years. That week when she got there after an unhurried drive up the coast, she had run out of state. End of the line. Also, she had forgotten that the Lewis and Clark bicentennial celebration was taking place and would be ongoing for months.

Everywhere there were new boutiques, new restaurants, fast-food chains and the town was almost garish with Christmas decorations ablaze with lights. There was even a new long pier. Everyone in town evidently anticipated a rush of tourists to rival the fur rush of the distant past.

Even the wide smooth beach was overrun, she thought with irritation as she walked. A dozen other people were out walking, most of them probably looking for a sunken boat that appeared only at the lowest neap tides, perhaps twice a year.

It wasn't raining, as it had been all along the coast until the day before, but a sharp, steady wind was blowing in and more rain was predicted for the weekend. She paid little attention to the other walkers, and less to the wind, and instead thought of her immediate problem. She had realized that morning, watching the news on television, that she had been gone for six weeks, and that she couldn't keep endlessly wandering, or she would go broke. She might have to get a real job, she had added mockingly. She even had a job offer. In San Francisco she had received an e-mail from an old acquaintance at Reed College. He had called the office, had written her a real letter and e-mail was a last resort, he had said. They wanted her to teach a class for the spring term starting in January, a class in criminal law. The idea was ludicrous, she had thought then. For her to teach idealistic students, soon-to-be attorneys, anything to do with the law had to be a joke.

She had not even decided yet if she would resume her law practice, she thought, scowling. She fingered the note in her pocket. It was getting frayed. Dr. Sanger's question kept repeating in her head—What are you afraid of? She walked faster.

As she approached the parking lot and her car, she scowled deeper at nothing in particular. Where next? It was Thursday, and she didn't want to be in Astoria when the weekend influx of tourists was due. Every weekend now was like the best weekend of summer, a waitress had informed her happily that morning. That time of year, she had gone on, they usually weren't even open during the winter months, but business was very good, even booming.

"Thank you, Captain Lewis, Captain Clark," Barbara muttered to herself. Then she stopped walking and stared. Ahead, leaning against her car was Bailey Novell, wearing his dreadful coat that he claimed made him look like a Sherpa guide, and she thought made him look like a yak. A woolen cap was pulled down almost to his eyes. He straightened up and waved.

"Hiya," he called. "It's freezing out here. Didn't you notice?"

"What in hell are you doing here?" she demanded, drawing closer.

"Waiting for you."

"What's wrong? What happened? Is Dad okay?"

"Nothing, maybe. I don't know. And yes. Your old man said for me to find you and deliver a message. Too important and personal for e-mail. You know how he is."

She knew. Frank believed sending an e-mail was like broadcasting to the world, and possibly he was even right about that.

"What message?"

"If you don't get yourself back to Eugene before Monday morning at nine, the cops are going to put out an APB on you." He rubbed his hands. "Cold. You don't hide very well, you know. I can give you some pointers."

"I haven't been hiding," she snapped. "What does that message mean?" Of course, if Frank told him to find her, he would do it, even if she had been trying to hide. Bailey was maybe the best private detective in America, certainly the best on the west coast. He could find a particular grain of sand on the beach if Frank told him to.

"Don't know what it means more than what it says," he said. "They want you. Accessory to kidnapping, aiding and abetting, miscellaneous criminal activities. It's a two-day drive, foggy down in the valley, unless you run the risk of adding to your criminal activities and get hauled in for speeding or something."

"I don't know what you're talking about. I'm going to my motel."

"Me, too. Too cold out here. I'll follow along, maybe get a room nearby."

"Bailey, for God's sake, you're not going to shadow me!"

"I got my orders."

He followed her all the way to Salem, where a dense fog made her stop and find a motel. He was there again Saturday morning, and stayed behind her all the way to Eugene. When she entered her apartment early Saturday afternoon, his old green Dodge, as disreputable looking as he was, made a U-turn and drove away.

Her apartment was cold and damp. She lingered only long enough to turn up the heat, then headed for her father's house.

When Frank opened his door, he simply embraced her and held her for a moment, then stepped back and closed the door. Both cats wound in and about her feet as if in greeting.

"Let me take your jacket," Frank said. "Go sit down."

He had made a fire, and there was the coffee carafe and cups on a low table. She suspected that Bailey had called in to say mission accomplished. She waited until they were both seated near the fire, coffee had been poured and the cats had each found a lap.

"What was that message all about?" she finally asked.

"I was hoping you'd tell me," he said. "State police are looking for you. Material witness."

"To what, for heaven's sake?"

Frank shrugged. "Seems you got involved with a woman who is being accused of kidnapping a child."

She gave him an incredulous look. "They're out of their minds." But even as she said it, she was thinking of the woman who had been attacked at the cabin just a week before. "For God's sake!" She told him about it. "If that little boy had been kidnapped, I'll sprout wings and take to the air. He was terrified because she was hurt and bleeding. He couldn't wait to get under the blanket with her and be held by her. He called her Mama."

"Family abductions are still abductions," Frank said. "Maybe we'll learn something more on Monday. Howard Janowsky, a state police lieutenant, wants to talk to you. In your office. I told him you would be available there, not up in Salem, or his office in town." He paused a moment, then added, "I'll be there unless you object."

She regarded him even more incredulously. "You think I might need an attorney?"

"Apparently the lieutenant is serious. That cabin belongs to Henry Diedricks, the founder of the Diedricks Corporation. They make replacement joints, hips, limbs, knuckles and they have a great deal of influence in the state. Apparently they've applied pressure to find a missing woman, the ex-wife of a grandson and her child, who would be Diedricks's great-grandson. They seem to believe that the missing ex-wife and the child were in that cabin. The ex-husband in the case is Terence Kurtz, and his father, Diedricks's son-in-law, died recently. The family gathered in Portland for his funeral, but the ex-wife and child were not among the mourners. It may be a matter of inheritance, wills, something of that sort, I don't know. But they want to find her and the child."

It wasn't difficult to talk Barbara into staying for dinner. Chicken and poblano chilies ready to go into the oven had been the clincher. He didn't ask her where she had been. He already knew. When he told Bailey to find her, the report had come back quickly. San Francisco, a week in a cabin owned by Samuel Norris, four days driving up the coast, and then Astoria. It had been a long six weeks. He didn't mention that either, nor did he ask her what she had been doing all that time. She would tell him, or not.

Then, lingering over apple crisp and coffee, she said, "I did a lot of reading on the road, here and there. And even watched quite a bit of television. C-SPAN, some talk shows. I haven't been paying a lot of attention to politics during the past few years, it was time to catch up."

He nodded, and waited silently, understanding that was simply background.

"I guess politicians don't change much, do they? I mean, you see corruption, interest groups, a lot of money being passed around, certain laws being enacted. I don't suppose that's changed over the decades, or even generations, except in scale possibly."

When he still didn't respond, she grinned slightly. "You're playing the wise, old laconic know-it-all, aren't you? Or you're waiting for an opening."

He laughed and poured more coffee for her. He had had his limit for the day.

"The question is," she said slowly, "if you decide for yourself which laws are allowable or for the good of most, but not all, people, who's to say that everyone else doesn't have the same right to pick and choose? And what finally does the law mean?"

He nodded. "Precisely the question. Did you come up with an answer?"

"No. I'm still wrestling with it."

Maybe just a little bit more coffee, he thought, pouring it, keeping his gaze on the carafe and his cup. Slowly, in a low voice, he said, "Bobby, no matter where you come down with an answer, you'll find the same question nagging at you decades from now. It doesn't go away."

"You gave up capital cases," she said, just as softly.

"Yes, I did."

That night in her apartment, sitting at her table, Barbara regarded a cardboard carton with distaste. It was nearly filled with mail—personal letters, flyers, credit card offers, invitations. She had started to sort through it all, only to stop and push it aside. It had waited all those weeks; it could wait a bit longer. Instead, she turned to look over the living room, then the small kitchen. It was bleak, all of it, cold and barren in appearance with hardly a sign of who lived there. Except for books on end tables it was as impersonal as the hotel and motel rooms she had been living in for weeks. The very nice gifts different people had given her over the years were for the most part put away in their own boxes, on closet shelves, even in her storage locker in the basement of the building. Too nice to keep out where it would collect dust, she had said of this or that, and packed it away.

But she could buy a few pillows, a colorful throw for the sofa, something to liven it up. Not a plant. They always died in her care.

Slowly she wandered to her home office and sat at her desk, and more slowly she took Darren's e-mail from her pocket and smoothed it out. Already frayed, it had been dampened at the Diedricks cabin when she took off her rain garb, and now the creases were starting to split.

My darling Barbara, I love you and it seems my fate to keep loving you. I got over the anger, and the hurt, and began to think, instead of just suffer gut reactions. You were right, Barbara. If that little bit of you was all I could have, I was content to live with it, or so I thought, without realizing what I was doing to you. How selfish we can be when we're in love—one of those mysterious puzzles we poor humans seem plagued with apparently. I want to be your friend, your companion, your lover. I want to be your husband, to marry all of you, not just the part I was too ready to settle for. I'm afraid it's all the way or not at all with us, isn't it? Will you marry me, Barbara? You can come home. I won't bug you, or call, or hang out on your doorstep.

She placed the e-mail message in a file folder on her desk, then sat with her eyes closed, remembering a session with Dr. Sanger. "When you confront what it is you fear, only then can you resolve it. But you have to find that elusive fear. No one can do it for you."

Abandonment? Betrayal? Unfaithfulness? She shook her head. Afraid of hurting him desperately. She knew that was part of it, but was it all? Marjorie Sanger had not thought it enough. Find a better answer, she'd said. Six weeks had not been long enough. She had brought home the same two problems that had resulted in her flight—her wandering, futile search for answers. Could she work within the law when she believed with every fiber of her being that the law often was wrong? What to do about Darren? What she had come home to face now was a possible warrant for her arrest, and finding herself suspected of aiding and abetting a kidnapper, or worse. And she still had no answers to anything, she added almost savagely.

5

Maria and Shelley were almost giddy with joy at Barbara's return on Monday morning, both talking at once, hugging and touching, as if to verify that she was really back. Shelley had several interesting cases, two from Martin's restaurant, one a real paying office case, and Maria was apologetic about so much mail in the office, and in the box at the apartment. No bills, she added, smiling. She had taken care of the bills, paid the rent and they'd had to have a repairman do something about a computer glitch.

Laughing, Barbara walked through the reception room to her office with Shelley close behind. Fresh flowers were on the round table, and a new plant in a new cloisonné urn near a window. She looked at Shelley accusingly.

"Well, your father said you'd be back today, in all likelihood. I thought a little something special would be nice. I have to run. Court at eight-thirty, shoplifting, seventeen-year-old brat...."

Barbara waved her out and went to sit at her desk. It was good to be back, she thought in surprise. Crazy, but it was good to be back.

Frank arrived minutes later. And promptly at nine Lt. Howard Janowsky appeared. He was a heavyset, middle-aged man with graying hair, wearing gold-rimmed eyeglasses, dressed in a bulky tweed suit and carrying a briefcase. His suit was too hot for indoors, Barbara thought, and not warm enough, or moisture proof enough, for outside. You wanted something you could shed inside, let drip, if necessary, or at the very least dry out a little before putting it on again. She imagined that heavy wool absorbed moisture and held it all day.

He nodded to Frank, and held out his hand to Barbara for a firm, no-nonsense handshake.

"Please," she said, motioning to the sofa and chairs at the low table. "I thought we would be more comfortable over here." She waited until he was seated in one of the chairs, then asked, "What can I do for you, Lieutenant? I understand you've been looking for me."

"That's correct," he said. "We have been asked to look into the assault you reported to the local authorities in Coos County on November twenty-fourth of this year. Will you please tell me about it?"

She repeated what she had told the sheriff deputies and then Frank. Janowsky listened making occasional notes. Then he asked, "Who was she?"

"I have no idea. I never met her before that day, and didn't meet her then, since she was unconscious."

"Would you recognize her again?"

"Probably not. Her face was swollen, covered with dirt, mud really, and bloody. Her nose had been bleeding, and a head injury had bled, and was still bleeding when I moved her. Her hair was muddy, wet and also bloody. And she never opened her eyes, so I couldn't say what color they were."

"But you had seen her before, down on the beach?"

"Yes, twice, each time at a distance, when she had on a head scarf and a dark rain coat or something. We simply nodded at each other, and I didn't stay on the beach after I saw her and the child."

"How about down in California, did you meet with her there?"

Barbara shook her head. "I told you, I never met her, never saw her close until after she had been attacked. I don't know who she is or anything about her."

"You said her computer had been taken. How did you know she had a computer?"

"I assumed there had been a computer," she said steadily, although she could feel her anger gathering. He was noncommittal, almost robotic in his way of putting questions, but each additional question seemed to imply disbelief. "There was a computer cable still plugged in, and there was a printer cartridge in the wastebasket. It doesn't take a rocket scientist to assume that there had been a computer and printer to go with them."

"Did you look in the other room, the one with the other table and chairs?"

"Later, when Mr. Norris and I went back. That door was closed, the room unheated and there was dust on the table. No one had used that room for a long time."

"How old was the child?"

She shrugged. "Little. I don't know how old. I don't know

kids that size and age." She held up her hand to estimate height. "Four, five, maybe six, maybe just three. I don't know."

"Would you recognize him again?"

"I don't know," she said. "His hair was wet, and he was so afraid, crying. I just don't know."

"What was he afraid of?"

"His mother was hurt, bleeding, on the ground in the rain. For God's sake, that's enough to terrify any child." Her voice was tight then, when she demanded, "Lieutenant, what's this all about? What are you looking for?"

"We think the child may be endangered, and we suspect the woman is, from your account. We're looking for them both."

"Well, obviously—" She caught a warning look from Frank and curbed her anger and impatience.

Imperturbably the lieutenant asked, "Is it possible that the child was terrified and trying to run away from something or someone when you caught him on the beach and took him back to the cabin?"

She shook her head. "I told you. He was looking for help. He grabbed my hand and started to pull me back up the trail. He said his mother was hurt, and he was crying."

"What else did he say?"

"Nothing. Not another word. He was shaking, soaked and freezing, staring at his injured mother."

"Where could he have found help on the beach if you hadn't been there, or if he hadn't expected you or someone to be there?"

The first time she had seen them, they had been down at the basalt stacks, scrambling on top of some of the shorter, flattened ones where there were many tide pools. He had been dressed in a yellow raincoat with a yellow hat, and high yellow boots, the kind of clothes she had seen little kids in Eugene wearing. She told him about it. "From up there you can see past the rocks and stacks, see the next beach with people and a few buildings. I think that's where he was heading that day, but the tide was coming in, and he couldn't have made it all the way before it caught him."

His questions continued with painstaking attention to the details, and then he asked, "Why did you leave the cabin the next morning?"

She glanced at Frank and caught his nearly imperceptible shake of the head. "I had rented it for a week only and decided to cut it short by one day since there was the possibility of a maniac in the area."

"Where did you go?"

She shrugged. "Nowhere in particular, up the coast."

"Did you meet up with the woman again?"

"No."

His questions went on for another hour until she finally stood up and said, "Lieutenant, I've told you all I can about that incident. What I did before and after it are irrelevant. I suggest that it's time to conclude this interrogation."

"One more thing," he said. He opened his briefcase, brought out a folder, removed a picture and handed it to her. "Is that the woman you saw?"

The woman had regular features, lovely dark eyes and long sweeping dark eyelashes. Her hair was black, shoulder length, thick and glossy looking, with a slight wave. She was smiling. "I can't be sure," Barbara said. "Possibly, but I couldn't definitely say it is."

"How about this one?" He handed her a second photo, a five by seven, apparently a school picture of a sober-faced little boy with dark curly hair, and the same kind of long eyelashes as the woman's. He appeared to be holding his breath.

"He looks too young," she said after a moment. "And the boy I saw didn't have curly hair, but it was so wet. Maybe when it dried it would be curlier. But that child looks too young."

"The picture's a year old, a little more," the lieutenant said.

He replaced them both, closed his briefcase and stood up. "We'll have to ask you to make yourself available for additional questions if it becomes necessary," he said. "Are you planning any more trips soon?"

"No," she said. "I'll be here."

He nodded, and didn't offer to shake hands again. She went to the door with him, saw him out of the reception area, then returned and said, enraged, "Good God! They think I'm either in collusion with that woman or that I attacked her! He thinks she may be in danger! Jesus! She was murderously attacked and left for dead or dying!"

"Simmer down," Frank said mildly and went to the door to the outer office, where he said, "Maria, we could use some coffee in here, and will you see if you can find Bailey. I want him."

When he closed the door and returned to the sofa, Barbara was pacing furiously about the office. "He thinks the kid was running away, maybe even from me, and I caught him and took him back!"

When Bailey arrived, Frank got right to the point. "I want everything you can find about that whole family, the ex-husband, his parents and the ex-wife and child."

Although Bailey often questioned what Barbara wanted, he simply jotted down the names Frank provided, and nodded. He did not ask if there was a paying client in sight, as he often did when Barbara sent him on his quest.

"And where she was just before she showed up at that cabin, and where she went afterward," Barbara added when Frank paused. To her annoyance Bailey glanced at Frank, who nodded.

"She might have needed medical attention," Frank said. "That could be a good starting place."

"She was wearing a lined hooded jacket," Barbara said. "The cut was about here." She indicated a place near her hairline over her eye. "I imagine she had the hood up when she was hit, and it probably saved her life, then came off when she fell. I think she needed stitches, and her face was swollen and discolored down to her jaw line."

After Bailey left, Barbara said, "Dad, you know this is going to cost a fortune, and I don't have a client."

"I do," he said.

6

Barbara had spent most of Monday catching up with mail, and on Tuesday morning, as Shelley looked in before leaving for a court appearance, she felt the first twinge of guilt when Shelley said, "I'll go straight over to Martin's after court. If it isn't too late, I'll come back here, but if it's after four or so, I'll just head for home. Try to beat the fog."

Barbara knew how busy she had been during the weeks that Shelley had been away on her honeymoon, and apparently Shelley was just as busy now, doing double duty at Martin's as in the office.

She started to say she would take over at Martin's that afternoon, then left the words unspoken. One of the letters she had yet to respond to concerned the job offer at Reed College.

Seated at her desk with the formal letter before her, she brooded about the offer. She might not be free to go, she thought sourly, and she was not at all certain she even wanted to teach, and doubted that she would be a suitable instructor in the first place. But neither was she eager to resume her own practice. She felt as if she were existing in a state of indefinite limbo, waiting for decisions to come from above. "Later," she muttered, putting the letter aside.

The next letter concerned new management at her apartment complex and an increase in rent. Three increases in three years, with no end in sight, and no recourse for the tenants. How much was she willing to pay in order to keep a location that was so convenient for her river walks?

She looked at the door in relief when there was a tap and Maria entered at her invitation. "Mrs. Sarah Kurtz is on the phone," Maria said. "She wants to come in this morning. She said it was about the woman who was attacked, and you'd know what she meant."

"Tell her sure," Barbara said. "About ten?"

Sarah Kurtz was accompanied by her son Terry. She introduced herself and him. She was dressed in a long black coat with a velvet collar, and a black velvet hat. Her son helped her off with the coat, then put it on a chair. He took off a black leather jacket and tossed it down, also. He was one of the most handsome men Barbara had ever seen, almost too good looking to be real and not signed up to a movie studio or a model agency. Tall and athletic, a nice tan, deep blue eyes, even the classic cleft chin. Although his mother was also tall, she was forty or even fifty pounds overweight, a fact that a simple gray dress with long sleeves did nothing to disguise. She wore a single strand of pearls, and had small gold studs in her ears. Her hands were shapely with long slender fingers, surprising on such a large woman, and she wore only a single ring with a diamond. What little hair showed from under her hat was blond. Everything about her was discreet and in excellent taste, Barbara thought.

Terry Kurtz held his mother's chair as she seated herself, then waited by the second client chair until Barbara was seated before he sat down.

"What can I do for you?" Barbara asked.

"Ms. Holloway, I want to retain you to handle a very delicate matter for my family," Sarah Kurtz said.

Barbara shook her head. "I'm afraid I'm not free to represent any new clients at this time. You told my receptionist you wanted to discuss an incident where I happened to be on the scene. I'm sorry she didn't realize you wanted to retain me, or she would have informed you accordingly."

Sarah's lips tightened slightly and she said, "Am I to assume that Elizabeth has already retained you? That I might represent a conflict of interest?"

"I'm sorry, Mrs. Kurtz, but I will neither confirm nor deny any assumption you might make. I'm sure your firm already has an abundance of attorneys you are free to consult. Now, if you'll excuse me…"

"Hold on," Terry Kurtz said. "Look, Ms. Holloway, we're desperate to find Elizabeth and my son. And we don't want any publicity. None. When she gets in touch with you, please tell her I have to know my boy is all right, that he's safe. And tell her I demand the right to see my son. Our divorce agreement gave me visitation rights, and she can't refuse to let me have access to him."

Sarah Kurtz was sitting straight upright, as if ready to get to her feet. "Ms. Holloway, I don't know what story she told you. No doubt a pack of lies. Now hear the truth of the matter. She trapped my son, pursued him relentlessly, that cheap Spanish dancer. As soon as she got what she wanted from the union, the assurance of a child, she abandoned Terry and brought her lesbian lover into their apartment. And now she's engaged in some kind of illegal activity that has put my grandchild in mortal danger. We handled the affair very quietly some years ago. It was too ugly to take public, and she benefited handsomely from her settlement. Blackmail is a more appropriate word for it. It will not be so civil this time, I can assure you." She stood up and Terry jumped up from his chair and retrieved her coat, then held it for her.

Sarah Kurtz started to walk toward the door, then stopped and regarded Barbara. "Yes, I have resources, Ms. Holloway, and I won't hesitate to use them. Tell Elizabeth I fully intend to gain custody of my grandchild and ensure that he has a decent upbringing, a decent home. If she resists, I shall crush her in the process, and anyone who comes to her aid, as well. Good day."

Terry reached the door before she did and held it open for her to pass through. Without another glance at Barbara, they left.

An hour later Maria tapped again, and this time she said, "Terry Kurtz is on the line, Barbara. Do you want to speak with him?"

Barbara spread her hands in a what-the-hell gesture. "Why not? Put him on."

She picked up her own phone a second later when Maria buzzed. "Holloway," she said.

He sounded hesitant when he said, "Ms. Holloway, I apologize for this morning. Would it be possible to see you again? Alone? Just me this time?"

"I doubt I can be of any more help than I was earlier," she said coolly.

"I'd like to talk to you about what happened with Elizabeth," he said. "This morning wasn't the right time, I'm afraid."

She said, "Sure, come along," and he said fifteen minutes.

Although when he arrived this time his manners were as impeccable as before, he looked more like a college boy dreading a confrontation with a wrathful mentor than a self-assured man of the world. He fidgeted in his chair and looked past her at the wall as he said, "I'm afraid my mother is a little off her rocker these days. My dad had heart surgery last month, and he lingered in intensive care for weeks before he passed away. It was tough on my mother, and then for Elizabeth to take off without a word just added to her misery. She keeps going on that Jason and I are all she has left. Grandfather, her father, is nearly ninety, and she knows he could go any day, any hour. She's pretty upset."

Barbara did not say a word. Then, after a moment, Terry said, "Norris called the house about the attack, and we all thought it had to be Elizabeth and Jason. She knew about the cabin. We went there once, she and I. She knew where the key was and could get in. We all assumed that it was her, and when he said you were in the nearby cabin and you had found her, Mother got it in her head that Elizabeth must have met you there. Why else would you both suddenly be at the same isolated place like that? I don't know what she thinks you had to consult about, but there it is, what she believes."

He stopped studying the wall behind her and looked directly at her then. "How badly was she hurt?"

She told him what she had told everyone else. "I don't know that it was Elizabeth Kurtz. I don't know who she is."

"Didn't she say anything at all? Didn't the boy?"

She shook her head. "All he said was, 'Mama's hurt.' Not another word."

"She didn't see who attacked her?"

"Mr. Kurtz, I've told you everything I can about it. She was unconscious, or semiconscious at the best. I didn't try to question her."

He got up and began to walk about the office aimlessly. Turned away from her he said, "It must be wrenching, Ms. Holloway, how a man feels when his wife leaves him for another man, I guess, but it's a lot worse when she leaves for a woman. Funny thing is, I care about her. She didn't pursue me. We were both pursuers and pursued. One month together, then married. I thought it was one of those made in heaven marriages, perfect playmates, perfect lovers. Then I heard her talking on the phone to Leonora and I knew. But, I'd take her back tomorrow. I'd beg her to come back and try again. And I want my son nearby, where I can see him, watch him grow, take him to the ball game, or play ball with him. Read to him."

He returned to her desk, leaned on it, and looked directly at her. "I don't care what she's done, or what she's mixed up in. I want her back. When you see her, or hear from her, will you tell her that? I want her back desperately." He reached into his pocket and brought out a little notebook, jotted something in it and put the torn out page on her desk. "That's where we'll be for the coming weeks, Mother and I. It's the house Dad grew up in, left to him when his mother died four years ago. He kept putting off coming here to go through things, but Mother decided it was past time. I'll be helping her. Tell Elizabeth I'll meet her wherever she says, and I won't tell Mother a thing about it. If we can just meet, talk things over. That's all I'm asking."

Barbara did not touch the note he had dropped on her desk. She stood up and after a moment he turned, picked up his leather jacket and put it on.

She walked to the door with him, where he said, without looking at her, "I know you won't tell me anything else, but give her the message. That's all, just give her my message."

She opened the door, and he added, "Thanks for seeing me."

"And that's how it was," she said to Frank in his study later, after telling him about her visitors. She had left the office early, tired of mail that she was reluctant to answer, or unable to answer yet. Now fog was moving in, thick and penetratingly cold. "I spent a couple of hours on the Internet and learned more about prosthetics than I cared to know." She had been filled with revulsion to learn that the per capita number of amputations during the Iraq War far exceeded the average for past wars. Somehow, the fact that more of the wounded survived, due to better medical care, airlifts from battle zones to hospitals, failed to alleviate the horror of thinking of all those young people missing arms, legs, hands. The Diedricks Corporation profits were at an all-time high.

"The founder," she continued, "Henry Diedricks, was a true innovator apparently, a genius. He'd been an orthopedic surgeon, gave up his practice and began to make better prosthetics. And the rest, as they say, is history."

Frank nodded. He had spent a good deal of time researching the company, also. Now Diedricks was eighty-eight or eighty-nine, blinded and left partly paralyzed in a single-engine plane crash—his plane, which he had been piloting. The company innovations had slowed precipitously with his injuries thirteen years before, with only a few more developed and patented since then.

"Any word from Bailey yet?" Barbara asked, gazing at the fog-shrouded garden moodily.

"He had to get some associates to do some digging in New York," Frank said. "He'll come around on Friday morning. Apparently Elizabeth Kurtz lives, or lived in New York City, and why she ended up in that cabin is anyone's guess at this point. I think we can assume the woman was Elizabeth Kurtz."

"Well, everyone else does, we might as well go along with it," she said. "They all also assume that we met there by design with some ulterior motive."

"Well, keep in mind that the crime was against her, not committed by her, and until and unless she lodges a complaint, as far as the police are concerned there's little they can do regardless of what kind of pressure the family exerts."

"It depends on what's in the divorce decree, doesn't it? A visitation clause, an agreement not to leave the area without prior notification or even permission. They could still press for a kidnapping charge."

The fog was getting denser even as she watched; bushes and

trees were taking on a ghost-like appearance. She shivered. "I'd better be on my way while I can still see the streets."

"Your old room's available, dinner's coming up."

She shook her head. "Thanks, but I still have some mail to clear up. See you Friday morning." Minutes later, as she drove through town, Christmas lights here and there were taking on an ethereal appearance, like an aurora dance, forming, blue, gold, pink, then fading, forming, fading. Christmas, she thought, almost in surprise. She kept forgetting that in little more than two weeks it would be Christmas, and she had not even thought of shopping yet.

7

By Thursday Barbara could not keep up the pretense of accomplishing anything, and her conscience overcame her reason when she heard Shelley outlining her day to Maria. No office appointments. She would be in court until noon at least, then Martin's and, if there was time, she had a little more shopping to do.

"I'll take Martin's today," Barbara said. "You have enough on your plate."

Shelley tried but failed to hide her relief. Neither she nor Maria had asked Barbara anything since her return, and if they had noticed how little she was doing, that went unremarked, also.

"It's really okay," Shelley said. "I mean, things have been slow at Martin's these days. You know, Christmas coming, people have other things on their minds."

"Fine. So I'll surf the Internet and gab with Martin. Go on to court."

* * *

Martin's restaurant was decorated lavishly for Christmas
with lights, tiny star-studded trees on the tables, special
candles in pretty little red and green holders. It smelled good
with pastries in the oven already, and the fragrance of fresh
pine. Martin and Binnie were delighted to see her, and Martin
wanted to ply her with a special wine, which she refused. "If
I start drinking this early in the day, where will it lead?" He
laughed his booming laugh and poured her coffee instead.

"You're putting on weight," she said, eyeing him narrowly.
"You're turning into a big black bear stuffed for hibernation."

"Binnie's fault. Her pastries. I'm giving them up after the
holidays." Binnie laughed silently, a laugh that seemed to illu-
minate her face. She was mute, but her expressions were
eloquent; she could hide little of what she felt.

"And here comes your customer," Martin said then, and he
and Binnie went into the kitchen to resume prepping for the
dinner crowd later.

It was slow that day, with only two clients. At three o'clock,
Barbara closed her computer and stretched. She really should
go do some shopping, she was thinking, when the bell over
the door rang again and a man and woman entered together.

"Ms. Holloway?" he asked. "Are we too late to talk to you?"

"Nope. Have a seat." She waved at the chairs at her table.
The woman was thin, dark and intense looking, with sharp
features, wearing jeans and a sweatshirt, a denim jacket, no
jewelry or makeup. Her hands were red and chapped looking.
She took off her jacket and draped it over the back of her chair.
She looked young, mid- to late twenties. He was at least six
feet, with scant pale hair, black-framed eyeglasses, a heavy

multicolored sweater and black jeans. He wore a wedding ring. She guessed him to be early forties, but his thinning hair could have made him look older than he was.

"I'm Brice Knowlton, this is my sister Rita," he said.

Barbara nodded. "What can I do for you, Mr. Knowlton?"

"That's a problem," he said. "I'm not sure exactly. I'm a teacher at the University of Oregon, biology. She's an artist, pottery, things like that. I guess we just want a little advice. I can pay you," he added quickly.

"Why here? Why not the office?"

"We've read about you, how you talk to people here, advise them, without their having to make an appointment first. And we wanted to see you now, not wait a week or two, so we took a chance." He glanced at the door, as if afraid it would open and another client would interrupt. "It's about Elizabeth Kurtz," he said.

"I see," Barbara said, lying. She saw nothing, and felt as if the whole world, strangers off the street, wanted to talk to her about a woman she had never met. "Hold on a second." She got up, went to the door, and took down the Barbara Is In sign, then returned to her own chair.

Brice Knowlton visibly relaxed a little. "A couple of weeks ago we read that Joe Kurtz died, and his funeral was being held up in Portland, and that Elizabeth and Terry Kurtz had been divorced. That much was in the newspaper here. Then we heard that she was missing and that she had been attacked and you were on the scene, and we thought that if you were in touch with her, maybe you were our best bet to get in touch with her, too."

He said this all in a rush, then ran his hand through his thin hair and shook his head slightly. "That's all we want from you, a way to get in touch with her."

Barbara regarded him thoughtfully. "I grant that the funeral, and perhaps even the divorce were reported, but that she's missing? That she was attacked? I don't recall seeing a word about either in the newspapers."

Brice glanced at his sister, who tightened her lips and leaned back in her chair. "Go on," he said. "Tell her. It doesn't make any sense otherwise."

He sounded like a big brother ordering his little sister around, Barbara thought, watching them. She looked defiant, and he kept his gaze on her steadily. Then she shrugged and said, "My boyfriend works in the records department at city hall. They posted her picture and the kid's and they've sent it up and down the valley and coast. They're looking for them."

"The attack? Is that posted?" Barbara asked.

Rita shook her head. "No, but there's been talk at city hall, because you're involved somehow. They like to keep tabs on you, I guess. My boyfriend knows we're interested in the Kurtz bunch and he told me."

Well, if they had been serious about putting out an APB on her, that would have caused some talk, Barbara thought. She stood. "Let's have some fresh coffee," she said, going to the kitchen to ask Martin for it. He was already preparing a tray with cups and the carafe.

"Okay," she said, resuming her seat. Martin followed close behind her and put the things on the table, then quietly withdrew again. "There's got to be a little more than that. What's the rest of the story?" She poured coffee for Brice at his nod. His sister looked at it with disapproval and shook her head. An herbal tea type, Barbara thought, and refilled her own cup. She watched Brice, who seemed to be holding an interior monologue the way she had seen professors do in the past, as if gathering too many facts, too much data into a package that students could grasp.

When he spoke, evidently he was choosing his words very carefully. "We have reason to believe that some years ago there was a serious mishandling of certain papers that properly should have been released to our father. If Elizabeth has had a falling out with the Kurtz family, there is a possibility that she could come to our aid, since she is a trained scientist, one who understands the importance of provenance in such matters, and who would recognize how important those papers could be."

"Oh, knock it off!" Rita said, giving him a scornful look. She leaned forward, and her cheeks were suffused with color as she spoke. "It's a simple thing, not the long way around a barn without showing anyone the door. They stole from our father and she might be the first chink in the high wall their lawyers and their money built. They stole from him, and ruined him financially when he tried to get his rights back, and they destroyed his reputation. They destroyed him in every way. If I could gather them all in one big rotting pile and drop a bomb on them, I'd do it. If she's a decent person who was around them more than a day or two, she must know what they're like, and she might know something about what they did. And if she feels about them the way they deserve, she'll help us. She might want to drop that bomb herself."

"Rita! That's enough," Brice said. His voice was quiet, but it was the voice of an authority that she evidently recognized, and she subsided, leaned back in her chair again and crossed her arms over her chest.

"None of that is material to what we want," Brice said then to Barbara. "I don't know what your relationship is to Elizabeth Kurtz, if she's your client, whatever, and we don't need to know. Neither am I asking you to compromise yourself as an attorney. Just a simple request. That's really all I came for. Just a request for her to talk to us. Here. In your office, wherever it's convenient for her, and whenever she will."

He pulled out his wallet and took out a card, put it on the table. "My address, phone number at school and cell phone number. I can write you a check now, or you can send a statement to that address, whichever you prefer."

Barbara shook her head. "You don't owe me anything. Mr. Knowlton, Ms. Knowlton, please believe me, I have no way to get in touch with Elizabeth Kurtz. I can't pass your message on to her. I happened to be in the same area when she was attacked, that's all. Synchronicity. Coincidence. Happenstance. Just not by design. I never met her, never talked to her and I'm not even certain that the woman who was attacked was in fact Elizabeth Kurtz, although everyone seems to assume that she was."

"You just happened to be over there, that out-of-the-way place that no one ever heard of before?" A look of disbelief, then a cold look of withdrawal crossed his face, and stiffly he stood. "Sorry we've taken your time. Let's go," he said to Rita.

She was already on her feet, pulling on her jacket. Her look was contemptuous as she glanced at Barbara. "You're in their pocket. Dad was right. Find out how much the other guy is paying a lawyer, up it by a buck and you've got yourself an attorney, at least until the money runs out." She had marched to the door as she spoke, she yanked it open and walked out. Brice was at her heels.

Barbara continued to sit still for a moment, then slowly rose, all thoughts of shopping gone. She went to the kitchen door to tell Martin and Binnie she was leaving, and drove back to her office in deep thought. She couldn't blame them all for assuming that she and Elizabeth had planned to meet. It was an unlikely place, deserted, private. But this was a whole new wrinkle. It seemed that every time she thought a picture was forming in her mind, something came along to shatter it into unconnected shards.

At four she entered the reception room and waved to Maria, as she headed for her office.

Maria stopped her at the door. "Oh, Barbara, I just hung up. Elizabeth Kurtz called. She said she'd try again in ten minutes, just in case you returned. I told her I wasn't sure if you would."

"Thanks. Put her on the minute she calls back. No other calls until then. Finally, the elusive Elizabeth."

Two weeks ago to the day, she thought at her desk. Just two weeks since she had dragged the unconscious woman into the cabin. Now, she thought, maybe she'd get a few answers to questions that seemed to increase dramatically day by day.

It was a long ten minutes, but finally Maria buzzed.

"Barbara Holloway," she said. "Ms. Kurtz?"

"Yes. I have to talk to you. Are you free? Can I come now?"

"I want to talk to you, too," Barbara said. "Your former mother-in-law, your ex-husband and today two people named Knowlton all assume that we're in touch. It's time to make that a reality."

"They've been talking with you? Terry, his mother? Oh, my God! They'll be watching. I can't come there!" There was a pause, then she said, "I have an apartment. Will you meet me at the apartment? Don't tell anyone! Please, don't tell anyone where I am! What time do you usually leave? Don't draw attention or anything. They might be following you! Oh, God!"

"Calm down, Ms. Kurtz. Take it easy. I'll leave at five as usual. Traffic will be heavy, and I'll make sure no one is following me. Where are you? What's the address?"

Traffic was as heavy as she had known it would be at that time of day. She turned off Chambers onto Twelfth, stopped at the curb to make certain no one was following, then continued to Polk and turned again, this time heading for Eighteenth. An apartment complex near an Albertson's supermarket, Elizabeth Kurtz had said. That would be at Chambers, Barbara knew, and passed the address to park in the Albertson's lot. It was packed, and the fog was heavy again.

She was certain no one had followed her, and she walked back on Eighteenth to the apartments, six of them in a line. Elizabeth had said hers was first, closest to Eighteenth. Barbara rang the bell. Traffic noise was loud, and Christmas music was blaring from one of the apartments. She rang the bell again.

When no one came, in exasperation she tried the doorknob. The door swung open and she entered a dark apartment. A light from another room provided the only illumination. Barbara gasped.

A woman was lying on the floor near the door to the lighted room. Barbara ran across the living room and dropped to one knee to feel for a pulse, but when she touched the woman, she knew she was dead. She stood up and backed away, fighting nausea. Again, she thought dully.

This time most of her face had been destroyed by a wound to the head. Her hair was wrapped in a towel with a spreading red stain and more blood was under her cheek. She was wearing a pale bathrobe, her feet were bare. A bigger pool of blood was under her body.

The door suddenly flew open, and two uniformed police officers, and a sobbing woman entered. One of the officers had a drawn gun pointing at Barbara. The woman looked at the body on the floor and screamed.

8

"You might turn a chair away from the body and let her sit down," Barbara said to one of the officers, as the woman continued to scream, staring at the body as if paralyzed, unable to turn away. "And you might want to look around for a child. He could be hiding in a closet or something."

The other officer was on a cell phone, no doubt calling homicide. It was apparent that neither of them knew what to do about the hysterical woman. The one Barbara had spoken to turned a padded chair toward the window and touched the woman's arm. She screamed harder and Barbara went to her, took her arm and pushed her down into the chair. She stopped screaming, buried her face in her hands and shook with sobs. Barbara sat down in a nearby chair, facing the room, watchful.

"What's your name? Who is she?" the officer asked, nodding toward the dead woman.

"I don't know who she is. I assume it's Elizabeth Kurtz. I'm Barbara Holloway, and I haven't a clue about who she is." She pointed toward the sobbing woman.

"Do you know what happened?" he asked.

"No. I had only just got here when you guys came in."

He let it go at that and stood by the door as his partner went through the apartment, turning on lights. They were careful to keep clear of the victim, and touched as little as possible. There was no child.

Barbara pulled her cell phone from her purse and the officer told her to stow it. "I have to call my father. He's expecting me and he'll worry." She hit the speed dial button and ignored the officer, whose hand had moved toward his holstered gun. "Dad, it's me," she told his answering machine. "I'll be delayed, so you two go ahead without me. I think Elizabeth Kurtz has been killed and we're waiting for homicide to get here. I'll tell you about it later." Frank picked up as she spoke, but she broke the connection as the officer came toward her, as if he intended to grab the cell phone. "See, just to keep him from worrying. All done."

The homicide unit arrived, and Lt. Vern Standifer regarded her with a dour expression. They had met before, and she had never seen him smile. He was tall and underweight, with a fair complexion and gray eyes, and he had a pale mustache. "They said you were on the scene. What's the story?"

"I had an appointment with Elizabeth Kurtz at this address and when I walked in I found her on the floor. The officers and this woman came in immediately after me. And that's all I know about it."

"Right," he said skeptically. He pulled a straight chair around and sat before the other woman. She had quieted, with both hands pressed against her face. Now and then a convulsive ripple shook her whole body. "Miss, who are you? What's your name?"

"Leonora Carnero," she said in a faint, dull voice. Barbara looked at her more closely, remembering what Terry Kurtz had said. He'd heard Elizabeth talking to Leonora and he knew. Leonora had black hair in tumbling curls about her face, nearly to her eyes, and she was dressed in jeans, a loose jacket, sneakers, the same kind of clothes Barbara wore when flying. She glanced toward the door where there was a roll-on suitcase with a garish red and yellow tie and an airline baggage claim on the handle, along with a small, wine-colored carry-on.

"I flew in and she said to come here and when I came in, she was..." She began to sob again. Then, brokenly, she said, "I was sick, vomiting, and crying, and I had to call Mother and tell her, but I couldn't find a telephone. And she said I had to call the police. I couldn't find this address. Mother said to call the police. I had to look in her purse for the address book, and she was dead and I had to call Mother..."

"Hold it, Ms. Carnero. You came here and found the victim, is that right?"

"She said to come here. I flew here. I didn't want the police to tell Mother or for her to see it on the news and I couldn't find her number. Her room, her things, on the floor, everywhere. I had to look in her purse for the number, and I was sick..." She lifted her head from her hands and stared straight ahead, with her nose dripping, tears running down her face. "I had to call Mother."

"Let it go, Standifer," Barbara said. "She's in shock, hysterical. Get her out of here and give her a little time." Then she said, "Ms. Carnero, did you fly here from New York today?"

"She said to come and bring the passports and I found her." She swiveled about in her chair, and said in a voice that sounded almost robotic, "Mother said not to let Terry touch her, or get near her. Mother will come. She said she will come." She stood, swayed and clutched the arm of her chair, then sat and began to sob again. "Mother will come."

Barbara shook her head at Standifer. "You'd better have someone take her to a motel or something, let her calm down. You know the drill here. The medical examiner, forensics, it's going to take hours and you're not going to get anything from her while all that's going on. Keep at her and she will collapse altogether. Flying all day, probably no food, vomiting, now this. She's ready to keel over."

Reluctantly he pushed his chair back and stood.

In a few minutes a female officer led Leonora away. After a short consultation with Standifer, a plainclothes detective took her bags out. When they were gone, Barbara stood. "It's going to be a while before the medical examiner gets here. I might as well go to Dad's house and wait for you there if you have questions for me. Or else, I have to sit in this chair in everyone's way, and cool my heels while you follow the proper protocol. You know where Dad lives. I'll be there."

For a moment he regarded her with a hostile expression, but he knew she was right; she would simply be in the way here, and there was nowhere else to wait.

"Tell me again how you came to be here," he said brusquely.

She shrugged. "We had an appointment, no one answered

the bell and I tried the door. It wasn't locked. I came in and saw her, felt for a pulse and then Carnero and the officers got here. I didn't go into any other room and doubt that I touched anything except her neck, the door, the bell and this chair."

He didn't like it, but she was in the way and would be more so when the forensics crew got there and went about their business. He let her go, and told her to wait at Frank's house as if it had been his own idea.

"Christ on a mountain," Frank said softly. "Shot?"

Barbara nodded. "Twice, in the midsection and again in the face, the side of her face." She shuddered. "I have to go wash my hands. I touched her."

He took her jacket and she went to scrub her hands. He was by the fire in the living room when she returned, coffee cups and a carafe on the table. He poured for her and motioned toward the chair nearest the fire, and she realized that she was still shivering, not just from the penetrating chill of the fog outside, but from deep inside.

"Bailey's on his way," Frank said, sitting opposite her. "You want to wait to tell us together?"

"I'm all right," she said. "Cold." She began to tell him about Elizabeth's phone call, and was still at it when Bailey arrived. She started over after Bailey was seated with a drink in his hand.

"That was at ten after four. I got there about an hour later, ten after five, and she was dead. From what she said, I assumed that no one knew where she was, or even if she was around. She said that someone could be watching the office and she was afraid to go there, and afraid someone would follow me. No one followed, they got there first."

"The window of opportunity wasn't open long," Bailey commented.

"Less than you think," Barbara said after a moment. "The call to me was at ten after four. She was ready at that time to come to the office, and changed her mind. Then she went in to take a shower. I could smell a shampoo fragrance, and her hair was done up in a towel. One light was on, probably in the bedroom, maybe the bathroom. She put on a robe, but no slippers after the shower. Let's say that took ten minutes at least, more like fifteen. About four-thirty by then, and we don't know when Leonora found her. Check the flights in," she added to Bailey. "Allow time to collect luggage, rent a car, find the apartment. Anyway, from four-thirty until Leonora got there was the window of opportunity. Half an hour? Maybe." She thought a moment, then said, "Leonora wasn't making much sense, but she said that in the bedroom things were on the floor, tossed around. A search? Could be. That's cutting it really close. If she had arrived minutes sooner, she might have become a second body on the floor."

And if Barbara had arrived earlier, she might have been there, too, Frank thought. He got up to give the fire a poke it didn't need.

"I can tell you a little about Leonora Carnero," Bailey said.

Barbara shook her head. "After I talk to the cops. I intend to tell them every single thing I know about all this. Let's not add to it yet. See what you can dig up about the Knowltons and their father."

He nodded. He had already made a note about Brice and Rita Knowlton.

"How old's the Carnero woman?" Frank asked then.

"I don't know," Barbara said. "Thirty, thirty-five."

"Thirty-four," Bailey said.

"Doesn't make much sense," Frank said. "Her first thought was to go call her mother."

"Good trick," Bailey muttered. "Her mother's dead."

Barbara stared at him. "She said her mother's coming," she said softly. "She said it several times."

"Even a better trick," Bailey said.

Frank glanced at his watch. "Let's have a bite to eat before the investigators get here. I suspect it's going to be a long night." Barbara had said that Standifer hadn't seemed to know about the attack from two weeks earlier, but whoever came to question her no doubt would. A long night was certainly in store for them.

Bailey looked hopeful and Frank nodded. "You, too. It's mostly leftovers, but of what there is, there's plenty."

He had combined leftover chicken and vegetables—green beans, peas, a little asparagus—added noodles and a cream sauce and put it in the oven after Barbara's call, and as he had said, there was plenty and it was delicious.

It was eight-thirty before the doorbell rang again. Bailey and Barbara waited by the fire for Frank to admit the detective. She groaned when she heard Frank say, "Evening, Milt. I'll hang your jacket. Nasty night."

Milt Hoggarth was in his fifties, overworked and looking it, and that night he was scowling fiercely, first at Barbara, then at Bailey. "I'll talk to you alone," he said. He had fading red hair receding fast and a florid complexion. The cold air that night had made his face redder than usual.

"Don't be silly," Barbara said, waving toward a chair. "Dad's my lawyer, and we'll tell Bailey every word said here, as you know. Do you want coffee?" She was having a glass of wine, but he always turned down wine, beer, or anything more potent than coffee. "What happened to Standifer? Did I scare him off?"

"I'm assigned to the case," he said, eyeing the cats that had gotten up to greet him. He seemed to believe they were closer to mountain lions than domestic pets, and that they might go into attack mode any second.

Grudgingly he sat down, leaned forward and said, "So, give."

"Right." She told him everything she knew without omitting a detail, and he was as disbelieving as everyone else had been. Absently he helped himself to coffee and did not interrupt a single time.

"So there it is," Barbara said. "I never met Elizabeth Kurtz, and the only words I heard from her were on the telephone this afternoon. But since I got home on Monday, there's been a parade of people demanding I produce her, or put them in touch, or something else. Sorry, no can do."

Hoggarth started at the beginning with his questions. Why did she stop at that cabin? Where had she been in California, doing what? Where did she go after leaving the cabin? He was as thorough as Janowsky, the state police lieutenant, had been, and as skeptical of her answers.

"Today, on the phone, tell me again exactly what she said."

Barbara did so. Just doing his job, she reminded herself more than once and kept her temper in check as she went over the same details again.

"So maybe still another person has been looking for her, and that one found her," she added. "Or—" She straightened in her chair and carefully put her wineglass down on the table. "Or someone could have a bug on my phone."

"I'll have it checked out," Hoggarth said, as skeptical as ever.

She glanced at Bailey and he nodded slightly. So would he.

"Was she your client?" Hoggarth asked.

"Listen to me, Hoggarth. I never met her. I never spoke to her until today, and never corresponded in any way with her. What about that is it you don't understand? I don't have a client. I'm thinking of retiring, maybe do some teaching."

He made a rude sound and his scowl deepened. He poured more coffee.

"Was it a bullet wound?" Frank asked.

"Yeah. No gun around."

"Had someone searched the apartment?" Barbara asked.

"What makes you think that?" he demanded.

"Something Leonora Carnero said. That things were on the floor, messed up in the bedroom. It sounded as though the place had been tossed."

He nodded. "Yeah."

"No sign of the child? His belongings, anything?" Barbara asked.

"She didn't have a kid with her. No one saw a kid around."

"If that was Elizabeth Kurtz, there has to be a child around somewhere," Barbara said. "Where is he?"

"What do you mean if?" Hoggarth asked.

"For God's sake! I never met her, remember? People keep telling me that's who she is. At the cabin her face was muddy, bloody, swollen. And you must have seen her face tonight. I couldn't identify her from what I've seen either time. But there was a child at the cabin. Where is he? What happened to him?"

9

Hoggarth left at ten-thirty, dissatisfied with Barbara, with her answers to his questions and not at all happy to have had a new homicide investigation dumped on him right before Christmas. At the door on his way out, he stopped and glowered at her. "You'd better plan to stay around for awhile."

"No travel plans in sight," she said. His frown deepened and he stomped out.

"Funny, isn't it?" Barbara commented. "This might be the first time in our cordial relationship that I came absolutely clean the first time around with him, and he didn't believe a word I said. So much for sticking to the truth."

Bailey downed the same drink he had been nursing all evening and set the glass on the table. "You want what I have now, or wait for morning?"

"Now, by all means," Barbara said and Frank nodded.

"Just the high points," Bailey said. "Elizabeth Littleton Kurtz. Thirty-four. Master's degree in zoology from Stanford. Undergrad at Johns Hopkins. National Science Merit Scholarship winner. Married Terry Kurtz in Spain about six years ago, divorced roughly two years later. Their son was six months old. Works as an editor for a publisher of science books, text books. Mother from Spain, father an undersecretary or something at the UN until his death when she was about eleven. Mother back in Spain now, remarried." He paused a second or two, then continued in the same kind of rapid-fire, nearly staccato recitation. "Leonora Carnero, also thirty-four, mother Puerto Rican, dad American. Mother took off when she was twelve, and she moved in with Elizabeth and her mother and grew up in their household. Divorced, lives in same apartment with Elizabeth. Works for an insurance group."

He gave Barbara a knowing look. "Elizabeth knew how to hide. Took off from her job, left the city with son Jason back in October and not a trace of her until she showed up in that cabin. If that was her. No credit card, no cell phone use, nothing, zilch."

"Your guys in New York looked beyond the obvious?" Barbara asked. "Not much time to check cell phone and such."

"There was time, especially when nothing was showing up. No airline reservations, train reservations, bus tickets in her name. Like I said. Nothing."

"She must have driven, used cash everywhere," Barbara said after a moment. "She knew someone was looking for her."

"After withdrawing ten grand in New York, she sold a BMW in Philadelphia, got cash, so she had plenty with her. Probably paid cash for something else somewhere else and headed for the west coast," Bailey said with a shrug.

"What about the company?" Frank asked. "Anything there?"

"Not much. Henry Diedricks started it, and apparently his inventions, innovations, whatever, made him famous in the prosthetics sphere. He's from Portland, the company started there, and the research and development bunch is still there. They opened a production plant in New Jersey seven or eight years ago, and moved corporate headquarters to New York City. Business is booming. Diedricks is out of the picture, old, demented, in a wheelchair, blind. Two kids. Daughter Sarah married Joseph Kurtz, a researcher in charge of R&D. She's a social creature, has nothing to do with the business apparently, and her son Terry is the original best catch bachelor of the year, even if he has been married. Diedricks's son Lawrence runs the sales department, hangs out on the East Coast for the most part. Kurtz was back and forth a lot over the years. He died in November. The whole family is in the state for now. They came for the funeral and are hanging around."

Neither Barbara nor her father had any significant questions. They both knew Bailey's full report would have whatever details his New York contacts had been able to provide.

"Okay," Barbara said, "let's call it a day. Tomorrow, the possible phone tap, and the Knowltons, all of them. The plane arrival time, if she rented a car." She glanced at Frank. "Anything else?"

He nodded. "Check all the phones, her apartment included," he said to Bailey, motioning toward Barbara. "And this one. She'll stay here tonight."

"Dad—"

He leveled his gaze at her. "Someone's putting a lot of resources into whatever is going on. If they tracked that woman to the cabin, they're both resourceful and willing to spend a good deal of money. And you were on the scene at the cabin. Then you both dropped out of sight again for days. They don't know if you and Elizabeth Kurtz planned that or not. If they learned her location from her telephone call to you, it means they were primed and ready to seize the opportunity instantly. Let Bailey check some things out before you go back to your apartment."

Her room in his house was always ready for her. The same old three-quarter size bed she had used from the time she left a crib until she went away to school. The same lovely patchwork quilt one of Frank's clients had made for her many years before, the same comforting Raggedy Ann doll forever sprawled on the wide window seat, a few clothes in the closet, things in drawers, a new toothbrush, her favorite Monet print on the wall.

In spite of what should have provided a return to the safety of another age, another self, she was a long time in settling down, in quieting her thoughts that night. Looking at it all from an outsider's view, she didn't blame anyone for not believing her. She could think of no less likely place for two separate women to have chosen to visit in winter. If only she had not seen that For Rent sign, if only she had not turned off the highway that day. She rolled over and tried another line of thought.

She should have pursued it, followed up, not just run from

the situation at the cabin, letting the locals handle it as best they could. She might have done something. What? She demanded of herself. There was no answer.

Where was the child? Out running away in the fog? Hiding in the neighborhood? Tears streaming down his face? Cowering.

The image of that shattered face morphed into the bloody face streaming water mixed with blood, morphed back to the ruined face in the apartment. Elizabeth had known how to run and hide, but someone had caught up with her in the end.

She rolled over again. How could anyone have managed that brief window of time? Someone close by? A mad dash to the apartment, two shots, a quick search, then out.

Her next thought brought a sharp pang of desire. What was Darren doing these lonely nights? Did he go into the little apartment over the garage where they had lost themselves time and again? Did he sit at the table, remembering?

She hugged her arms about her chest and squeezed her eyes shut as tightly as possible and willed sleep to come, to stop the whirlpool of thoughts that, regardless of where the maelstrom started, always ended up with Darren. She rolled over again, then again.

Frank took one look at her the next morning and without a word motioned to a chair at the table and poured a cup of coffee. The newspaper was open on the table with Elizabeth's picture, and the headline Murder Victim.

Below it was the picture of Jason Kurtz with its own headline, Where is Jason?

Frank removed the newspaper, poured a second cup of coffee and sat down opposite her.

"It will keep until later," he said, indicating the newspaper. "Are you up to eggs? Pancakes? French toast?"

"Later," she said. She sighed. "It's an unholy mess, isn't it?"

"Yep. I issued a statement in your name. 'No comment at this time.' That's enough, but it won't hold them. I think you'd better stay away from the office today, let things cool off a little. I turned off the telephone ringer, but messages are piling up. Also, I called Shelley and told her if she has to get in touch, to use her cell phone and call mine. I left the same message for Bailey. At least my number isn't public, and I know damn well it hasn't been tapped."

She nodded and sipped her coffee. After a moment Frank stood up. "At least a piece of toast. The rest can wait a while." He crossed the kitchen and put bread in the toaster, poured orange juice and put it down before her.

She drank the juice, but when he brought the buttered toast, she had little appetite for it. An unholy mess, she kept thinking. The newspaper accounts, television accounts, everyone would think exactly what the police thought, that she was lying, that she knew a lot more than she was telling, or, worse, that she was criminally involved somehow. And there was not a thing she could do about it.

Frank pulled his cell phone from his pocket and spoke into it. It must have buzzed him, with the ring muted. She knew how much he hated the things, and realized again how seriously he was taking this if he was willing to use his. He said it wasn't natural to hold it to his ear and speak into the air. He wanted something he could really hold, a mouthpiece and a real ear piece. He listened without comment, then said, "Right. Thanks." He broke the connection and replaced the phone in his pocket.

"Bailey. Hoggarth's team found a tap on your office line. No receiving station nearby. They packed up the tent and left apparently. Also, Leonora Carnero's plane landed at three-thirty."

"How long could it have taken to claim her bag and rent a car? Drive to the apartment?" Barbara said slowly. The drive would not have taken more than twenty minutes, not at that time of day. Another twenty at the terminal? She should have reached the apartment no later than ten or fifteen minutes after four.

"I think that window of opportunity might be closing all the way," Frank said.

"But where the hell could she have gotten a gun? She couldn't have brought one on the plane."

He shrugged. "Maybe it was Elizabeth Kurtz's gun."

At ten Shelley called. Frank answered his phone, then found Barbara in the living room pretending to read a book. He handed her his cell phone.

"Barbara, are you all right? Is there anything I can do? Or that Maria can do? Except dodge reporters, I mean."

"I'm fine," Barbara said. "Just staying out sight for now. What's up?"

"A woman called, Ashley Dakota. She says she runs a shelter for women in Salem, and she wants to talk to you about Elizabeth Kurtz."

Barbara closed her eyes. Strangers off the street wanted to talk to her about Elizabeth. It was still happening. "Did she leave a number?"

"Yes. She said she's on her way down here, on I-5. She'll be in town by eleven." Shelley read the cell number. "I just told her I'd see that you got the message, that's all."

"Exactly right," Barbara said. "Thanks. I'll call her."

Ashley Dakota was what Barbara thought of as a feather-duster type of woman, with soft fluttering hands that seemed to itch to reach out and smooth, pat, stroke, minister to whomever she was talking to. She was slightly built, in her sixties, with gray wispy hair in an untidy bun. Frank took her coat and hung it up and they went to the living room, where she stopped moving when she saw the two cats.

"My, my," she murmured. "They are gorgeous! I'm envious."

Seated with Thing One on her lap, she said to Barbara, "I know about the work you do down here, of course. I imagine everyone connected with shelter houses does. Such good work. Anyway, I read about the murder in the paper this morning. That poor woman. And the account hinted that you had secreted her away somewhere after she was attacked the first time. I just felt I had to tell the police it isn't true." Thing One was purring loudly as she stroked him, and she smiled and used both hands. "But it's a difficult problem. They must be discreet if I tell them. I can't have the public know the location of the shelter, of course."

"What can you tell us about her?" Barbara asked.

"Well, I thought I should tell you first, in case they say I must not talk about it. If I already told you, that is moot, now isn't it? But I kept thinking that if you were her attorney, you have a right to know, and they don't always divulge what they learn, do they?"

Before Barbara could repeat what she had said so many

times that it was sounding like a mantra, Frank said heartily, "Ms. Dakota, you are correct. She has a right to know."

"Perhaps I should speak to you alone," Ashley said to Barbara. She smiled at Frank, as if to soften it, not to offend him.

"My father is my colleague," Barbara said. "We often work together. You are perfectly free to speak with him present."

"Well," she said doubtfully. Frank smiled at her and she went on. "I know where she was from November twenty-fifth and the next five days. She was at the shelter. She came to the door on Friday in the afternoon, nearly falling down, stagger-ing and deathly pale. It's a wonder she had been able to drive in that condition. The little boy, Jason, was fine, just tired and hungry. We put her to bed, and I called the doctor. He put stitches in a cut and looked her over. She slept all afternoon, and much of the next day, and then she was much, much better. Jason is a little darling. Everyone fell in love with him. I didn't ask any questions, of course. I assumed a domestic bat-tering, you know. And we moved her car out of sight. Some-times they come looking, you know. She didn't say anything about what happened, who did it or anything else. But she was really nice. I suggested that she should call the police, get a restraining order, you know, but she said she would take care of things. When I came down on the sixth morning, they said she had gone before dawn. She left five hundred dollars on the table by her bed, and a note that said "Thank you." That's all it said."

Frank stood. "Ms. Dakota, can I get you a cup of tea? Coffee?"

Barbara knew what that meant. He wanted to ask some questions.

Ashley said, "Tea would be lovely."

She had little to add, however. She was positive it was Elizabeth Kurtz, no doubt about it. That lovely hair. "They had to cut a little, for the stitches, you know, but after she had a shampoo, it was beautiful hair, a little wavy. And those eyelashes! Lashes to die for, one of the girls said." They cleaned up her car, did a little laundry, just little things. She had not looked inside Elizabeth's purse, she said, clearly shocked by the question when Frank asked it.

"We respect the privacy of women who need our help," she said sternly. "That would be most inappropriate. They tell as much or as little as they are comfortable with, and they are safe. That's what matters. They are safe." She stopped, looking stricken. Then she said faintly, "At least, they are safe for a time."

That afternoon Bailey came to inspect the telephones, and the outside wire. "You're clean," he told Frank, then said to Barbara. "You had a tap on the office line and the apartment, too."

"No operators around?" Frank asked. A tap meant someone was listening to the calls, not just taping them.

"Nope. A green closed panel van was parked over by the REI store all week, gone now. And an SUV was at the apartment complex, also gone."

"So someone knew at four that Elizabeth was trying to get in touch, and that she would call back in ten minutes," Barbara said. "That opens the window a little more, doesn't it? Make plans, get ready to act, whatever."

"Maybe," Frank said.

"Do you know where they took Leonora?" Barbara asked Bailey.

He shook his head. "They're keeping her under wraps. Not arrested, just out of reach. The manager of the rental apartments said Kurtz got there Tuesday afternoon, and there was no kid with her. And she said she was expecting a woman friend to join her so she wanted a two-bed apartment for one week. That's the kind of place it is, weekly rentals for vacationers, people here on business or conventions, things like that, families that don't want a hotel room. She paid in cash and he handed over the key. Done."

"The question now is where was she from Wednesday when she left the shelter until she showed up in Eugene on the following Tuesday? And what did she do with Jason?" Barbara said.

"Remember, she had stitches that had to come out," Frank said. "Apparently they were both too distinctive looking not to be noticed along the way. I expect they'll track her down." He fervently hoped that was so, and that wherever she had been made it impossible for her to have met Barbara during those days.

Late that afternoon Hoggarth and the state investigator showed up. Janowsky was again in his heavy tweed suit that now had beads of moisture on it. The fog had returned, so thick that droplets formed on surfaces, like rain that didn't fall so much as materialize.

"Shelley said you were staying over here," Hoggarth said by way of explanation. "We have a few questions for you."

"I thought that was the case," Barbara said, motioning

toward the living room she had just wandered out of, after spending another hour trying to focus on printed words in a book that she forgot the instant she put down. Thing One and Thing Two were on the two chairs nearest the fire, and to all appearances not willing to yield them to newcomers.

Hoggarth eyed them warily and chose the end of the sofa, and Janowsky unceremoniously pushed one of them off a chair and took it himself. Frank joined them, and without any preliminary discussion, Janowsky asked, "Did you tell Elizabeth Kurtz to go to the Dakota Shelter House when she left the cabin? Did you give her the address?"

10

"I told you everything I know about Elizabeth Kurtz. I've already told you every word I said to her, that I was going to go get help, she needed a doctor and my name. And that's all I said to her." Barbara's voice was steady, but there was a furious set to her mouth and a dangerous gleam in her eyes.

Frank cleared his throat. "Gentlemen, I suggest that you get to the point of this visit."

Hoggarth spoke up for the first time. "Why did Ashley Dakota come straight here after she read about Kurtz's death?"

"Ask her," Barbara snapped.

"I did. She said because you were Elizabeth Kurtz's attorney."

"Ms. Holloway, if you know where Jason Kurtz is, tell us now, for your own sake as well as his," Janowsky said.

"How many ways are there to tell you the same thing?" she said coldly. "You want it with music?"

"You checked into your Astoria motel on Monday night. Did you meet Elizabeth Kurtz on the following days?" Janowsky asked.

"No."

"Can you explain how Kurtz drove straight to that shelter house?" Hoggarth said, not really a question, since he seemed to know she would not treat it as such. "She was in Oregon one time in her life according to her ex-husband, and they drove down the coast that one time, nearly six years ago. Never in Salem in her life, yet she went straight there. Someone told her about it."

Barbara stood up. "I've told you all I can. Excuse me." She walked from the room without a backward glance.

Hoggarth did not appear surprised, but Janowsky was clearly infuriated. He stood, almost unnaturally stiff and rigid. "Mr. Holloway, please advise your client that withholding information in a kidnapping is a very serious charge, obstructing justice even more so."

"I'll be sure to tell her," Frank said. Hoggarth rose then and unless he was very mistaken, Frank thought, the lieutenant was suppressing a grin. Well, they went back a few years and little that Barbara did would surprise him, but more, no doubt he was sore that the state investigators were intruding on what he thought of as his turf. As little as he wanted one more case, he wanted state investigators to take over even less.

Frank saw the two lieutenants to the door and out, then waited as a delivery man with a large floral arrangement approached.

"If they come back, don't let them in unless they have a warrant," Barbara said, coming from the kitchen. She stopped when she saw the flowers.

"For you," Frank said, handing her a small envelope with a card.

She removed the card and read it silently. "If there's anything I can do, I'm here."

That was all. No name, no salutation. Without a word, she turned and went back through the hall, then up the stairs, taking the card with her.

A few minutes later, when she came down again, she was wearing her jacket, carrying her laptop and her keys were in her hand. "I've imposed long enough," she said at the door to the kitchen where Frank was considering dinner.

"Barbara—"he started, but she cut him off. He didn't offer to give her the flowers, or even to mention them. And she did not refer to them.

"I'm going home. With the fuzz popping in every hour or so, I think it's safe enough," she said brusquely.

He didn't argue with her. There were times when it was a mistake to argue, he knew, and this was one. He nodded. "Sunday night as usual?"

"Sure," she said.

After she was gone, he cursed softly. If he was a kicking-the-cat sort of man, he knew both cats would be behind the moon by then. Darren had sent the flowers, he knew without a doubt, and there had not been a call, not a word about or from him until now. And he would never know what had happened between them. He cursed again. She had become almost rigid as she read the card, an attitude of inflexible rejection, or else withdrawing as far as possible in order to hide whatever she was feeling. And he didn't know which was the right interpretation.

He had a great deal of sympathy for Darren, and a growing frustration with his stubborn daughter. Not just frustration, he realized with surprise. Anger. The more sympathetic
he felt toward Darren, the greater his anger at her grew.
Darren's son Todd was going on fifteen. In a few years he
would be off to school, then gone, and Darren would be
kicking around alone in his nice house. She would be alone
in her barren apartment. "Damn fools!" he muttered.
"Goddamn fools!"

On Monday morning Bailey was as morose as always,
swathed in his hideous yak coat and equally hideous woolen
cap. "It's going to snow," he said gloomily, shedding the coat.
"They're saying it will miss us, a sure cue that we're in for it."

Frank, already seated with coffee in his hand, nodded agreement. It was snowing in Portland, and as far south as Salem.
In Eugene it was a freezing rain, with the temperature not
quite cold enough for it to start coating everything in a glaze.
Just right for snow. Barbara had said earlier that Shelley called
to report it was snowing out at their place in the foothills of
the coast range. She wouldn't make it in that day.

Bailey helped himself to the coffee and pulled his old duffle
bag closer to his chair.

"Okay, so that's the weather report for the day. What do you
have?" Barbara asked impatiently.

"Lot of stuff," he said. "One, Elizabeth Kurtz's mother
Beatriz Cortezar flew in from Spain on Saturday and identified and claimed the body yesterday." He shrugged. "She
ordered cremation, and she'll take the remains home to Spain
for a burial in her family plot."

Barbara knew Bailey had a contact at the police department, one who served up reliable information from time to
time. She had no idea what the payoff was, although it was one
of the charges included under miscellaneous when Bailey presented his bill. She never questioned it. Neither would Frank
now, and it was his party, she reminded herself. He had a
client, she didn't.

"Cortezar insisted on removing Leonora from the place
they were keeping her and putting her in an apartment, one
they'll share until she returns home. I have the address." He
motioned toward the duffel bag. "Leonora calls her Mother,
and is treated exactly like a daughter. And get this, Cortezar
is loaded. Her family's had an olive plantation for generations, and she married this guy named Fernando Cortezar, and
his family had an even bigger olive plantation, and now they
have an olive empire or something." He drank his coffee and
said, "King of the olives. I guess the kid is an olive branch."

Barbara gave him a murderous look, and he shrugged.
"Okay. Knowlton. Might be something there. When Diedricks cracked up in his plane, he wasn't expected to make it,
and probably shouldn't have. Really banged up, needed a lot
of surgeries, like that. Seems he and Jefferson Knowlton had
worked together on some stuff they got patents on. Then
when it was clear that Diedricks would never work again,
Knowlton claimed the company stole his ideas. It was kept
pretty quiet by a pack of attorneys, but it made the business
section of the newspapers. Knowlton didn't have a leg to
stand on. No paperwork, no notes, nothing but his word, and
no one believed him. Diedricks didn't back him up. Knowlton
kept at it for a couple of years, then dropped out of sight. Left

Portland, had a breakdown or something, and moved to Eugene with his wife and kids, dead broke. That was his son, Brice, and daughter, Rita, that you met."

"Other employees must have seen them working together," Barbara said.

"They went to that cabin, or worked in Diedricks's house. There's a big spread in the hills southwest of Portland, sixty or seventy acres. The family said Knowlton was a draftsman, not a coinventor. Then Joseph Kurtz finished a couple of the ideas Diedricks had been working on, and his name is on the patents along with Diedricks's. Knowlton was all the way out of it."

He pulled a notebook from his pocket and consulted it. "They're scouring the neighborhood around that Eighteenth Street apartment for a gun. A Luger. And they have a crew going up and down I-5 trying to find out where Kurtz bought gas, where she and the kid ate. Paying a lot of attention to the Astoria area. And, finally, Leonora Carnero made arrangements for a car rental at the same time she made plane reservations, a package deal. All she had to do here was sign papers, five minutes."

And that would put her in the apartment even earlier, Barbara thought, before Elizabeth called about an appointment possibly. If they found a gun, that would be it. How the gun got there—Elizabeth's or smuggled on board the plane by Leonora—would be irrelevant.

"Along about now you should be glad she isn't your client," Bailey said, closing his notebook, returning it to his pocket.

She nodded. She was glad. "There is still that green van and the guys who took off the minute they got the address," she said.

He shook his head. "I doubt it. Guys who do surveillance don't usually fill in for hit men on the side." He drained his cup, then opened his duffle bag to get his full reports. "Anything else?"

"Not for me. His show." Barbara jerked her thumb toward Frank.

"Let us know if they find a gun, or if they track down the child," Frank said. "Then we wait for developments."

Bailey left to hole up at home, he said, and wait for the snow to fall and then to melt.

As Frank put on his overcoat Barbara said, "I wish I knew what Elizabeth told Leonora. This thing will wind down and I'll never know a thing about what was going on."

"None of your business," Frank commented. "Leave it at that."

"It's the little boy," she said. "Where is he? If she didn't have pals here, didn't know anyone, here just once in her life, what could she have done with the boy? They're making a case that I'm the only one she could have talked to about him, and everything else apparently."

He nodded. It wasn't the child she should be concerned about at the moment, he thought. He fully expected Janowsky to demand a formal sworn statement from her, possibly even a deposition, and how well she would handle it could be a problem. He knew without a second thought that she would be a terrible witness for herself.

After Frank left, Barbara stood at the office window watching for snow, but it was still rain or sleet, no matter what her weather expert said. She remembered that as a child she had called sleet silver rain. Exactly right, she thought at the window. Shopping, she said under her breath. There wasn't a thing to do in the office that needed doing today, but there was shopping to be done. Decisively she stuffed Bailey's reports into her briefcase, then paused momentarily wondering why she had them and not Frank. No matter. She told Maria to take off.

"Go bake Christmas cookies or something. I'm closing shop for the rest of the day."

It felt like snow, she thought outside, and it smelled like snow, but not yet. She got into her car and headed for the university bookstore where she usually found books the chains didn't stock.

For the next two hours, she chose gifts. A book of dolls from around the world down through the ages was perfect for Shelley. The Russian doll within a doll within a doll, Japanese geishas, straw and wood fetish dolls from the Yanomamo tribes of Brazil, porcelain dolls from China—she started to read the text, and forced herself to stop. But she would read it before she wrapped it, she decided. For Dr. Minnick, Darwin's exploration, notes and drawings from the Galapagos. The world's most fabulist natural places for Todd—waterfalls, mountain lakes, an underwater grotto. The two-volume set by Jared Diamond, *Guns, Germs and Steel,* and *Collapse* for Alex. Suddenly she stopped scanning the shelves. A book for Todd? She bit her lip but did not remove the book from her basket. She moved on to a complete Sherlock Holmes collection for Maria. An audio book for Maria's mother, who could not sit still to read, but would listen as she did mending, ironing, cooking, knitting or something else useful. For Maria's daughters? She didn't even know if they were readers. Busy teen-agers, did either of them actually sit down and read? Ask Maria, she decided and moved on.

Then she stopped again. Halfway down the next aisle Brice Knowlton stood, regarding her with a cool appraising look that, while not overtly hostile, was not friendly, either.

She took another step forward, then said, "Mr. Knowlton, can we talk a few minutes?"

"Why? What's to say? Elizabeth Kurtz is dead and out of reach. I don't have any other business with you."

"She's dead, and everyone keeps trying to involve me whether or not I belong in the picture. I'd like to learn the truth about your father and the Diedricks Corporation if you're willing to tell me about it."

"Again, why? If you're not involved, what's it to you?" They both moved aside as several other customers came down the aisle. She waited until they were past.

"I don't know. I assume you read the newspaper and know that they keep pulling me in in spite of what I say. I'd just like a little more information than I have." Three students, talking, turned down the aisle.

After they had passed, he nodded. "Sure. Quid pro quo. Isn't that the term?"

"It is."

"Where are you parked?"

She told him behind the store, and he said, "You can't stay there or they'll ticket you. Let's go to the Excelsior for coffee. You can drive and then bring me back to get my car. It's just a few blocks."

She checked out her purchases and they both pulled up

hoods against the steady silver rain and hurried to her car. He directed her the few blocks to the alley behind the restaurant where there were half a dozen parking spaces, all but one empty now. The lunch crowd had left and it was too early for happy hour or dinner arrivals.

Inside the restaurant, with coffee at hand and the carafe on the table, he said, "You first."

She told him what she had told everyone else. "That was the extent of our meeting. She called to ask me to meet at her apartment at five or a little after, but when I got there, she was dead."

"At her apartment," he said. "Strange, or was it?"

"It was. At first she asked if she could come to the office immediately and I told her that various people had been asking about her—Sarah Kurtz, Terry Kurtz, you and your sister. She was afraid someone might be watching the office and that's why she asked me to come to the apartment. She told me to make certain no one was following me. She was running away from someone, Mr. Knowlton, but it wasn't me."

His expression changed subtly as she spoke. He looked more thoughtful and slightly more believing perhaps. "Your turn," she said, refilling her cup.

"Okay. We lived in California near Caltech where I was enrolled and Dad worked with a group on robots. They had been at it for years. Diedricks got in touch with him and wanted to have a meeting, and Dad agreed and flew up to Portland. Next thing, he was working with Diedricks on a prosthetic knee or something. For the next five years they worked together. My mother moved to Portland to be with him, and Rita and I stayed behind to finish school. She was still in high school and I was going after my Ph.D. I sort of took charge of her and we both accepted that. Then, thirteen years ago Diedricks crashed his plane and it was touch and go for him for a couple of years. It left him blind and partially paralyzed."

He turned to gaze out the window. "I don't know what they were thinking of during those years they worked together. No contract, no written agreement, nothing except two driven men doing the work they both loved. After the crash Dad tried to see Diedricks and couldn't. Intensive care, no visitors allowed. Dad wasn't allowed in the house where they had done a lot of their work, and at the plant, where the main R&D is still done, his workspace had been cleared out over one weekend. He had nothing to show for the previous five years. He finally saw an attorney, and that started two years of hell for him."

He looked directly at her and said slowly, "They robbed him, Ms. Holloway, and he couldn't prove a thing. He could replicate some of the work they had done together, but the attorneys said so could anyone else familiar with the field. It wasn't enough. He made some sketches of ongoing work, and they were called pie-in-the-sky fantasies, science fiction stuff. They ridiculed him at the hearings, said he should go back to playing with his robots, try to get work in the movies making science fiction horror films. And so on. Then a new patent was granted and it had Joe Kurtz's name as well as Diedricks's name, and that probably was the tipping point for Dad. He always said Joe Kurtz was not a scientist, he was a hack, a second-rate thinker, laughed at behind his back by the real developers and researchers. They all revered Diedricks and understood that Kurtz was vice president of R&D only because he had married the boss's daughter. They pretty much ignored him. Anyway, Dad lost the first trial and wanted to start an appeals process. His attorneys tried to talk him out of it and told him how much it was likely to cost and he fired them and started over with a new bunch. Six months later he was broke, and he had a nervous breakdown."

"After Diedricks began to recover, didn't he intervene, make a statement or anything?"

"Nothing. For a couple of years I guess he couldn't, and later—I don't know why not. He and Dad formed an instant friendship, a bond. They understood each other perfectly from the first meeting, and Dad always said that was a first for them both, to find someone else that compatible with the same work. I don't know why Diedricks didn't take a stand in the matter. That was one of the things I wanted to talk to Elizabeth Kurtz about."

He looked out the window again. "It's turning into snow."

Big oversized flakes were falling, and staying where they fell. "Time to get on the road," Barbara said.

"One more thing," Knowlton said. "Something Elizabeth Kurtz said, that someone might be watching you. Someone followed Rita and me when we left the restaurant that day. She spotted him first and I thought she was just being paranoid, more conspiracy theory stuff, which she's pretty much into. But I looked and after I dropped her off and headed for my house, I saw that same car again. It was pretty foggy and he was staying in close. There's no other way to explain why another car would have gone to her apartment on Tenth near Jackson, then turn to head out to the Santa Clara area where I live. She was right. We were followed when we left you last week."

11

Barbara sat in traffic at a red light near the corner of Sixth and High and watched, holding her breath, as a car started to turn onto Sixth, began a tortuously slow sideways slide and pulled out of it less that a foot from the car in front of hers. The sliding car straightened, wavered back and forth for several feet and completed the turn. It seemed a long time before another car moved.

When she reached the corner, she didn't continue straight, the way to her apartment, with numerous stops between here and there, instead, she eased around it in low gear and inched forward the next few blocks to the foot of the slight hill that led to Frank's house, a hill hardly noticeable as an inclined slope normally. She did not try to negotiate it. Still in agonizingly slow motion, she pulled over to park, and let out a long breath when her wheels came into contact with the curb.

No longer the big lazy flakes that drifted to earth, a tease more than a meaningful snowfall, the snow now was coming down with a rainlike intensity that suggested it was serious. The temperature had plummeted, freezing the earlier rain to a thick coating of ice on the streets, sidewalks, everywhere, a glaze now hidden by snow.

She left the bag of books in the car, shouldered her purse, took her laptop in one hand, her briefcase in the other, and started the treacherous walk to Frank's house. Slipping and sliding all the way, sometimes perilously so, by the time she reached his front door, she was freezing. She didn't try to get the key from her purse, simply rang his bell and waited.

"For God's sake! What are you doing out in this weather?" Frank demanded when he opened the door. He took her laptop and briefcase, pushed the door closed with his foot and led the way to the kitchen. "Sit down, let's get those boots off."

"I can do it," she said. "It's okay." The boots were caked with snow, her hood was covered, her shoulders and both legs.

Minutes later, wearing fuzzy warm slippers and a heavy wool robe, she told him about her talk with Brice Knowlton. "How many people are they using?" she said. "The green van, and the SUV by the apartment, a guy who followed Brice and Rita, maybe another one who stayed behind to keep an eye out. Why? Why all that effort? And the expense! My God, it's costing someone a fortune. Or it was."

He hoped *was* was the operative word. Barbara moved back a little from the hearth. He had made a fire while she changed her clothes and it was starting to heat up. He seldom had a fire when he was alone. He much preferred to sit in his study with his books and his old chair that was past saving by a repair shop, but was still the most comfortable one in the house. But she liked a fire, and she had been icy.

He left and returned with a bottle of wine and two glasses. She was surprised, since he rarely drank anything alcoholic except with a meal, and very little then.

"Let's take it from the top," he said, after pouring wine for them both. "Whatever is going on must have started back in New York, since she apparently began her flight there."

"Right. But why head for Oregon? She had no friends here. She knew about the cabin, though. But again, why go there?"

"Why did you?" he asked. "Maybe her reason was as innocent as yours, just a place to have some peace and quiet for a time."

That made as much sense as anything else. "Okay. So whoever attacked her either didn't know about the child, or didn't care." She paused. "And why take just the computer? She wasn't robbed. She left five hundred dollars in cash at the shelter. It wasn't a migrant or a casual pickup who attacked her, but someone specifically after her. Or after her computer and whatever she had on it. How did anyone know where she was if she had stayed hidden for weeks by then?"

She sipped her wine thoughtfully, then said, "They didn't find it, whatever it was they were after. Leonora said, and Hoggarth confirmed, that the apartment bedroom had been tossed. They were still looking for it. For something." She looked at him. His face was set in a hard expression. "You've been going through this, haven't you? Thinking about it?"

"All afternoon. I tried to call you, but you must have had your cell phone turned off."

She had turned it off when she went to the bookstore. It was in her purse, still turned off.

"Take it the next step, Bobby. They searched the apartment. What if they still didn't find what they're after?"

"They could continue to look for it, or they might give it up now that she's dead." She thought a moment, then added slowly, "Or they could think I have it, or know something about it."

"Exactly. They can't know any more than Janowsky does how much contact you had with her, if you actually met out at the cabin by arrangement, if she talked to you or passed something to you. I don't think it's going to stop here, not unless they found the missing link, and we can't know if they did." He drank the little bit of wine in his glass and stood. "I'm going to put on some dinner."

Barbara continued to sit near the fire, trying to make sense of what was happening, and when that failed, she wandered out to the kitchen to stand by the door and watch the snow. It was falling as hard as before. Four inches by morning, she thought, at least that much, maybe more. And nothing would be moving in town for the next day, two days or even longer. Some of the main streets would be plowed or sanded, but the side streets had to wait for the thawing rain that inevitably followed a snowfall. She knew very well that Frank would want her to stay there in his house until he was satisfied of her safety. But that could be a long time, she also knew, since they didn't know what the killer was after, where that wanted thing was or anything else about it, including who was doing the looking. In any event, to stay or not to stay was a decision to be put off by necessity for a day or two.

"It must have been Leonora who pulled the trigger," Frank

said, pausing while chopping carrots. "The time won't work for anything else."

"Or at the very least she was in the apartment when that trigger was pulled," Barbara said. "Elizabeth rented the apartment the day before, and she must have been in touch with Leonora, to give her the address. She must have known when Leonora would get in, yet she decided to take a shower. It doesn't add up. It's hard to believe that she would have left the door unlocked to go shower. She must have admitted Leonora, then she went in to shower, came out and was killed. Her own gun? Left out for someone to see and use on her? I know security is a matter of hit and miss at the airports, but you'd better not count on sneaking a loaded gun through." She remembered the roll-on and the carry-on bag still by the door of the apartment and added, "I don't think she had unpacked a thing yet, or even opened her suitcase."

"Leonora could have been met by someone at the airport and that person gave her a gun," Frank said. "She handed it back or tossed it when she went out to call Elizabeth's mother." He was frowning, apparently rejecting that scenario even as he voiced it. "And the first attack? A separate, unrelated incident?" He frowned harder and resumed chopping. "Or Leonora Carnero could have been the one searching for something while Elizabeth was in the shower, found the gun and used it."

"Could be the likeliest idea so far," Barbara said a bit uneasily. She didn't like for him to be chopping anything while talking. Knives were too dangerous, but he had started this and she continued. "But if Leonora had the address, and was in cahoots with the other attackers, they didn't need to tap my line to get the address and they could have gone there earlier. Was she working alone, or with a second group? Talk about conspiracy theories! God, I'd like to have half an hour with Leonora."

He didn't repeat that it was none of her business and to leave it alone. Circumstances were making it her business. It appeared that as far as Lieutenant Janowsky was concerned, she was part of whatever was going on. And someone had been watching her office, probably followed her to Martin's, tapped her phone line and might even then be watching to see if she remained here overnight.

That night on the local news a segment was devoted to the missing Jason Kurtz, starting with a summary of his illustrious great-grandfather, Henry Diedricks. There was an account of his service as a field surgeon during World War II, followed by two years at Walter Reed, a brief private practice, then his breakaway to pursue better prosthetics. He was quoted as saying, "Those fine young men deserved better than peg legs, and Captain Hook claws, and that's about what it amounted to in those days." There were clips of his two children, Sarah and her brother Lawrence, when they were both good-looking athletic youngsters. A brief mention of the recent death of Joseph Kurtz. A rather breathless account of the murder of Elizabeth Kurtz, followed by a more recent photograph of Jason than the one Barbara had seen earlier. The segment ended with an impassioned plea by Terry Kurtz for anyone who had seen Jason, who knew his whereabouts, to please get in touch with the authorities.

Barbara turned off the television. "Interesting, isn't it, that they're no longer suggesting a possible kidnapping? They're implying that Elizabeth took him somewhere and entrusted him to another party. They want whoever has him to feel they won't face serious charges if they simply call in, hand him over and claim they were doing her a favor."

Frank agreed, then said, "But they'll be in over their heads if they do that. How long's it been now? More than a week since she left the shelter and took him somewhere. You can't keep a youngster hidden indefinitely. School, doctors, immunizations." He gazed at her with a somber expression. "It can't be any commercial child-care organization. They wouldn't keep him a second after she was killed. And she didn't know anyone in the state, apparently, much less have a good friend here who would go out on a limb for her like that."

"And that leaves a kidnapper, possibly a child homicide, or me," Barbara finished the thought. "I know a lot of people, some who might even owe me a favor. How do you think they'll play it? Keep the two separate, the murder a local affair, the missing child state business, maybe FBI eventually if not already?"

"Maybe," he said. "Hoggarth will try for that, at least."

She stood. "Well, not much I can do about it, is there? Wait and see." How often had she told her clients exactly that, she wondered, walking out. She veered from the living room where she had been headed, and went instead to the dining room, and stood gazing at the lovely flowers on the table.

Janowsky probably would demand more sessions, more questions, a formal statement. And eventually he would want her e-mails, other correspondence, telephone records. She knew the routine and, again, there was not much she could do about that, either. But Frank was right about the Internet, she thought, looking at the flowers. Sending an e-mail was like broadcasting, out there for anyone, everyone to see. Including Darren's letter. The thought of anyone else reading his message, his love letter, snickering, casting knowing glances not just her way, but also at him, made her hands clench until she realized her nails were cutting into the flesh. It would be leaked, she knew without a doubt. Too juicy to keep secret, the notorious criminal defense lawyer and a highly regarded therapist in charge of the most prestigious physical therapy center on the west coast. It would be leaked. Abruptly she left the room and went upstairs.

In her room, with her back pressed against the door she opened and closed her fingers. *No,* she thought, then said it aloud, "No! I won't let them do that to him!"

When she returned to the kitchen, she was dressed in a sweater and jeans, but still wore the fuzzy slippers. With a determined effort Frank began to talk about coming invitations for dinner, the office party, getting a tree. He gave up when he realized that she was paying little, if any, attention.

"Have you seen a weather report?" she asked.

"No. It's snowing, that's all we need to know."

"Maybe. I'll go see what they're saying." She went to the study, tuned in the weather channel and watched weather for more places than she cared about before they got to the local scene.

"Front coming through late tomorrow, snow turning to rain and then we'll have a day or two of slush," she said, back in the kitchen. "But navigable, at least." It was usually like that. Snow seldom lasted more than a day or two. And then what? she asked herself, going to the back door again.

"I really want to see Leonora," she said. "How can I do that without making like an ambulance chaser?"

"You can't. She calls you or she doesn't."

"I know. But there must be a way. Probably not while Mrs. Cortezar is on the scene. I wonder how long she plans to stay around."

Frank shook his head. "Barbara, you can't take her on as a client. That would be inadmissible."

He was speaking to her as an attorney, not as father to daughter, she realized with a shock.

"You're going to be called as a witness. You will be the one to establish the time that Elizabeth Kurtz called you, possibly the last call she ever made. You could be the last person she ever talked to, and you're going to be the state's most important witness against Leonora Carnero. You can't also act as her attorney. Stay away from her."

"I wasn't even thinking of her as a client," she said. "I just want to know what Elizabeth told her, if she'll talk to me. Believe me, Dad, I don't want a new client, a new murder trial to go through. In fact, on Friday we're closing the office until after Christmas, and Bailey and Hannah are going down to San Diego to visit her family over the holidays, leaving this coming Monday. I don't want Carnero, and even if I did, no judge would allow me to represent her. I know that. I just want to talk to her."

"And you can't. So forget it."

She gazed at the snow. It was very beautiful with city lights reflected in eerie patterns, softened, other worldly. Snowbound, she thought. At least temporarily, they were all snowbound. At a standstill. For now.

12

All through the following day Frank had a growing sympathy for zookeepers watching their charges pace cages endlessly. Barbara was upstairs and down countless times, from the back door to a window to the front windows, as if the snowscape might change depending on where she stood. Between her weather checks, she worked on her computer, read and channel-hopped on TV. The two cats were as restless as she was. They exited through the cat door several times and kept to the snow-free sections of the porch, sniffed snow, backed away, sniffed somewhere else. Finally, they gingerly stepped out into it. When they came inside again, they complained bitterly and roamed some more.

Late in the afternoon the wind began to blow in from the southwest, bringing clouds, then rain, and snow dripped from tree limbs, from the roof, from the fence, and fell now and then in clumps that splashed when they landed.

It was nearly dark when Barbara came down in her heavy jacket and boots, her hood up. He did not comment when she walked out the front door, nor when she returned after a few minutes with one whole side covered with slush and snow, and without a word went straight upstairs.

Still later, she said, "I looked up the robot research Knowlton was involved in at Caltech. Pretty interesting. They were developing a robot with sensors and a feedback mechanism so the robot hand could pick up a feather, or turn a wrench or do a number of other tasks. And computer-assisted articulated legs with feet that could sense differences and adjust to them in the floor level, stairs, risers, just bumps. That's probably the expertise he brought to Diedricks's prosthetics. It's hard to tell now just how far the research had gone eighteen or twenty years ago, about when he joined forces with Diedricks. It's pretty much a reality now."

"Visionary," Frank said softly. "No more peg legs and Captain Hook claws."

"According to Brice Knowlton, his father was the one who understood computers and how to make them work with prosthetics. They must have made a terrific team, Knowlton and Diedricks. Why would a company freeze out anyone who opened a whole new avenue, with almost guaranteed profits down the line? And why didn't the old man speak up? That's the real question of the day."

They watched the late news but there was no mention of the murder or of Jason Kurtz.

"I'll go on up," Barbara said, going to the door of the study, where she paused. "Dad, if Janowsky starts pushing, how long can we keep him from getting my records, computer files, everything? If he's convinced that I know something, he'll go after them."

"I know he will," Frank said. "But we won't make it easy. And I'll try to limit it to that one issue, if you were ever in touch with Elizabeth Kurtz."

She nodded. "Good night." *Try,* she thought, going up the stairs, not that he would limit it, or that he could. He would try. A lot would depend on how hard Janowsky pushed, or whether Jason turned up and if there was an explanation that left Barbara all the way out of it.

In the upstairs hall, she walked back and forth for a long time, trying to think of a way to see Leonora Carnero, and once there how to force her to tell whatever she knew.

The next morning Barbara brought in the newspaper while Frank made French toast. "Two for one today," she said, tossing a newspaper down on the table unopened. The delivery boy had not made it the previous day. She unfolded the current paper. On the front page, in the lower half, was a picture of Sarah Kurtz, and one of Terry. The headline read Where Is Jason Kurtz?

She read the item. It included a statement and plea by Sarah Kurtz.

Barbara Holloway was present when she was attacked the first time, and she was present when she was murdered. Why won't she tell us what she knows about Jason? If her father were not the senior partner of the influential law firm of Bixby and Holloway, would she be granted such immunity? Does her privileged position place her above the law? Why are the investigators not using the authority of their office to demand an explanation? Please, whoever you are, wherever you are, please, my son and I beg of you, bring Jason back to his family.

She threw the paper down and cursed.

Frank brought a platter of French toast, and a bowl of warmed blueberry preserves and sat down, picked up the newspaper and read the article. He put the newspaper aside and helped himself to breakfast. "Used to add a lot of butter and even whipped cream for the top," he said. "Remember? The good old days, before we knew about cholesterol."

"Dad! Cut it out. You can't just ignore something like that!" She pointed to the newspaper.

"What do you think we should do about it?" he asked, and poured coffee for them both.

"Sue them. Bomb them. Hire a hit man. Run her down with your car. God! I don't know."

"Exactly. Try the French toast. Organic blueberries."

"If Sam Bixby had any hair left, he'd be pulling it out along about now."

"Well, he doesn't. Don't worry about Sam. I can handle him."

He and Sam Bixby had started the law firm nearly fifty years before, and Frank's criminal practice had sustained it for a long time, until the corporate, business and other wealthy clients had come along. These days Sam wanted the firm to have nothing more to do with criminal cases; too much bad publicity, he had said. And he had a point, Frank had to admit. He did have a point.

Barbara ate in silence, seething. What could she do? She could think of nothing. Darren, Frank, anyone associated with her, no doubt, would be smeared, ridiculed, maligned. She remembered clearly Sarah Kurtz's parting words—"I'll crush her, and anyone who comes to her aid."

She left Frank's house not long after breakfast and headed for the office. The streets were not bad, once she walked down to her car, but the side streets were slushy, and even frozen where shadows were deep. It would all freeze over again after dark, she suspected, but she intended to be in her own apartment well before that.

Maria handed her a memo with several calls listed, and bemoaned the loss of another shopping day, with Christmas crowding in so close now. She said Shelley had called in; their roads were still blocked by snow.

"Take off whenever you're ready," Barbara said, walking to her office. "Dead time around here. You might as well be out shopping."

But she knew Maria wouldn't do it, not as long as Barbara was checking in, and the possibility existed that there might be something for her to do. In her office, she took off her boots to let them dry, and put on old sneakers she had brought from her closet at Frank's house. She looked over the messages.

Two reporters, a TV producer, nothing urgent, she decided, then she stopped and regarded the last message, clocked in just minutes before her arrival. Mrs. Beatriz Cortezar. She would call back.

Elizabeth Kurtz's mother, she thought, and looked impatiently at her watch. Call back when? Her message didn't say.

She had to wait an hour and a half for the call, and it seemed much longer. "Ms. Holloway, I'd appreciate having a little time this afternoon to talk to you," Mrs. Cortezar said without bothering with any amenities. She had a slight accent and sounded self-assured and, while not exactly demanding, as if she fully expected her wishes to be accommodated.

"Fine," Barbara said. "When would it be convenient?"

"It is now eleven-thirty. I can arrive at twelve-thirty."

She arrived promptly, and was likely the most elegant woman ever to walk into Barbara's office. Dressed in a dove-gray hooded cape with an iridescent sheen, dove-gray gloves, hat and matching boots, she looked to be anywhere from forty years old to over sixty. Wearing little makeup, and needing little with unblemished ivory-toned skin, her black hair unstreaked with gray in a bun held by a tortoiseshell comb, she was a timeless woman. But she had dark hollows beneath her eyes.

Barbara offered to take her cape, but the woman simply tossed it over a chair back. "That will do, thank you," she said, then sat in the other client chair.

"Thank you for this impromptu meeting," she said. "I feared that you might be unavailable today, and tomorrow I leave. I am grateful."

"Mrs. Cortezar, I am very sorry about your loss. You have my deepest sympathy."

She bowed her head and took in a long breath. Her lashes against her pale cheeks were the same long, sweeping black eyelashes that Barbara had seen on the photographs of Elizabeth and Jason.

"Thank you," she said, and drew off her gloves and laid them along with her purse on the other chair. "I read that piece in the newspaper this morning. That made me seek a meeting with you. We have told the authorities—and you should know also—that Jason is safe. Elizabeth told Leonora that he is safe and cared for."

Barbara regarded her for a moment, then said, "Mrs. Cortezar, please tell me what you know about this. When did Elizabeth tell Leonora anything? What did she tell her?"

"Yes, of course. She called the day she rented the apartment and asked Leonora to come, to bring their passports and asked if she wanted to go to Spain. Leonora said yes. Elizabeth said she would explain everything after Leonora got here."

"When did she say Jason was safe and cared for?"

"That call. Leonora asked about him, and that's what she said. And that she would explain, that it was a long story, not one to relate on a telephone."

"Leonora called you Mother," Barbara said slowly. "Her first thought was to call you. It must have been the middle of the night in Spain when she called."

"She was like a second daughter from the time she was twelve," Mrs. Cortezar said. "Her mother was ill, homesick, abused and she fled and returned to Puerto Rico. Leonora came to live with us and became my daughter, Elizabeth's sister, in all ways. I was mother to both girls, just as both of them were mother to Jason from the time of his birth."

"Who will gain custody of the child if the police locate him?" Barbara asked. "You saw that article. Mrs. Kurtz and Terry Kurtz are anxious to find him."

"They can't claim him," she said firmly. "I'll fight them for custody. Ms. Holloway, Terry abandoned my daughter during her pregnancy and did not return until Jason was months old. I don't believe his mother has ever seen Jason, and the family cut off Elizabeth totally when she filed for divorce, charging desertion. They couldn't contest it, there was too much proof, but they have never shown any interest in Jason. He knows nothing of that side of the family. His father is a stranger to him. I don't know why they are making a public display at this time, but it is not out of affection or duty. He spends most of the summer months with me, and we visit back and forth several times a year. He is my grandchild, and they cannot have him."

"Do you know where he is?" Barbara asked.

"Elizabeth said he is safe and cared for," she answered steadily.

For a moment they regarded each other, Mrs. Cortezar turned away first. "I had a purpose in asking for this meeting," she said, "as you may have surmised. I fear for Leonora. I wanted to take her home with me, but the police say she can't leave until their investigation is complete. They have returned several times to question her. They apparently are convinced that she knows more than she has told them, but she has nothing more to relate." She was gazing at the cloisonné urn with a distant expression. "I must leave tomorrow, but I am concerned. From all accounts you saved Elizabeth's life, and Jason's, as well, when she was attacked the first time. I want to retain you to watch out for her interests, Leonora's interests, if the authorities persist in harassing her. At the first opportunity, she will come to me in Spain, of course."

"Why isn't she here instead of you?" Barbara demanded. "Hasn't she been informed that she has the right to consult an attorney?"

"She hasn't been accused of anything," Mrs. Cortezar said. "There seems little need for an attorney at this time, unless they persist in questioning her relentlessly. She doesn't believe she needs an attorney. It should not be difficult to determine that she was in New York when the first attack occurred. We believe they will find the murderer and release her passport, tell her she is free to leave."

Barbara shook her head. "Mrs. Cortezar, that is not going to happen. From what little I know, it's clear that the police are focusing on Leonora as the only possible suspect they have for the murder of your daughter. The time element makes it impossible for her not to have been inside that apartment when your daughter was shot. The conclusion is that either she is the one who killed your daughter, or she knows who did, and in neither event are they going to release her. As for the first attack, no one knows what happened that day. No one besides me even saw her, and the local authorities dismissed the incident as a case of domestic violence, a man and woman traveling together, fighting, then leaving together. Or, they suggested that the attacker could have been a vagrant. There is no direct connection between the two events."

Mrs. Cortezar had grown pale down to her lips as Barbara spoke. "What do you mean about the time element?" she said in a near whisper. "What you are suggesting is madness!"

Barbara told her about Elizabeth's call at ten past four. "At that time she was prepared to come to my office and changed her mind when I mentioned that people had been asking about her. Instead, she asked me to come at five. Leonora's plane arrived at three-thirty, and the police will have an exact record of when the rental car was timed out—the companies keep such records. And they will determine if there was a delay in unloading luggage. They will know nearly to the minute how long she was at the airport. And it isn't hard to figure out how long it would take to reach the apartment at that time of day. In fact, she should have arrived at the apartment even before your daughter was getting ready to take a shower. Elizabeth Kurtz was too afraid to have left the door unlocked, and who but Leonora would she have admitted only to leave to shower? That's the case the police are putting together, Mrs. Cortezar, and it's hard to refute it. They'll simply dismiss the first attack as coincidence."

Mrs. Cortezar appeared frozen, immobilized by shock. Barbara leaned back in her chair and waited.

Finally Mrs. Cortezar shook herself slightly and moistened her lips. "I see. We'll have to discuss this. Leonora and I." She picked up her purse, and drew out a slim gold case, removed a card from it and handed it across the desk to Barbara. "That is my Barcelona address and telephone number. I wrote the apartment address here and her cell phone number on the back. Will you notify me if the police arrest her? Will you help her if they do that?"

"I can't promise to represent her in a criminal trial, Mrs. Cortezar, but I will assist her in every way I possibly can. And if I find that I cannot be her attorney, in the event she requires one, I can promise to see that she has someone who will serve her well. But, Mrs. Cortezar, she will have to initiate a meeting herself. I can't impose myself on her. Is that sufficient?"

Mrs. Cortezar closed her eyes briefly, then nodded. "That's really all I can ask for at this time," she said. "If she requires an attorney, she will call you. Thank you." She reached into her purse again and this time brought out a check. "It was presumptuous of me, but I wanted to have this prepared in the event that you agreed to help her. For preliminary expenses." She placed the check on the desk.

Barbara picked it up and read the note on the stub. "For services rendered to Beatriz Cortezar."

The check was for ten thousand dollars.

"It's insufficient if she is charged," Mrs. Cortezar said in a low voice. "I wasn't thinking of that, only that you might be able to intervene if they kept questioning her or refused to release her passport. Tomorrow I must go to New York City to settle affairs for my daughter and from there I must return to my home. I shall arrange a transfer of funds to Leonora's bank so she will not find herself penniless when her expenses increase. I assume they will if the scenario you've outlined is correct. However, such transfers often require days, or longer, to be finalized. After that period, she will be responsible for her own financial needs. If she is arrested, if there is a trial, I shall return at that time to be at her side."

"Mrs. Cortezar," Barbara said, "you have to understand that the authorities will not accept your statement that Jason is well and being cared for without proof. There is a massive search ongoing, an Amber Alert and no doubt the FBI has become engaged."

"Of course, I understand. In New York I shall contact my attorney's associates and instantly begin the process of establishing custody of the child. That will be settled in a civil court in the state that issued the divorce decree, of course. Meanwhile, I have told your local authorities all I know about the situation."

"If his father has visitation rights, he can pressure the police to pursue this as a criminal matter, one of abduction. Do you know the terms of the divorce?"

"I shall learn that in New York when we open her safe-deposit box. I know that her will names Jason as her beneficiary and names Leonora and me as joint guardians, that will be our starting position. As for an abduction, I can tell them no more than I have already done."

Barbara was feeling a mounting frustration with Beatriz Cortezar. Only her pallor, the hollows beneath her eyes and a hard to define expression in her eyes that could have been fear or sorrow, betrayed emotional distress.

Quelling her impatience, Barbara said, "You say you read that article in the newspaper, and you must appreciate the position I find myself in. Presumably you were in Spain, and Ms. Carnero was in New York, but I was on the scene here during the first attack as well as the fatal attack, and the assumption seems to be that I was in the confidence of your daughter, and may have information about her son. Neither assumption is correct, but I am in a difficult position. If I am to assist Ms. Carnero I must have some information. I have to have a copy of the divorce decree, and access to Ms. Carnero in order to ask her questions."

"Of course," Mrs. Cortezar said. "If I may have your card, I shall fax you a copy of the divorce papers, and I shall speak to Leonora. We must discuss what you have told me. I assure you that she will be cooperative. Ms. Holloway, I sincerely regret your becoming involved through nothing more than a Good Samaritan deed, for which I cannot express enough gratitude. Whatever I can do for you will be done."

"You could tell me where the child is," Barbara said coolly. She passed her card across the desk.

"I'm sorry. Now I should be getting back to the apartment before Leonora begins to worry that I skidded into an accident. Thank you for seeing me on such short notice." With quick, decisive motions she slipped the card into her purse, pulled on her gloves, stood and drew her cape about her shoulders and walked to the door.

After seeing her out, and ordering Maria to take off for the rest of the day, Barbara sat at her desk for a long time thinking about the meeting. Mrs. Cortezar had not realized that Leonora was in danger of being suspected of the murder, she thought in wonder. It had been like a thunderbolt, jarring her to the marrow. In control of her expressions and her movements, she had not been able to control the pallor that had swept her.

13

That afternoon Barbara went straight to an import shop where she bought gift certificates for Maria's daughters, a few small items and a mammoth clamshell with a pedestal for Frank. "Bird bath," she said under her breath when she spotted it. Ideal. Finished in record time, Christmas shopping done, she wandered through the store toward the exit when she was stopped by a lovely game table, inlaid with white marble and black onyx squares to form a chessboard. Two small drawers on opposite sides held jade and bone chess pieces. She put down a piece that she had been examining and started to move on, but stopped again and returned to look for a price tag. Far too expensive, she decided, and took a few steps away.

"Pretty, isn't it?" a salesman asked.

"It is, and much too awkward to do anything with."

"Oh, the legs are detachable. Actually they're held in place with those decorative nuts and bolts," he said.

Half an hour later, with the clamshell on the backseat of her car, and the boxed game table in her trunk, she drove home. Fog had moved in again, and the streets that had not been cleared were starting to freeze in ridges and dips where slush had been left by traffic. She was cursing under her breath on her own street as her wheels slipped, found traction, slipped again. It wasn't the dangerous slide that had underlain the earlier snow, but still annoying.

"Home, soup, read a novel," she ordered herself, finally parking. The birdbath could stay exactly where it was until Frank took it out himself, and the table was perfectly safe in the trunk, she decided. Carrying the smaller bag, she entered her apartment building.

Darren was sitting on the top step. She stopped moving.

"Hi," he said.

"How did you get in?" Her voice was little more than a whisper.

"I came to return the key you gave me months ago. You returned mine. Fair's fair." He stood up and stepped back to the landing out of her way.

She climbed the stairs, then hesitated at her door. "Do you want to come in?"

"No. How serious is the trouble you're in? Is there anything I can do to help?"

She shook her head. "I happened to be in the wrong place at the wrong time, twice. There's nothing to be done."

His gaze roved over her face, her eyes, her hair. "I sent you an e-mail. Did you get it? You didn't answer."

"I got it," she said. They were both whispering, neither of them moving. "I didn't know how to answer it."

"It would be a gamble, Barbara, for both of us. I know that. I'll be waiting for your answer." He unlocked her door, turned the knob to release the latch and moved away from it, leaving the key in the lock. He went down the stairs swiftly, without looking back at her.

She pushed the door open with her foot, entered and put down her purse and purchases, then retrieved the key. It was still warm from his hand. She leaned against the door holding the warm key for a long time.

Under her breath, she said, "Stay away from me, Darren. You have to stay away. They'll crucify you." She finally moved away from the door, but the thought persisted—they would crucify him. Dig up his past, juvenile detention camp, sister married to a gangster, father a corrupt police officer. Darren once under suspicion of murder. It would all be rehashed, twisted. She couldn't let him come near her, had to keep him away, out of their sight and she couldn't tell him why, or even hint that there was a reason. *Just stay away,* she willed. *Stay away.*

It had been a long, restless night and she felt grumpy and out of sorts when she mounted the stairs to the office on Friday morning carrying a shopping bag with gifts to be exchanged later that day. Two men were lounging in the hallway outside the office door. She knew one of them slightly, Gary Nichols, a reporter, and she guessed his companion was another reporter.

"I'd like to ask you a few questions," Gary said, straightening up.

"Why not? Who's your pal?"

"Herb Newton, from the *Statesman Journal*, Salem," the second man said promptly.

"Come on in," she said.

"Your secretary wouldn't let us," Gary complained.

"Orders, just following orders. Nothing personal."

She motioned them to follow and opened the door, nodded to Maria, whose lips tightened when she saw them and led the two reporters to her office.

"I'll tell you what I've told the police," she said, taking off her jacket, then sitting at her desk. "Have a seat."

She told them almost exactly what she had already repeated many times, and concluded, "I never spoke to Elizabeth Kurtz until she called for an appointment on the day she was killed. I did not arrange to meet her anywhere ever before that time. I never knew her name until the authorities told me. I don't know who she thought might be watching my office or whom or what she was afraid of. I don't know where the child is. I have no information other than what I've just told you. Period."

They asked a few questions and, as long as they referred to what she had already told them, she answered truthfully, aware that their skepticism persisted. Finally she stood and said, "I think we've covered it. Like you, I'm awaiting developments."

As soon as she had ushered them from the office and closed the door Shelley emerged from her own office. "Maria said you were talking to reporters. Is there something new?"

"Nope. Just getting my own statement out there, for all the good it will do."

"Maybe I'll come in next week," Shelley said. "You know, just in case..."

"I certainly will be on hand," Maria said.

"Nope. Holiday. If they arrest me, Dad will let you know. Then it's time enough to show the flag. Bailey's coming around at about four, and Dad said he'll pop in. Cookies and hot chocolate time, or something." She waved at them and reentered her office.

Wine, booze for Bailey, a tin of cookies that she had picked up, and she knew Maria would bring something to eat. She always did. Party time at four.

She sat at her desk, brooding over Elizabeth Kurtz, who was proving to be a pain in the neck, dead or alive.

And that was how various innocent clients had felt over the years, she realized—helpless and cornered by circumstantial evidence they could not disprove.

She had not yet moved from her desk when Maria buzzed to say that Lt. Janowsky and an FBI agent were in the office and wanted to see her. Barbara said to send them on in, and she got up to open her door for them.

Janowsky might have owned another suit, she thought greeting them, but he seemed to prefer the heavy tweed. His companion was very young looking, with carefully parted dark hair neatly combed, wearing a conservative dark gray suit, white button-down, discreet blue tie, shined shoes. He looked like an insurance auditor.

"Special Agent Gerald Whorf," Janowsky said inclining his head toward the younger man. Barbara did not offer to shake his hand, and he didn't extend his.

Today, instead of the chairs around the low table, Barbara motioned toward her client chairs, and sat behind her desk.

"All right, what now?" she asked. "Do I need my attorney to be present?"

"Of course not," Whorf said. "No, no. I mean, this is informal, just information gathering." He smiled, and looked like a college sophomore trying to con a professor into a higher grade.

She nodded.

"I'd like to hear from you about your various encounters with Elizabeth Kurtz," he said, and drew a notebook from his breast pocket.

She glanced at Janowsky, who had crossed his arms over his chest, and looked patient and somewhat pained. "Don't you guys share information yet?" she asked. "In spite of all the admonitions and warnings?"

"We like to get it firsthand," Whorf said quickly. "If you don't mind."

She shrugged. "Whatever you say." She retold the same story once more.

"You say you were in San Francisco for several weeks before you returned to Oregon," he said when she finished. "Do you mind saying where you stayed there?"

"Agent Whorf, what I did in San Francisco has nothing to do with my encounters with Elizabeth Kurtz. I was on vacation, stayed in a hotel apartment, went to shows, visited museums, had dim sum and rested. Then I headed for home."

"Did you meet, even casually, with Elizabeth Kurtz during that period?"

"Nope."

"Will you tell me the motels you stayed in after you left Mr. Norris's cabin?"

"After my credit card statement arrives. I don't remember."

She bore with it for an hour, then stood. "I've told you all I can."

He pursed his lips in disapproval. "Ms. Holloway, the state police and my own bureau take the possible kidnapping of a child very seriously. He may be in grave danger, may already be dead. It is our sworn duty to try to locate him, and your responsibility as a law-abiding citizen to aid us in any way we ask."

She nodded solemnly. "I understand, Agent Whorf. Since I have already told you all I know, now would it please you for me to start telling you stories about how Elizabeth and I sat over a campfire conspiring to get rid of the little bugger? Or about the slave-trade marketer we met at midnight on Fisherman's Wharf and dickered with over a sale price? Give me a minute or two and I can probably come up with several additional scenarios for you to follow up on."

Agent Whorf flushed, and Janowsky's face turned a shade darker brick red. He stood first. "Let's go," he said to the young FBI agent.

"Yes, of course. Yes." Whorf stuffed the notebook into his pocket and gave Barbara a look that she assumed was meant to be threatening. "I'll be in touch with you."

"I'm sure you will," she said, and walked to the door, opened it and waited for them to leave. Before the hallway door closed all the way, she said to Maria, "They're going out to get a malted milk shake or something. No more visitors today until Dad and Bailey get here."

It was not much of an office party, Barbara had to admit later, with only the small crew of her team present, but they ate the empanadas that Maria produced, and some of the cookies, drank wine or coffee, and Jack Daniel's for Bailey.

They talked about coming events, a party, a dinner party, music at the Hult Center, and exchanged presents. By five-thirty it was over. Bailey pulled on his ugly coat, wrapped a six-foot-long scarf about his neck, then paused on his way out. "Almost forgot," he said. "Looks like they've found out something about the gun. They sent someone down to Sacramento to check out a gun dealer at a show just about the time they figure Kurtz was in the area. If they nail that down, it's curtains for Carnero."

"Gun show when?" Barbara asked.

"Weekend of November eighteenth. Puts her in the cabin a few days later, with a gun in her possession."

"One she didn't use," Barbara commented.

"Oh, well. Who goes armed to take a shower?" He wished them all a Merry Christmas and Happy New Year and left.

After the others had gone, Barbara took one last look about and left also. She had a date with friends for dinner.

She had not mentioned the visit by the FBI. What would have been the point? she asked herself. Nothing to be done about that. Bailey had gloated about the coming week and a half, fishing, playing golf, taking in the sun, and Shelley was brimming over with holiday spirit these days. Not a good time to introduce gloom and doom. She felt that she was being pressed tighter and tighter into a corner, now especially if they could put Kurtz in Sacramento that weekend, while she, Barbara, had been in San Francisco. Forget it, she told herself sharply. Leonora Carnero was the one being put in a box. If Elizabeth Kurtz really had bought a gun, and if that gun turned out to be a Luger, that would cinch it, as far as the police were concerned, no doubt. Where Carnero disposed of it would matter little.

* * *

Barbara was home again that night by eleven, after dinner with two good friends. Janey, a child psychologist, had asked at one point, "Did you know that there are more suicides this time of year than any other? People get depressed. But also, some people who are at death's door just don't go through until the holidays are over and done with. Go figure."

That had dispelled the good cheer, at least for a time. Three single, professional women, never married, and as Janey had said in the past, they couldn't keep a flame alive long enough to get warm all the way through. Why not? Barbara asked herself in her apartment that night. Why not? What was lacking in them? Was anything? The question posed by Dr. Sanger came to mind again: "What are you afraid of?" Nothing, she snapped back at that voice in her head.

They would prod and prod to learn where she had spent the days in San Francisco, she knew, and there was no way on earth she would ever tell them. But if Elizabeth Kurtz had been in Sacramento that weekend while she had been in San Francisco, they would come back to it again and again. Account for your time down there. Where were you? Who did you see? Did you return to Oregon by Interstate 5, go through Sacramento? She knew the process well, having watched it play out with clients many times. They were not likely to leave it alone.

She drew a bath and used a lovely new bath oil Janey had given her. Years before, they, the single women, had all agreed—no more things to be put away for safekeeping—give consumables. The oil was expensive, the fragrance elusive and faintly spicy. It felt wonderful on her skin and the steam smelled wonderful, but instead of relaxing, Barbara kept coming back to the problem of Elizabeth Kurtz. Where had she taken the child? Who would dare keep him with the FBI on the case, the state investigators, the Amber Alert? And how to account for Mrs. Cortezar's acceptance that he was well and being cared for, when presumably she was deeply attached to him? And why was Sarah Kurtz, who had never seen him, the one publicly demanding, begging for his return?

There were too many unknowns, she decided, and left the tub only when the water had cooled. But still not ready for sleep, she put on her robe and slippers and went to her office to jot notes of those few things she did know, instead of worrying over the many she didn't. Kurtz had been savagely attacked, and probably left for dead, or at least left to die un-attended in the cold rain. She had gone to the shelter and stayed for five days, left with stitches in her head. Jason had been with her. Next she showed up in the apartment. Why had she come to Eugene? And where had she left Jason?

She shook her head impatiently. Just the things she knew, she reminded herself. Kurtz had called at four, then again ten minutes later. She had been afraid, terrified. She had called her friend from childhood, her almost sister, or her lesbian lover, depending on whose story was to be believed. Leonora had flown to Eugene, rented a car and had gone to the apartment, and should have arrived by the time Kurtz was making her second call to Barbara.

She stopped writing, and gazed at the wall, thinking. It didn't make sense. If Elizabeth Kurtz had known when Leonora was due in, she would have expected her by the time she called. Why choose that time to go take a shower? Especially since only a few minutes before she had been ready to go to Barbara's office. And that didn't make sense, either. If she was expecting Leonora, why call Barbara at that time? She didn't know when to expect Leonora, she decided, but then why was the door unlocked? If it had been locked, how did the killer, Leonora or someone else, get into the apartment?

Would she have left her door unlocked? As terrified as she had sounded on the phone, it just didn't seem possible. She must have opened it herself, admitted perhaps the one person she trusted, then showered.

Moving on, she reminded herself. Just the things you know. Leonora had found her friend dead, or so she said, and she had run out to call her friend's mother, who was her adopted mother as well. Barbara couldn't even imagine what that call had consisted of. But Mrs. Cortezar had left almost instantly to come to Leonora's aid, to identify her daughter, have her cremated and take her ashes home for burial. And she accepted that a beloved grandchild was well and being cared for, accepted the word of the woman who was very likely going to be accused of murdering her biological daughter.

Barbara scowled at the timetable she had jotted down, but it was inescapable. There was not enough time for anyone except Leonora to have committed the murder. Just what you know, she thought, and nodded. Elizabeth Kurtz had been terrified on the phone, and Leonora's hysteria had been real. Her runny nose, uncontrolled sobbing, her pallor, they had been real.

She left it at that and went to bed, but it wouldn't stop going round and round in her head. She hoped that Mrs. Cortezar had warned Leonora of her danger, advised her to seek counsel right away. Her shock and dismay at hearing Barbara say that Leonora was in danger of being accused of murder had also been real, she thought. She was certain that Mrs. Cortezar had not even considered it before Barbara said the words.

It was a long time before she began the drift into sleep. Then, more asleep than awake, she was dreaming that she was in the witness chair and the questions were being flung at her with a furious intensity. Who did you see? What did she tell you? Why did you go to the cabin? Who was she running away from? Where did she put the boy? Exactly when did you first meet Elizabeth Kurtz? She looked across the courtroom at Leonora Carnero, whose head was bowed, her curls thick around her face.

Barbara twisted and turned in protest and flung her hand up, and the motion woke her up entirely. She sat up, shook herself violently, but before she could lie down again, her mind cleared.

Wide awake now, she got up and put on her robe and slippers and went to her office, where she stared at the time-table she had made earlier. "Oh, my God!" she said.

14

At nine in the morning Barbara called the cell phone number Mrs. Cortezar had provided for Leonora Carnero only to get the voice mail. "Ms. Carnero, this is Barbara Holloway. I have to talk to you. I don't think Mrs. Cortezar realized the danger you may be in. Call me back as soon as you can." She gave her number and hung up.

The return call came five minutes later. "I have to talk to you," Barbara said crisply. "You must not make a statement to the police until you have consulted counsel. We need to talk."

"But I... They had me make a statement yesterday," Leonora said. "They said it was routine."

Barbara drew in a breath. "Stay right where you are. I'm coming over there."

The condo apartment was in one of the newly sprouted glass and black high-rise buildings behind the sprawling mall, and mall traffic was backed up to the access streets as cars circled trying to find parking spaces. Stop-and-start traffic for a mile or two, frustrated drivers, a light rain, it was not a good morning, with little evidence of Christmas cheer. A sign in front of the building Barbara was looking for had a Leasing Now sign out front, and flags beckoning. It also had a security desk in the lobby with a bored attendant. She gave her name and waited impatiently for him to call the apartment, then motion for her to go on to the elevator. Leonora's apartment was on the third floor.

Everything smelled new and vaguely of cheap perfume and plastic. Off-gassing like crazy she thought, wrinkling her nose, wanting to hold her breath.

Leonora opened her door and stepped aside to admit Barbara to a room with ultramodern furnishings, molded pale wood, a lot of chrome and striped drapes in shades of pale blue and silver. Cold and expensive, Barbara thought.

"What do you want?" Leonora asked, staying by the door.

"To save your neck if you haven't already put a noose around it," Barbara said, taking off her jacket. "Did you sign a statement? Were you under oath?"

Leonora nodded. "They said it was routine in an investigation."

"Right." Barbara walked through the living room, glanced into an adjacent dining area and kitchen, then returned. "Is anyone else here?"

Leonora shook her head. "What do you want?"

"It's time to stop playing games," Barbara said coldly. "I don't know how much damage you've done, but considerable. Your mother retained me to look out for your interests, and

I intend to do that, if possible." She moved closer to Leonora as she spoke, and without warning she reached out and lifted the woman's hair from her forehead and face to reveal a fresh-looking scar above her eyebrow, nearly at her hairline. "We'd better sit down," Barbara said. "And don't give me any bullshit about who you are. It's too late for that."

Leonora looked as if she might faint, and clutched the doorknob. Barbara took her by the arm and pulled her away from the door, shoved her onto the sofa.

"I think you'd better do some pretty fast talking, Elizabeth," Barbara said furiously, standing over her. "That woman in the apartment, that was Leonora, wasn't it? And your mother identified her as you. Jesus! Are you both insane?"

Elizabeth closed her eyes and drew in a long breath. Her eyelashes were short and blunt, not the long sweeping lashes of her photograph. "I sometimes think I must be mad," she said. She put her hands on her face, her hair, as if reality checking. "I may be mad."

"Well, snap out of it and tell me what the hell you think you're doing."

"I panicked," Elizabeth said. She touched the scar, hidden again by her curls. "They thought I was dead. If they knew I wasn't they'd be back and make sure next time. I didn't know what to do."

"Hold it," Barbara snapped. "Start further back. You called Leonora to fly out and meet you. Then what?"

Elizabeth drew in another deep breath. "That day I met Leonora at the airport but we didn't have time to talk. I wanted to see you before you left the office, and I thought she and I would have all night to talk. I collected her suitcase

while she signed for the rental car, and I gave her the apartment key and told her I had to see you and I'd come as soon
as I could. I told her how to get to the apartment. She said she
wanted a shower and a drink, and I said there was sherry."

She bowed her head. "She liked a good sherry."

Standing, she glanced about the apartment in a distracted
way, then sat down again and folded her hands. Her voice was
low when she continued. "I couldn't call you right away. One
pay phone was out of order and people were using the others.
While I waited I tried to think how much to tell you. I hadn't
decided yet. Then your secretary said you were out, and I had
to wait even longer. When you said they had been asking
about me, I was afraid they'd be watching. I had a coffee,
thinking, and I decided that might even be better, to see you
and Leonora together, tell you both. I didn't expect you until
five, and I knew Leonora would be taking a shower. There was
no rush. Then I went back and I...I found her."

She stood again and this time she began to move aimlessly
about the room, touching a table, the back of a chair, the
window drape. "I was sick at first, but suddenly I seemed to
turn to ice, like in a dream, just watching myself, not really
there. I looked at her again and I thought, that should be me.
They thought it was me. If they realized I was still alive, they
would try again, and again until..."

She stopped her aimless movements and pressed her forehead against the outside door. "I became Leonora. I took her
purse, got some money from mine and left it there. I had to
call my mother. She was expecting us by Monday and I had to
tell her. I drove until I saw a pay phone and I called her. I lost
the ice, lost all control while we were talking. It hit me that

someone had shot Leonora, that I had sent her there. I hadn't warned her that it was dangerous, that people were trying to kill me. I didn't tell her and she must have left the apartment unlocked so I could get in while she was in the shower. It was my fault."

Her voice thickened and she began to shake, as if weeping. Drawing long shuddering breaths she continued. "I should have told her. It was as if for the first time, while I was on the phone, it hit me that she was dead and it was my fault. Mother said she would come on the first flight, and I kept saying I'm Leonora now. She said let them think that, so I'd be safe until she got there. I ran out of change while we were talking and I didn't know what she was saying, except that she would come. Then I dialed 9-1-1 but I couldn't stop crying and I didn't know where I was. They said to stay right there. I waited in the car and they came and got me and took me back. And you were there."

Barbara regarded her with mounting fury and frustration. "Jesus," she muttered again. "I'm going to make some coffee and we're going to talk." Elizabeth didn't move from the door, shaking.

Her fury unabated, Barbara strode to the small kitchen, yanked the coffeemaker and coffee forward on the counter and spooned in the grinds. As the coffee dripped through she found mugs in the cabinet, banged them down on the table and added a sugar bowl and a container of half-and-half. She put it down hard enough to cause some to spill, and she cursed, then ignored it.

Count to ten, count to ten, she kept telling herself, but she was too furious to follow the advice, and instead she glared at the coffeemaker and willed it to finish. As soon as it was ready, she poured coffee, then went back to the other room, where Elizabeth had not moved. She still stood with her forehead pressed against the door, her shoulders sagging, both hands loose at her sides. Barbara took her arm and pulled her around.

"Come in and sit down," she said. She kept her hold on Elizabeth's arm and half pulled, half led her to the kitchen and seated her, then put a few tissues in her hand. She waited until Elizabeth blew her nose and wiped her cheeks and eyes. "Now tell me about it, starting with page one."

Elizabeth started with the day Terry had gone to her office and they had gone to his parents' condo. Disjointed, often nearly incoherent, she told it all.

After she realized what she had found in the files, she knew she had to get away, to read through it, see if it meant what she thought it did. She drove to Philadelphia that evening, and the next day she sold the BMW, a wedding present from his parents. She bought a used Hyundai, paid cash and headed west.

"I didn't have any place in mind, just far away. I knew I couldn't use a credit card, or my cell phone, and I had to have money. I'd need a printer and a scanner, motels, meals. I couldn't drive far any one day. Jason would get restless, and I stopped a lot for him to run around and play, or we'd go to a movie or something. And at night, as soon as he was asleep, I read the material, and did some research on the Internet. I couldn't do much, too tired, and we got up so early. It took a long time to get to Las Vegas, but eventually we did, and I rented an apartment for a few days just to have time to scan material, copy it to a disk, so there would be a record. I put all the original material in a locker at the airport and kept the copies and a copy of the disk."

"Then what?"

"I didn't know what to do," Elizabeth said. "They had cheated Jefferson Knowlton, and I had proof, but I didn't know what to do with it, or even if I should do anything. I kept thinking of Terry's grandfather. I liked him. We, Terry and I, came out here soon after we married and we stayed at the big house for a week or so, and I liked the old man. He was so happy that I could speak French. He's into ham radio, and there was a Frenchman he really wanted to talk to, but language problems made it hard. I translated for him several times. That pleased him. He's partly paralyzed, and he's blind, but he's sharp, and even funny. I couldn't believe he knew what had been going on, but if I went public, he'd be in the thick of it along with Sarah Kurtz, Joe and all of them. I just didn't know what to do, and I was so tired by then, driving, taking care of Jason, worrying, afraid all the time, watching over my shoulder.

"I was so tired. I read in the newspaper that Joe Kurtz had died and the family had gone to Portland for the funeral, and that made me think of the cabin. Isolated, private, safe. When Terry showed it to me years ago, he said no one ever used it, but his grandfather refused to sell it. He wanted it ready if he ever decided to go there. It seemed ideal, a place where Jason could run around on the beach and I could relax for a few days and think."

She gazed past Barbara and shook her head slightly. "It seemed so simple there. I knew they were looking for me.

Early on I called Leonora and she said they were, and I thought they would stay in Portland for a few days, maybe a week, and then go back to New York, and I'd just wait in the cabin and rest. Then I thought I'd go to Portland myself and talk to Grandfather Diedricks and let him make the decision. If he said to leave it alone, I would. It seemed so simple.

"I went out to get firewood that day," she said after a moment. "Jason was taking a nap, and I went out for firewood but I didn't have anything to carry it in, and I turned to go back for a paper bag or something, so I wouldn't have to go out in the rain again later. I didn't really hear anyone, but I started to look behind me. Maybe I sensed someone was here. I don't know. It was raining. My hood was over my head, and I got hit when I started to turn to look. I didn't even get a glimpse of him. And you came and I began to wake up while you were moving me, but I was so groggy, I just wanted to sleep. I heard you say your name and something about getting help, then Jason was with me and he said are we going to sleep here now? That's when I really woke up. The computer was gone, the envelope with all the papers, everything. I was afraid he would open the envelope and see that they were copies, not the original drawings and notes, and he would come back. I gathered everything and threw it in the car. I was staggering and blundering into the wall, the door frame, but I had to get out, get Jason out, and we left."

She had pulled into a dirt road, she continued, and they stayed there overnight, slept in the car and in the morning she started to drive again, but she didn't know where to go. She was dizzy, disoriented.

"I must have been weaving back and forth on the highway.

A truck driver was blasting his air horn at me, and I knew I had to get off the road, stop driving."

She had pulled off at a rest stop and had taken Jason into the restroom, where two women were ready to leave. They skirted around her, no doubt thinking she was stoned, or drunk, but one of them stopped and took a closer look.

"She wanted to call the police and I said, 'No, no police,' and she said I needed a doctor. They thought my old man had beaten me," Elizabeth said with a shrug. "Anyway, they talked a minute or two, then one of them said she knew this place in Salem that took care of battered women. She told me the address, but when I started to leave, I nearly fell down, and one of them grabbed my arm and held me. She went to my car with us, put Jason in his car seat and drove to the shelter. The other woman followed in her car. They made sure I got to the door, and they left. I don't even know their names."

She didn't know how many days she remained at the shelter, but she knew she had to leave, had to get Jason to safety. She left before dawn, and drove to Tacoma that day, and there she took Jason to a multiplex theater, bought popcorn and juice for him, and parked him with a few hundred other children at a movie. Mothers all around were doing the same thing, leaving the children in order to shop. She found a telephone and called her own mother in Spain.

"I told her everything. I was desperate to get Jason someplace safe, and I didn't dare go anywhere near Grandfather. They might all still be there. I didn't know another soul in the north-west. I couldn't just fly out with him to Spain. Our passports were back in New York. My head was bandaged, my face bruised…"

Her mother had told her to check her watch, and give her an hour to come up with a plan, and she would call back at that number. The plan she devised was simple enough. Her mother had a cousin in Vancouver, B.C., who had several grandchildren, one about Jason's age. Her mother flew into Vancouver, met the cousin and the two women drove to Tacoma together. The cousin removed the stitches. "Mother couldn't bear to do it, and we couldn't go to a doctor. I'd been keeping my hood down low when I went out, but that wouldn't keep working, so they cut my hair and gave me a perm." She ran her hand through her curls. "And they trimmed my eyelashes."

They cut Jason's hair short—almost a burr—trimmed his eyelashes, and the day they took him back to Vancouver, they painted his face. "You know how they paint children's faces," she said.

Barbara didn't know, but she let it go. They had painted his face. He loved it, grinning like an imp at everyone.

"They had the passport belonging to the cousin's grand-child, and it was close enough if anyone had asked to see it. No one did." He became the cousin's grandchild as far as customs was concerned. Her mother used her return ticket, and the cousin booked the same flight for herself and her *grandchild,* and that was that. They all three went to Spain.

"It worked," Elizabeth said. "It seemed so far-fetched, so unlikely, but it worked. I waited in the motel until they reached Barcelona. Mother called the room from there so I would know. And then I headed back down to Eugene. I planned to get an apartment, call Leonora and have her bring our passports and take her on a vacation to Spain. I looked you up on the Internet in a cybercafe and read about your work and I thought you might be willing to help. I was going to ask you to take charge of the original file, and after we were gone, to decide the best way to handle the material—go to Knowlton, or to his attorney, or to the police, whatever you thought best. I wanted nothing more to do with any of it. I just wanted Jason to be safe, and to be with him."

"You thought as Leonora you'd just waltz away from it all? Leave the hunt for Jason up in the air, give a statement to the police and be on your way? God! There's an Amber Alert out for that child, his picture's plastered everywhere you look! And you're going to be charged with murder! Jesus!"

"It never occurred to either of us that they might think Leonora did it," Elizabeth said in a near whisper. "She was in New York when he attacked me the first time." She looked at her hands, twisting and retwisting, and put them in her lap. "We thought they'd check on that, that she was in New York and just flew in. We thought they'd have a lot of questions, maybe want a statement, but then say she could go back home. This is insane, for them to think she'd do that. There's no reason. We were best friends ever since preschool…"

She was weeping and seemed oblivious to the tears running down her cheeks. "I was going to go to Las Vegas when they said I could leave, and I was going to send all that material to you with a note. And go to Barcelona to live with Mother and Jason." Her voice faltered, and she jumped up. "Excuse me." She hurried from the room.

She returned with tissues and a washcloth. "I keep doing this," she said, wiping her eyes. "I keep thinking it was my fault."

"Why on earth didn't you tell them the truth? My God, did you really think you could keep up the charade forever?"

"I was afraid to tell them the truth. They wouldn't have kept him away if he knew I was alive. I knew they would kill me. First the cabin, then the apartment, I couldn't hide. And they couldn't keep him away."

"Who? Who's after you? Why? Stolen ideas? Is that it?"

Elizabeth shook her head. "That's just part of it. They're in negotiations with a Swiss pharmaceutical company, a big company that wants to buy out the Diedricks Corporation. It's not just stolen ideas and drawings. Millions of dollars, hundreds of millions of dollars are at risk if it falls through." She sounded firmer as she said, "That deal will fall through because it's based on fraud, stolen patents, stolen ideas. There will be lawsuits, scandal. There won't be a deal when it comes out. They will hunt me down and kill me if they suspect I'm still alive."

"Who?" Barbara demanded. "You're talking about your ex-husband, his mother, someone connected to the Diedricks Corporation?"

Elizabeth nodded. "Someone in the company. I don't know who. It's a huge amount of money. Elizabeth Kurtz has to be dead until the fraud comes out in the open, until it's settled. I'll tell them when it's safe."

"So why didn't you tell the police about it, have them go get the stuff, just turn it over to the authorities?"

"You don't understand," Elizabeth said tiredly. "Joe Kurtz was using Knowlton's work, claiming it as his own, but he wasn't capable of it. I knew him. I studied science, and I've edited a lot of science books. I knew what I was seeing, but a nonscientist? They would see the initials on the drawings, the schematics, and even if some of the preliminary sketches and concepts had Jefferson Knowlton's full name, they would claim that he was simply executing Grandfather Diedricks's ideas. That's what they claimed before. Sarah Kurtz would swear it was Joe's original work, that I had stolen it. And I did. I took it from his files. That work needs to be authenticated by scientists who can understand what they're looking at and what it means. That's going to take expertise and time. The police might just hand it back to Sarah Kurtz and add robbery, possibly an extortion charge, against me. But they wouldn't protect me." She shuddered. "Maybe if they know they have the original documents in their possession again, they would forget about me, but I don't believe it. They couldn't be certain I hadn't made more copies and put them somewhere."

Barbara leaned back in her chair and took a deep breath. "Well, the police have your sworn statement, and God alone knows what kind of corroborating evidence they think they have, and they intend to charge you with murder. And if they bring you to trial, you're going to be found guilty. That's the bottom line."

Barbara stood and walked the length of the kitchen, back, did it again. Then she stopped at the table. "Were you and Leonora lovers?"

"No! Of course not. I'm not gay and neither was she."

"Did you stop at a gun show in Sacramento?"

Elizabeth looked bewildered by the question and shook her head. "I drove straight up to Oregon."

"When did you put those papers in the locker in Las Vegas? The date."

"I don't know the date, the day before I left Las Vegas, then two days on the road, a couple of days at the cabin. I don't know the dates. Why?"

"Because it may be their policy to clean out lockers after thirty days if material isn't claimed. Where is the key?"

Elizabeth stood up. "I'll get it."

Barbara was trying to count days back. Elizabeth had been attacked on November twenty-fourth, after two days in the cabin. She could have left the material around the eighteenth or nineteenth. It was December sixteenth. Time was running out fast if anyone was going to retrieve that material.

"What are you going to do?" Elizabeth asked when she returned and handed the key to Barbara.

"I don't know. I need to think, and we have to get that material and stash it somewhere safe."

"What should I do?"

"Nothing. Your hands are tied. You can't do a thing now. You can't leave the state, or even the city. You have to sit tight and sweat it out." She sat again, then said, "I have a lot of questions and I want some straight answers."

Elizabeth nodded. "Are you going to represent me?"

"They wouldn't permit me to," Barbara said after a moment. "I may well be a state witness in a trial of the state versus Leonora Carnero for the murder of Elizabeth Kurtz." She shook her head. "But I'll see to it that you will get an attorney."

15

It was nearly four in the afternoon when Barbara finally went to Frank's house. She had not called first. He would be home or he wouldn't, and if he wasn't there, it would save arguing. He was home but the argument was postponed when she saw that he had brought in a Christmas tree, and boxes of ornaments were on the living room floor.

"Well, just in time," she said. "Or do you want me to sit back and watch?" She always helped him decorate his tree.

"This is as far as I intended to go," he said. "Ready for tomorrow. What brings you around now?"

"Premonition," she said. "I closed my eyes and saw an old man cursing a tangled string of lights. Let's do it."

The lights not only were not tangled, he had already tested them and replaced those that were burned out. They began the ritual of trimming the tree. She knew every ornament, some of them painted by the three of them—her, her mother and father; some from her mother's own childhood; two received as gifts. The tree, when completed, was exactly how it had been as far back as her memory stretched.

"Beautiful," she murmured. "It's just beautiful."

Frank nodded. "Smells good, too. Now, eggnog or wine?"

That, too, was part of their tradition.

They put the empty boxes in the hall closet and went to the kitchen where he poured eggnog into pretty little crystal cups and raised his own in a toast. "Another year," he said.

She touched the cup to her lips, then said, "I have to talk to you, lawyerly sort of talk. Maybe in the study?"

He stiffened. "Are they harassing you? Why didn't you give me a call?"

"In the study," she said and led the way.

There, with him behind his desk, and her seated before it, she told him first about Beatriz Cortezar's visit. She paused for a moment then continued, "I called Leonora Carnero this morning. She had already made a signed statement, and I went over to talk to her."

He listened with no change in his expression, his lawyerly face, she assumed, the face his clients had seen over the many years as they talked about various crimes—murders, blackmail, assault, whatever had taken them to a criminal defense attorney in the first place.

When she finished, he said softly, "Christ on the mountain. Insanity."

"That's what I said."

"They'll trace that flight her mother took," he said after a moment. "They'll widen the net and it will come out, and after that's exposed the rest will follow."

"In time," Barbara said. "Both of them are smart, Elizabeth and her mother. Mrs. Cortezar's passport was still in the name of her first husband—Littleton. She remarried just three years ago and hadn't got around to changing the name on it. She booked a round trip to Toronto, and took a domestic flight from there to Vancouver, then flew back to Toronto. Her cousin booked a flight to Toronto for herself and her *grandson* and a separate flight to Barcelona. They thought of that. As soon as Mrs. Cortezar got back home, she had the name changed, so now the passport reads Beatriz Cortezar. In time they might run it down, but not right away."

"It wasn't very smart to pull such a stunt," he said. "How much alike were they? Elizabeth and Leonora?"

"Similar, that's about all, but no one here knew either one of them. I said from the start that I couldn't identify the woman in the cabin—bloody, dirty, swollen, a washcloth on that head wound, partway down her face, black hair dripping wet and bloody. The only one who might recognize her is probably her ex, Terry Kurtz, and he has no way of getting close enough. Sarah Kurtz hasn't seen her for about six years, and now with curls and her eyelashes trimmed and stubby, it's doubtful Sarah Kurtz would make any connection if she had the opportunity to see her. She probably never even met Leonora. Then, for her mother to make a positive ID and claim the body cinched it. Who was going to dispute it?"

"You can't represent her," Frank said almost absently. "They'll arrest her in the next week or two probably. No bail. An unknown here, without ties or family."

"We could try for house arrest," Barbara said. "A bracelet, anklet, I guess. They might go for that."

"Don't say *we*," he said sharply. "You're out of it. You're going to be a state witness against her."

"I can't represent her, but Shelley can."

He shook his head. "A transparent dodge they'll swat right down."

"You could defend her," she said. Before he had a chance to respond, she added, "Dad, we have to face it. I'm implicated, like it or not. I shouldn't have let it go after the first attack. I could have raised a hell of a stink, insisted that they go look for her. I knew she was in no condition to drive away, but I didn't do anything. I let it go. And if she hadn't called me at the office Leonora wouldn't be dead. No matter what I say or do now, I'm involved. I could be arrested myself, as you well know, as a material witness. There is that.

"But also," she continued, without letting him get in a word, "we can't let it proceed to a trial, no matter who represents her. We can't let her go on the stand as Leonora Carnero accused of the murder of Elizabeth Kurtz. She'd be found guilty and spend the rest of her life in prison under an assumed name. And that means she can't bring in outside counsel. No one who knows the truth can defend her in a trial and without the truth she'll be found guilty. But if the truth comes out too soon, she's dead. Period. I agree with her that whoever carried out both attacks wouldn't hesitate to strike again, or get the child and use him to find her. We're stuck with her. At least, I'm stuck with her. Also, I want to see discovery, find out what they've come up with. Did they even question Sarah and Terry Kurtz? And what's that nonsense about a gun dealer in Sacramento? Elizabeth never bought a gun in her life."

Frank gazed at the ceiling silently and she waited. At last he said, "We have to get those papers from Las Vegas."

"I was with her for hours this morning, then I spent an hour trying to get a flight to Las Vegas. Best I could do is a nonstop to Phoenix, connecting flight to Las Vegas. I'll return on Monday, Las Vegas, San Francisco, Eugene. Get in around eleven."

"No! Bailey work."

"He can't, Dad. He and Hannah are going to Portland tomorrow to fly down to San Diego Monday morning."

"We'll find someone else then. Not you. Barbara, think. If the kind of money is involved that Elizabeth says, they'll pull out all the stops to keep any fraud from being disclosed. They likely are watching your every move."

"Let's put that aside for now," she said. "We agree we need to get those papers before they're tossed out. Then we'll need to see Knowlton. And he'll need a team of attorneys willing and able to take on the Diedricks Corporation, knowing Knowlton lost the first time around. Also, we need to find out who has a financial interest in the corporation. It's a closed corporation and Elizabeth doesn't know. Some people could have backed Diedricks in the beginning and their heirs kept an interest over the years, and they'd certainly be concerned now, if they know what's going on. One or more of them might be extremely concerned. Enough to commit murder? Who knows? Plus, we have to try to keep Elizabeth out of jail, but safe. Full plate, isn't it?"

He scowled and stood. "I'm going to put on some dinner.

But, Barbara, stop saying *we*. If you make a move toward Knowlton, you'll confirm that you have something or know too much." He picked up his cup of eggnog and walked out.

Neither of them had really drunk any of it, she realized, and tasted her own. Too sweet for right now, she decided, and followed him to the kitchen and got out the good dry pinot noir instead.

He stopped whatever he was doing at the sink and said, "We can give Alan McCagno a call, let him go."

"No way. I got the last seat out tomorrow, and the tickets aren't transferable. I have to get to that locker by Monday, and just hope that isn't already too late."

He resumed working. She did not say another word until he had put chopped onions aside. She was afraid to distract him when he had a sharp knife in his hand, for fear he'd take off a finger. She knew that on those few occasions that she actually cooked, any distraction could prove fatal, if not to her personally, at least to whatever dish she was preparing. Cooking required absolute concentration in her opinion.

"I'll put one of the office interns to work to root out the major shareholders of the Diedricks Corporation," he said, opening the refrigerator.

"If Sam finds out, since he's got no hair of his own to pull out, he could come after yours," she commented.

He closed the refrigerator door and snorted. "What's he going to do? Fire me?"

He'd have a fit, she thought, but she said nothing. She suspected Sam was a little afraid of her father. She smiled slightly. He might come after *her* hair.

"One day next week let's get Brice Knowlton to take his dad

to lunch, maybe in one of the booths at the Electric Station. Nice and quiet, and private back there, and we could meet them. What do you think?"

He didn't answer, and she suspected he was concentrating on the food he was preparing, and said nothing more. She got up and wandered back to the living room to gaze at the Christmas tree for a time, then walked into the dining room and touched a yellow rose in the flower arrangement from Darren. "This is why," she said under her breath, as she realized how thoroughly she had put him out of mind as she had become more and more preoccupied with the problems she had stumbled into—murder, a missing child, corporate fraud, hundreds of millions of dollars at stake, Elizabeth, the coming day or two. *It wouldn't be fair,* she thought.

Repeatedly, she let her work override everything else. No one would stand for that after a time, no one. Playing second fiddle to someone else's work. But she seemed to have no choice in the matter; it happened over and over. She drank the rest of her wine and went back to refill her glass.

Frank was entering the kitchen at the same time. "Something I had to do," he said. "You want to set the table in the dinette? Dinner in ten minutes."

She no longer asked, or even wondered much, how he could prepare a delicious meal in half an hour, with virtually no warning ahead of time. He could, and that was enough. That night it was a spicy stir-fry of pork strips and crisp vegetables, a touch of ginger, garlic, soy sauce.

The phone rang as they were eating, and Frank stood. "I'm expecting a call," he said, leaving.

When he returned, he resumed eating his dinner without

mentioning the call. Only after the table had been cleared and they'd both had coffee did he mention it.

"Bailey's putting us in touch with an operative he sometimes uses in Las Vegas. He'll meet your flight and take you to your hotel. Pick you up in the morning and go with you to retrieve that material. You'll have an envelope ready, addressed to me at the office and he'll take you straight to the nearest post office where you'll put it in the mail, overnight delivery, registered and insured. Then he'll take you back to the airport in time for your flight out. You won't carry those papers any longer than that."

She stared at him in amazement. And she had thought he was concentrating on chopping vegetables. "That sounds good," she said without argument. "How do we get in touch with his guy?"

"I have his number. He's waiting for us to call and give him flight times and such."

Later, after they had made their arrangements with Bailey's operative, they sat by the living room fire, with a golden cat on each lap, and royal fir fragrance heavy in the air, and discussed the rest of the week.

"I'll wait until you get back to meet Elizabeth," Frank said. "Let's make it on Tuesday. And we'll wait until those papers arrive, are copied, and put in the safe at my office before we arrange to meet with Knowlton. The originals should stay locked away until he has his own attorneys. Agreed?"

She nodded. "That pretty much covers it for now. Do you think they'll wait until after the holidays to arrest Elizabeth?"

"Possibly, or it could come tomorrow. They might want your statement before they go after her. Let me know if they do."

"You bet. It's going to be a tricky statement to make," she said. "I haven't told Hoggarth a single fib or dodged a pertinent question to date, but now? Oh boy, will I have to dance around things."

"We'll rein him in." Then, more grimly, he said, "Bobby, if they're having you watched, and we have to assume they are, this is going to be a tip-off, to have you met and escorted to the post office. We have to assume they'll suspect you mailed the documents, but they won't know where or to whom."

"We have to assume a couple more things, as well," she said, equally grim. "Whoever is behind this isn't hesitant to spend big bucks on a bunch of detectives, we know that. We have to assume they'll find out as soon as anyone gets in touch with the right lawyers and prosthetic experts. But once they know the research papers are in the hands of a law firm, and/or experts in the field, I think the program will change. I doubt they'll worry much about me any longer. They can make a case that Elizabeth stole the papers with extortion in mind and that they were Joe Kurtz's work, his research, as the first trial determined. The only one they'll really have to worry about is Jefferson Knowlton. No one else has a claim on that research."

He gazed at the fire and shook his head. "You're going to bring the whole roof down. If what Brice Knowlton said is correct, the Diedricks' attorneys maligned, mocked and smeared his father, and broke him. Don't expect any better treatment when they come after you. And," he added, "I have no doubt that you're going to be charged with making false statements to the local investigators, the state and the FBI, and that makes it a federal offense. You've told them all that Elizabeth never talked to you, except for that one phone call, and if they can trace that research documentation to you, they'll decide that's a lie. Make the return address on the envelope mine at the office. I'll hold them off for a time by declaring the papers came in anonymously."

He hadn't said *if* they came after her, she reflected; he had said *when,* and that was exactly right. The first hint of the approaching storm had already come when Sarah Kurtz was quoted suggesting that Frank's influence had intervened with the police in their questioning of her. The barometer was on its way down, she thought then, storm warning out. Get on your dancing shoes, she added to herself, for when they come back with more questions. Including her trip to Las Vegas? Probably.

"I'll tell them I went down to Vegas to make some Christmas shopping money on the slots," she said. He grinned slightly; they were still on the same track, she thought, and that was followed swiftly by another thought, one of appreciation. He had not suggested that she should get out of this mess any way she could. He knew she had to get the research papers, that she had to take on Elizabeth Kurtz—even if that could never be acknowledged publicly. He accepted as much as she did that there was no way to extricate herself from a situation she had not looked for, had not wanted, but found herself in. She knew the best advice was that if you found yourself in a hole to stop digging, but there were times, she also knew, when the only way out was to keep digging.

16

Going down the escalator in the Eugene airport on Monday night Barbara scanned the people waiting below. Frank had insisted on taking her to the airport despite her objections, and he had said he would be there when she returned. She didn't see him, but to her surprise she spotted Bailey leaning against a wall, back from the others, who were moving forward as passengers descended. Then, to her greater surprise, she also saw Alan McCagno holding a hand-lettered sign with the name Rogers on it. He was Bailey's best operative. His gaze met hers and moved on without a sign of recognition and she realized that he was working and did not acknowledge him, either. As she walked forward with the rest of the passengers, Bailey stirred and came toward her.

"Why aren't you in San Diego?" she demanded as he reached for her carry-on.

"You have more than this?" he asked.

"No. That's it."

"Good. Ready to go?"

"You bet." They walked from the terminal and across the access road without speaking, and he motioned toward the parking lot. "Over there."

He had brought his SUV. That was another surprise since he very rarely used it in town. After they were seated and buckled in, she repeated her question, "Why are you still here? You should be in San Diego."

"It's this way," he said, starting to drive. "Hannah's cousins from Kansas decided to spend the holidays in California, and along with the rest of her family it becomes too much. Yakking all day and night, and teetotalers, most of them, and those who aren't off alcohol tend to be real boozers, and there's always a brawl, so I said I'd come along later."

He was keeping an eye on the rearview mirror and making it easy for anyone who might be following. "Is Alan part of your changed plans?" she asked, resisting the impulse to look behind them. "And a Mr. Rogers?"

"You got it. Just trying to peg the guys. Not local, but maybe Portland or Seattle, or who knows? Anyway, they had two guys watching for you in Vegas. Busy little bees, aren't they?"

"Bailey, you won't be able to get a flight out," she said in a low voice. "They're booked solid this week."

In the same slow speed he drew in at the tollbooth, paid the parking fee and drove from the parking area on to the Airport Road. Car after car passed them.

"Wrongo," he said. "Know the best day to fly over the

holidays? Christmas Day. No problem at all. And our return is still on for Tuesday. No sweat."

They turned onto Highway 99 heading toward town and at that time of night the road was almost deserted. "There he goes," he said after a minute or two as another car passed theirs. "He'll dawdle and I'll pass him in another block or two. Wanna bet?"

She didn't. The other car was slowing at the next intersection, as if the driver was trying to read a street sign, and Bailey passed him. "Back in parade formation," he said soon after that. A few minutes later he turned off at Roosevelt instead of taking the more direct route, then at Blair he turned again, this time going to Fifth Avenue to complete the trip. He didn't turn at Monroe, which would have taken them to her apartment, but kept going.

"Where now?" she asked.

"Your dad's place. Orders. Our guy is hanging right in there, back two blocks, probably wondering where the hell we're going."

"And Alan?"

"Oh, he's around," Bailey said. "See, the game plan is for me to go in with you, and eventually our guy will either settle in for the night, or he'll take off, and if he takes off, Alan will be there. This guy is pretty good, but Alan's better, and he knows every alley and driveway in town, to say nothing of the streets. Just want to know where that guy's going, how many there are, little things like that. Figured he wasn't likely to tell us. Just doing the best we can."

"You're spending the night at Dad's house?" she asked.

"Yep. Turned off the water heater at our place. Hannah

won't leave it on if we're taking off for more than two days. Frugal or something. Your dad said I could hang out awhile."

"Right," she said. Hang out and guard her, she thought miserably, at least until those damn research papers were in the safe, or in some other attorney's hands. If she had driven to the airport alone, she wondered, would this return home trip have been so uneventful? Or if her driver were her father, a man in his seventies? No doubt they knew by now that Bailey was a private investigator, not an amateur easily intimidated.

Earlier that day when Bailey showed up, Frank had been as surprised as Barbara was later. "What's up?" he asked.

"Just thought you should know that my pal in Vegas said two locals were waiting for her, and that they're not nice people. She never would have gotten to the post office with whatever she was carrying. My pal and his associate changed the equation, so that part's done. But maybe she should have a couple of escorts when her plane gets in, just in case. You know. Insurance."

"How did they know?"

"Five minutes on the Internet, all it takes. Anyway, I can't stand some of Hannah's relatives. Rather be here."

Bailey didn't ask any questions, he rarely did, but Frank gestured toward a chair and proceeded to tell him what was going on. He always said they shouldn't hold out on Bailey if they expected him to do his job. They never did. Bailey whistled softly when Frank finished. "Big bucks," he said. "Real big bucks."

That night when they entered the house, Bailey nodded in satisfaction. "Like clockwork," he said. "He's out there."

Frank embraced Barbara. "Did you win at the slots?"

"Eight dollars. I'll hit the Dollar Store for my shopping spree."

After Bailey had gone up to the guest room, and Barbara up to take a bath and prepare for bed, Frank sat in his study for a time. He repeated Bailey's words under his breath, "Big bucks."

On his desk was that morning's newspapers, and again the story of the murder of Elizabeth Kurtz was making headlines, not on the front page this time, but on the front page of local news. Along with a plea for the return of Jason Kurtz, now with a reward of twenty-five thousand dollars for information leading to his recovery. But, worst of all, the smear campaign was in full swing. According to a *reliable source,* Elizabeth and Leonora Carnero had had a stormy lesbian relationship, with vicious fights over Jason, over money, jealousy. The same source had no doubt that Elizabeth and Barbara Holloway had met in that isolated cabin with an equally stormy relationship, that probably Elizabeth had fled from Barbara herself. There had been more along that same line. Well, he reflected, Barbara would learn about the article soon enough. Let her get a good night's sleep first, then hit the ceiling.

The article was not unexpected, he thought, but at lunchtime that day Darren Halvord's visit had been. He had come carrying a Christmas cactus in full bloom.

"An early present," he said at the door, holding out the plant.

"Come on in," Frank said. "It's a beauty. Thank you." He suspected that Darren had stopped at a supermarket and bought it for an excuse to drop in.

"Frank, is there anything I can do?" Darren asked.

"Join me for lunch," Frank said, turning back to the kitchen where he had been heating leftover soup. "Yesterday's soup, but it's better the second day. Always make enough to last most of the coming week, it just gets better."

He already had a baguette on the cutting board in the dinette, and now put a second place setting on the table. "Want to wash your hands? It's just about ready."

Over steaming chicken vegetable soup, he'd said, "Guess the answer to your question is probably not. She stumbled into a real mess that's going to take some maneuvering to get out of, but we're working on it."

Darren broke off a piece of bread, put it down. "How's she taking it? That article?"

"She hasn't seen it yet. She'll blow when she does."

"I'd like to strangle that reliable source," Darren said bitterly.

"Well, hold your fire. It could get worse before it gets better."

Darren turned to gaze out the window. "She's on the tight-rope again, isn't she?"

"Well, we do have a situation on our hands."

"I'd better get back to the clinic," Darren said. He had eaten very little.

"Darren, why don't you and Todd come over for dinner on Christmas Eve? No presents, just home folk and food."

"Todd's going to be at his mother's for Christmas Eve, my place Christmas Day."

"All the more reason. Don't sit in that house alone on Christmas Eve, too depressing."

Darren hesitated, his broad face betraying both yearning and resolve. "I told her I wouldn't bring any pressure while... She has a decision to make. She'd think it was pressure."

"Son, this is my house, my dinner I'm planning and I invite whom I please. At the moment that's you."

Abruptly Darren's features relaxed and he grinned. "You're on. Thanks. I'll bring wine or something."

"Or nothing. My idea at this time of year is to stay as far from any retail establishment as I possibly can, and that includes wine aisles in markets." He got up to walk to the door with him.

Darren had paused there. "You know I don't have a thing to offer her except to be there, a safety net or something if she ever falls from that high wire."

Sitting at his desk, Frank replayed that little scene, then cursed softly. What Darren had to offer was the world's riches. He would always be there for her, if she'd open her eyes and let it happen.

The cats were prowling about restlessly, the way they did when it was past bedtime. "Okay, fellows," Frank said, turning off his desk lamp. "Let's go." They raced him to the bedroom door.

All three settled down, the cats at his feet, purring at first, then snoring gently. It was a long time before Frank drifted off. He kept thinking of the incident on their hands and what an ungodly mess it was, and the likelihood it could get worse. He shifted and the cats complained, then shifted also. When he realized he was going through the possible ways it could get worse, he shifted again, and determinedly began to plan the coming year's garden.

17

"Where's Bailey?" Barbara asked the following morning when she joined Frank for breakfast. "Has he heard anything from Alan yet?"

"In my study, on the phone, checking with Alan at this very moment," Frank said grumpily. "And good morning to you, too."

"Oh. Good morning, Dad. Today, after I introduce you to our—your—new client, I want to see Hoggarth. But I don't want to lead a pack of goons to Elizabeth. Bailey work."

"I have to see Patsy first thing," Frank said, pouring coffee. "After that, Leonora Carnero. And let's call her that—and nothing else—until this is settled. What's on your mind for Hoggarth?"

"I want to cut a deal with him," she said with a grin. "He'll love it."

"You're going to give that man a heart attack," Frank

muttered. "I'm going to put on an omelette," he said as Bailey slouched into the kitchen. "Help yourself to coffee."

Looking as gloomy as usual, Bailey poured coffee, and took a chair at the table. "Three guys," he said. "Holed up in a motel suite, kitchenette kind of place." He looked out the window and looked even gloomier. It was raining. "Our pal hung around until nearly two and took off for home base. Pal number two is on the job this morning. Alan says if you want them taken out of the frame, let him know. He'll put a couple pounds of dope in their room and call the cops or something."

"That's a thought," Barbara said. "Maybe it will come to that, but not yet. Meanwhile, we have to see Dad's client today without having company tag along. Can do?"

"No sweat."

Later, Barbara sat in the rear seat of the SUV, where the dark windows hid her from view, not an important detail for now, since it was more than likely that someone had seen her getting in. She waited with Bailey when Frank went up to his office to give Patsy instructions about the package he was expecting. She would guard it with her life, he said when he returned, and he meant exactly that.

Taking his time, Bailey drove through town, across the bridge and on to the big mall, where the parking lot was already filled. "Now we wander about a little," he said. "Be ready to go when I give the word." He drove up and down the lanes the way others were doing searching for a parking space. "Just about ready," he said. Barbara was already holding the sliding door pull, ready.

"Now," Bailey said and came to a stop. Coming toward them

was Frank's black Buick with Alan at the wheel. The transfer was made quickly; Barbara slid into Alan's place at the wheel, Frank got in the backseat, and Alan stepped into the back of the SUV. Both vehicles crawled forward in opposite directions.

Once she left the parking lot it was only a five-minute drive to Elizabeth's apartment where they checked in with security, and were waved to the elevators. The attendant was a different one, but equally bored, Barbara thought, and wondered how efficient either of them would be in the case of an unwanted caller.

After the introductions, and they were all seated in the rather uncomfortable chairs, Barbara said, "I was able to retrieve those research papers and they're on their way to Dad's safe. After we know they're secure, we'll consider the next step."

"Thank God!" Elizabeth said. "It would have been too ironic if they had been thrown out as trash at this point." Then she asked, "How did you jump to the conclusion about who I am? I began to worry about it after you left. Will others do the same?"

"I don't think so," Barbara said. "There were several things. Your mother didn't ask a single question about the attack at the cabin but she should have been full of questions. And her easy acceptance that Jason was safe and being cared for. The police have his passport, and even if you were allowed to leave, as Leonora, what about him? It could only mean that he was already out of the country and wouldn't need a passport, or else that she knew exactly where he was and there were definite plans concerning him. And that meant there had been extensive communication between the two of you, but when?

It seemed to me that it had to have taken place after the attack at the cabin and before you came to Eugene, before the murder, before your phone call the night it happened, especially since she came prepared to claim Leonora as her daughter. And finally, although I knew your hysteria was real, the tears real enough, you were coherent about two things— your mother was coming, and Terry must not be allowed near the body. I had to wonder at that. But, of course, he would have known it wasn't you. None of it added up. I gambled."

She paused, then added, "As I told you, I can't represent you, but Dad can. He taught me everything I know about the law. You'll be in good hands."

Elizabeth moistened her lips and nodded.

"Your story will hold until you reveal the truth," Frank said. "Your mother's positive identification of the body insured that. No one else is likely to question it. Now, if you're up to it, I have a few questions of my own. Background on you and Leonora."

His questions were to the point, and her answers equally decisive for a long time. Then, after many specific questions, she summarized, "Leonora's father was abusive, first to her mother, and then to her. I couldn't even imagine what it must have been like for her at her own home with her father beating her mother, and turning on her. My father was employed at the UN, and there were times when he had to be away for a week or two weeks at a time, but when he returned, he was such a presence. He always listened to me as if it were significant, important. No matter how little it really mattered he acted as if it meant something to him. It was like that with Mother, too. It's hard to explain, and maybe that's common, but I never saw it with other girls and their parents. Terry was like that for over a year. We both were. Attentive, paying attention, real attention. He told me his mother and father had never heard a thing he said, that he would try to tell Sarah something, and she'd remember a phone call she had to make or something and leave in the middle of what he was saying. He said they were always too busy for him. There were nannies, summer camps, boarding school, university, then out. Like growing up alone." She shuddered. "He walked out on me, and that was that."

"Let's move on to the day you left New York," Frank said when she stopped. "What exactly did your ex-husband tell you about shares in the company?"

"Apparently his parents owned a percentage of the company. I'm not sure how much. His father assigned part of their share to us, a guaranteed lifelong income, or we could sell it back to the company at any time. Also, he said a sale to another corporation was being negotiated and our share value would rise drastically as a result. We were searching for the document Joe had drawn up and signed because if Sarah found it first she would burn it."

"Why would she do that? What did she have against you?" Frank asked gently.

"She called me a half-breed Spanish dancer who had seduced her innocent son and lured him into a marriage in order to have a child by him. She claimed Leonora and I were lovers and my plan from the beginning had been to get rid of Terry and resume my relationship with Leonora." She spoke in a flat, near monotone, but there was a furious gleam in her eyes and her cheeks were aflame. "Those were the two worst things she could say apparently, I was a half-breed and a lesbian."

"And exactly what were you planning when you found the Knowlton material?"

"I had heard just a little about that whole affair, not much. But I could tell at a glance that the research was not original work done by Joe Kurtz. I had talked to him a few times, and I didn't believe he was capable of such intellectual effort. I just wanted to make certain. I wasn't thinking of righting an old wrong. I think I wanted to get even for the way Sarah had treated me and my son. She refused to acknowledge him, to see him. Later, I knew I had to tell Knowlton, or at least Grandfather Diedricks. But I didn't have any real plans when I took them."

"But you knew from the beginning that it was dangerous," Frank said.

"At first it was the scandal that I thought Sarah especially would hate. For this gay half-breed seductress to point an accusing finger at her racially pure family would be more than she could bear. What I was most afraid of at first was that they might find us and seize Jason, and use him as leverage. I would have done whatever they demanded if they took him and secreted him away somewhere. When I realized how very much money could be involved, I knew how dangerous it really was."

"Do you think Sarah is behind it?" Frank asked then.

She shook her head. "Whoever attacked me at the cabin was willing to leave a small child in the wilderness to die. He's her grandson! I can't believe she would do that or condone it."

"Why do you suppose she's making such a public display about finding Jason now?" Barbara asked.

"She has to," Elizabeth said. "It's part of her image, the grieving widow and bereft grandmother. She has to play her part."

During that long morning she said she had little memory of Sarah's brother, Lawrence Diedricks, whom she had met only once, and recalled him as being very slick, very smooth. As vice president in charge of marketing he was used to dealing with Washington officials, committees, corporate executives. "You have to understand," she added, "Terry despised his family, the whole lot of them, except for his grandfather, and I never had a chance to get to know any of them. We were like two children on an extended recess with plenty of money and the world for our playground and no time left over for a boring family. Perhaps his Uncle Lawrence and his wife, Moira, are both fine and interesting people, but I never got to know one way or the other."

She gazed past Frank and said thoughtfully, "I think because they are all so extremely proper, Terry felt compelled to do more and more outrageous things. Like appearing in gym shorts at a formal dinner once, little things like that as a youngster. And marrying someone like me as an adult." She shrugged.

The hurt was still there, Barbara realized. She had been stung hard by that family, and deeply wounded by Terry and the hurt persisted after so many years.

Before they stood up to leave, Frank gave Elizabeth a few instructions. No more questions from the police unless he was present, no comment to any media person, no contact with Sarah, Terry or anyone else from the family. "We may send our own detective, Bailey Novell, but never without calling first to alert you. Don't admit any strangers, no matter what reason they might give for coming around."

He pulled on his topcoat and Barbara her jacket, and then Frank said, "Christmas Eve can be a lonely time if you're separated from your loved ones. Come to dinner. I'll ask Bailey to pick you up and bring you home again later."

Elizabeth blinked hard and nodded, "Thank you. I'd like that. I spent an hour in a toy store yesterday...and didn't buy a thing."

"What do you think?" Barbara asked when they were back in the car, heading for his office.

"She'll do," he said, high praise from him when it concerned a client. "She's intelligent. I just wish she had not flown apart when she found the body. Is she likely to do that again?"

"I doubt it. She was emotionally and physically exhausted. 'Last straw' syndrome. Weeks of fear, worry about Jason, his near death at the cabin, as well as her own. A probable concussion. She was overdue." After a moment, she said, "All that time she did everything exactly right. Finally, the only mistake she made was when she called my office." It was a disquieting thought.

Frank's secretary, Patsy, was overjoyed whenever Frank appeared at the office, and she made it clear that she welcomed him as a successful, published writer well on his way to completing a second book, with her aid and assistance. She was happy to see Barbara that early afternoon, also, but her welcome was muted, as if by a deep suspicion that, as usual, a string of trouble was certain to be trailing along at her heels.

"It came," she said. "The package you expected."

"Let's have a look," Frank said and he and Barbara followed Patsy into her office. She closed the door, then unlocked her desk drawer, withdrew a thick manila security envelope and handed it to Frank.

He opened it, and with Barbara crowding in close, he began to scan some of the sheets of paper.

"Greek to me," she said after a moment.

"And me," he agreed. "They'll take a little time I expect." He handed the stack to Patsy. "I'll need a copy of everything, then put both sets in envelopes. You can shred that one," he added, pointing to the envelope it had come in. "I'm going to order in some sandwiches, and we'll do a little work, but when you're done you can leave. Just tell whoever's on the front desk that I'm expecting Lieutenant Hoggarth and to let me know as soon as he gets here." He glanced at his watch. "About an hour from now."

"Tell me what you want. I'll place the order," Patsy said. Her expression had become grim and the look she cast Barbara's way was accusatory.

Frank knew she was unlikely to leave as long as Hoggarth was in the office. After they placed their own orders, he said, "And two pastrami on rye. Milt fancies them, and something for yourself." He also knew there was no point in arguing with Patsy. She had been with him too long and would wait him out in silence, and then do exactly what she had planned.

In his office he sat behind his desk and pretended an interest in the morning mail while Barbara paced. Although it was no more than ten minutes before Patsy tapped and brought in the research papers and copies, it was a long ten minutes.

"Sandwiches will be here in about half an hour," Patsy said on her way out. "The delivery boy isn't back from his last order."

Frank put the original papers and disk in his safe, and he and Barbara sat side by side on the sofa across the room and began to try to make sense of what they were seeing. Some of the notes and sketches were fairly comprehensible, and the final drawings, all very fine and detailed, often were also, but the middle steps were a mystery. There were pages of computer code as well as the drawings and notes.

Some of the notes had the name Jefferson Knowlton, some had initials, JK, and some had Hank Diedricks scrawled on them.

"Look, Dad," Barbara said turning a new page face up. "He was practicing the initials." An entire page had JK's that came closer and closer to looking like the JK on the whole name of Jefferson Knowlton.

"Why the devil did he keep such incriminating evidence?" Frank muttered. "That was insane."

"I expect he believed they were safe from prying eyes and he needed to practice and keep comparing copies to the originals. How much more proof would be needed?"

"Let's think," he said, and leaned back with his eyes closed.

Barbara returned the papers to the envelope and put it on his desk along with the other mail.

"As a Diedricks Corporation attorney my line would be something like this," Frank said. "We don't know where those papers came from. Knowlton's had ten or more years in which to follow the progress the company's made, plenty of time to duplicate whatever work they've already patented and produced. And he's a dreamer with all that stuff about computers and nanotechnology. The man was proven to be a fraud years ago, and this is a crude attempt to revive his old, properly dismissed charge of company theft of his work. For those fraudulent research papers to appear now, so closely following the death of Joseph Kurtz, suggests that Mr. Knowlton was simply waiting for the most propitious moment to renew his claim, knowing Dr. Kurtz no longer can protect his work. We respectfully suggest a psychiatric review of Jefferson Knowlton is in order at this time."

From across the office Barbara said, "It will take the testimony of Elizabeth Kurtz to establish where they came from."

Soberly Frank nodded. "She's the missing piece in the equation."

"It wasn't going to be enough just to get the research back. She had to be dead, as well," Barbara said. "And now more than ever she has to stay dead."

18

Frank had long suspected that over the years during one of the many remodels the offices had undergone Patsy had had a secret closet of her own built in, one that from time to time she visited to bring forth some of her treasures. That day it had yielded a lacquered tray, small plates with cloth napkins, china cups and saucers and a platter on which she had arranged the sandwiches. She had even purloined a red rose from the reception desk and placed it in a cut glass vase.

She put the tray on the low table by the sofa, then said, "That man just got here."

Frank suppressed his smile. "Well, bring him on back. And thank you for the spread." He was very much afraid that Lt. Milt Hoggarth would never rise higher in Patsy's mind than *that man*.

Frank met Hoggarth at the door and ushered him into the office. "Have a seat, Milt. You're just in time for a late lunch."

Hoggarth stiffened slightly when he saw Barbara on the sofa. She waved a greeting and he nodded without speaking, walked across the office to sit on the edge of one of the easy chairs.

"What's on your mind?" he asked Frank.

"A couple of things. I thought we could clear the air like this, an informal little meeting, save time later on. Chicken salad on wheat?" he asked Barbara. "I think that's yours. And pastrami on rye for you, Milt. I think the pickles go with that one."

"I already had lunch," Hoggarth said, eyeing the sandwiches.

"Call it high tea and have some more," Barbara suggested.

He took a sandwich. "So clear the air," he said to Frank.

"Right. We had a long talk with Leonora Carnero this morning."

Hoggarth, chewing, shook his head. He swallowed the bite then said to Barbara, "You can't defend her. The D.A. will have you tossed off her case."

She smiled. "Lieutenant, every single word I said to you in my office was the absolute truth. No embroidery, nothing left out, just the whole truth. I told you then I don't have a client. I still don't."

His look was openly skeptical. "The whole truth, like always," he said derisively.

"Well, put it this way, as usual."

"I'll represent Leonora Carnero," Frank said.

Hoggarth stopped his motion of taking his sandwich to his mouth. "I thought you were retired."

"Retirement's like a water mirage on the desert," Frank said. "Always just up ahead, never quite in reach. Anyway, the point is that I instructed her not to answer any more questions or make another statement unless I'm on hand. You might as well tell your fellows to come to me directly if they want more from her, and we'll set it up."

"Okay. Frank, why lower your batting score at this stage of life? Why this one? Open and shut, and she proves it with her statement." He jerked his thumb toward Barbara.

"We'll see," Frank said. "Another thing, I want a copy of the statement Ms. Carnero made, for reference. Just to keep us all in the same script, you understand."

After a moment Hoggarth nodded. He had become very watchful, his suspicion almost visibly mounting. "What do you know that we don't?" he asked. "I can't remember a tighter case unless a shooter was videoed pulling the trigger. The only question now is do we bring her in before or after *her* statement, before or after Christmas?" Again he jerked his thumb toward Barbara as he spoke, keeping his gaze on Frank.

Barbara answered. "We know she didn't do it, Hoggarth. And speaking of my statement, in order to save a little time, I went ahead and made a statement and printed it out for you." She reached for an envelope on the end table by the sofa, withdrew the statement and handed it to him. "I made it quite detailed," she said, "at the risk of its becoming overly long, but I wanted it all down in black and white. Exactly what happened on the two occasions that I encountered a woman later identified by others as Elizabeth Kurtz."

He put on his reading glasses and, holding the sandwich in one hand, eating as he read, he carefully read the statement. It was long. She had made certain to dot every *i* and to cross every *t*. Finally he tossed the papers down on the sofa, finished his sandwich and glared at her.

"Clever, but it won't do. We want a real statement, answers to real questions."

She shrugged. "I'm going to ask Patsy to notarize my signature, and that's the only statement you'll get from me. If you want to ask questions, shoot, and we'll add a postscript, but I'm telling you up front I won't answer any questions about what I did in San Francisco because it's irrelevant and none of your business. And I won't be more precise about what I did driving up the coast to Astoria or where I stopped because I can't. I found one receipt for a motel and included that one, but I don't know and won't know the others until I see my credit card statement early next month."

"What's that business, that the woman who called you claimed to be Elizabeth Kurtz? You told us she made that call."

"I misspoke. I should have said that's what she claimed, because I didn't recognize her voice, having never heard her before. All I can swear to is that she claimed to be Elizabeth Kurtz."

He reached for his second sandwich and bit into it as if it were raw meat and he a tiger.

"If you have no questions to add to that, I'll get Patsy to notarize it and make some copies, three I think. One for you, one for my attorney and one for the press if it becomes necessary."

Hoggarth put down his sandwich and wiped his mouth on the napkin, wiped his hands thoroughly, and, she suspected, counted to ten a number of times while doing so. His voice was even, but mean, when he asked, "What game are you playing this time out? Let's have it all in the open. What are you after?"

"I don't want Leonora arrested and charged with a murder she didn't commit. It's that simple. You know as well as I do that the two attacks are related. The first one didn't kill her, they came back to finish the job. Her computer and printer were all that were taken the first time, no car, no keys, no cash, credit card, nothing else, just the computer and printer and whatever she had printed out. They searched her room again the next time, so they hadn't found it yet. Leonora said Elizabeth was running and hiding from her ex-husband and his mother. You want it all on the table, out in the open, ask them a few questions. Ask Sam Norris whom he called when she was staying in the cabin. He's the caretaker and he knows that's the only cabin over there. He must have seen smoke from the chimney and made a call. Ask him. And he called the Diedricks house after the attack."

"What about a statement for the press? What does that mean?" he asked in the same hostile tone.

"If you arrest her, I go public. They'll have my statement linking the two attacks, and no doubt there will be a lot of questions, which I'll answer on the condition of being quoted as a *usually reliable source*. Carnero was in Manhattan when the first attack happened. Where were the Kurtz crew? Who took those phone calls from Sam Norris? What did Elizabeth Kurtz have that made it necessary to kill her? Why was she running and hiding from her ex-husband and his mother? Lots of speculating to be done, don't you think?"

"Jesus," he said in a low voice, "you're accusing her ex and his mother of murdering her? Leaving the kid to die? You're out of your mind."

She picked up the statement and stood. "Just wondering,

Lieutenant. Just wondering. I'll ask Patsy to get out her stamp. You want to witness it?" He didn't move and she walked from the room carrying the papers with her.

"She's out of her mind," Hoggarth repeated and if it was addressed to Frank or himself was not clear. He looked at Frank. "The locals are satisfied that it was a guy she was traveling with at the cabin."

"We're not, and neither are you," Frank said. "Admit it, Milt. You know whoever left her for dead the first time was the one who went back with a gun the next time." He leaned back in his chair and said, "You have to hold Leonora Carnero here, of course. But you can keep her as a material witness, even house arrest if someone over you demands it, but you heard Barbara. If there's a premature arrest and murder charge, she'll go public, and this case will be tried in the media. I know some damn powerful people are applying pressure and there will be more, but we'll fight fire with fire if it comes down to it."

Hoggarth shook his head. "It's the time element, Frank. There's no time for a third person to get in on it."

"Finish your lunch and let's talk about it when Barbara comes back. I think we'll need more coffee." He got up and went out with the carafe.

Frank and Barbara returned together. She handed an envelope to Hoggarth, put a second one on Frank's desk and the third one in her purse. Hoggarth tossed his copy down on the table. Frank poured fresh coffee and when they were all seated again, Barbara said, "Lieutenant, I understand the spot you're in. I've gone around and around with it myself. Let's speculate. What if the murder had already occurred before

that phone call to me? A search had already been made, then
the call, just to muddy the waters, made it appear that the
killer got the address at that time. Since I had never heard Elizabeth Kurtz's voice, there was no way I could tell who was on
the phone that day, as I made clear in my statement. The killer
could have left seconds before Carnero came on the scene. She
has no idea how long she was there, throwing up, panicking,
running around trying to find a telephone, the call to Spain.
No telling how long that all took. So certainty about time is
an illusion. And the two attacks are no longer separate inci-
dents."

"Now you're claiming the tap on your line didn't mean
anything," he said in disgust.

"I'm saying I don't know what it meant, or who put it there
or when. And neither do you."

She was giving him an out, Frank knew, and he also knew
that Hoggarth recognized it as such. Basically he was a good
detective, and clearly he was not happy with the two attacks,
one successful, one not. How much pressure he was getting
from above would be the key. Hoggarth drank some coffee,
put his cup down and shook his head.

"The M.E. will shoot it down," he said.

"He won't," Barbara said. "I was there for an hour and he
hadn't arrived yet. Another hour? Two more? No medical
examiner can pinpoint the exact time of death unless he's there
with a watch in his hand. We're talking about a difference of
minutes."

"Too many loose ends. What about the boy? Where is he?"

"A separate issue that has nothing to do with Leonora
Carnero. Let Janowsky have it. You're in homicide, not abduc-

tions. At this stage in an investigation aren't there always loose ends? At any stage that's true."

Before Hoggarth could respond, Frank said in a meditative way, "I'd appreciate seeing the autopsy. If you arrest her, I'll get it eventually, of course. Curious about two shots. Didn't the first one take her out? Barbara said there was a pool of blood around the midsection of the body, and another by her head. Curious."

"Yeah, curious," Hoggarth said. "The first one would have done it soon enough through loss of blood. From across the room, the first shot. The one in the face was close, two feet at the most. From above her. They figure she might have moved some after she hit the floor, the second shot was to make sure."

"Someone stood over her and shot her in the side of the face?" Barbara asked, horrified at the idea. It accounted for the condition of the face she had seen, shattered bones, unrecognizable features and so much blood. It accounted for Elizabeth's hysteria. She had seen that same destruction of her best friend.

Hoggarth stood up, then reached for the envelope with Barbara's statement, and put it in his pocket. "Thanks for the sandwiches. I'm thinking we won't do much until after the holidays. Too damn many sick-leave absences this time of year. Year after year, same thing, guys suddenly get sick along about now." He shook his head and walked to the door with Frank at his side.

When Frank returned after seeing Hoggarth out, Barbara said, "At least that puts it off for now. She won't get fingerprinted and put down in the books as Leonora Carnero."

"We'll see what kind of pressure's being applied. The next few days will be telling. Are you done with all that?" He indicated the tray.

"All done."

Before he could pick it up, there was a tap on the door and Patsy came in. "I'll take that," she said.

Frank called Bailey. "He'll take us home, let Alan bring the Buick later on. Keep it for a getaway car," he said.

He put the copies of the Knowlton material and Barbara's statement in his safe while they waited for Bailey. It wasn't long until they were in the SUV, taking an excessively long time to cover the few blocks to Frank's house, a route he routinely walked.

"Where did you lead the guys?" Barbara asked Bailey.

"Oh, we drifted around the mall parking lot for a time, then wandered over to the Gateway Mall and did some more drifting. I checked out a new subdivision or two. Listened to a replay of the Orson Welles broadcast of the *War of the Worlds*. At some point I dropped off Alan so he could get his bike. I think that covers the last few hours. Had to stop for gas." He was actually smiling. "No secret about where your dad's office is, and they're behind us now, watching me take you home. Busy day."

She grinned back at him. "Good work."

But in Frank's driveway her grin vanished when she saw Shelley's pretty little red Jaguar with Shelley inside.

Shelley was out and waiting before Bailey got parked. She looked anxious and even afraid, near tears. "Oh, Barbara! Are you all right? What's going on? Why are they doing this to you? There must be something I can do!"

Helplessly Barbara looked at Frank. He shrugged. "Come on in, Shelley." He said it regretfully, afraid that the little pink-and-gold fairy princess would become another target of a smear campaign, but it couldn't be helped. Barbara couldn't hold out on her any more than they could hold out on Bailey.

19

Inside the house, Bailey went off to use Frank's phone. He used his cell phone only for emergencies, or when he had no other choice, unconvinced as he was that they didn't result in brain cancer. Frank stirred the fire into new life and added a log.

Barbara turned to Shelley, "You first. Who's doing what to me?"

"You know. That awful article yesterday. And today, that filthy talk show. Our own local raving rant. Alex listens for ideas for his cartoons, and he called me to come hear what they were saying. You and Elizabeth Kurtz were lovers, you beat her up in that cabin and she ran away from you. Callers demanding an investigation, how do you disbar a lawyer, femfascists taking over the city. On and on." She said it in a rush, nearly a wail.

Barbara cast an accusing glance at Frank. "An awful article yesterday? Strange, I didn't come across it."

"I saved it for you," he said gravely. "If I'd known they were going to air that broadcast today, I would have taped it. We'll need a clipping service to keep up."

She snorted. "Right. So it's started with a bang. Big surprise." Then, turning to Shelley she said, "As for what's going on, you'll love it." She told her.

Shelley was as stunned and disbelieving as Frank had been. "She can't get away with it. What happens when they find out?"

"Good question," Frank said. "Wish to God I had a good answer."

Bailey had drifted in while Barbara was talking, and now he said, "Jefferson Knowlton has his own two tails. Knowlton and his wife live in a semiretirement community, and the two guys rented a house about half a block away. Supposedly fixing it up for the parents of one of them. Don't know if they have a tap on his phone. I told my guy not to push it. We'll just assume they do."

"Another big surprise," Barbara said. "They'll be watching for a special-delivery package, or if I get in touch with Knowlton, or something."

Bailey shrugged. "You going to stay put the rest of the day?" She nodded.

"Things to do," he said. "See you later."

"Dinner at seven," Frank said. Bailey saluted and ambled out in his usual slouching way.

"There goes the restaurant idea," Barbara said sourly. "We have to find a way to talk to Knowlton and I thought we might all accidentally show up in the same restaurant," she said to Shelley, "but not with four pets at our heels. Who knows? They might even compare notes."

"Someplace big and really crowded," Shelley said.

"Not the mall," Barbara said hastily with a shudder. "Something like the Hult Center."

"We could all go see the *Messiah* tomorrow night," Frank said. "Half of Eugene will be there."

"They have meeting rooms," Shelley said. She flushed slightly. "I sort of contribute, and I bet I can get a room for a meeting."

Barbara laughed. It was anyone's guess how much of a contribution Shelley made, enough to give her a little clout apparently. "That's it. Shelley, if you can get a meeting room, and tickets for four Knowltons, Brice and his wife, and the parents, plus two for Dad and me, I'll give Brice Knowlton a call and let him arrange it with his dad. Separate sections, nowhere near each other."

Half an hour later, with an air of triumph, Shelley said it was done. "The tickets will be at the ticket counter, and I'll drop in and make sure the room is okay."

"Great. Now for Brice Knowlton." Barbara called his cell phone. When he answered, there was too much music and laughter in the background to talk, and he moved to a quieter room evidently. "Sorry about that," he said. "Kids. What's on your mind?"

"We have the research material your father needed years ago to prove his claim," Barbara said. "We have to meet with your father and you, and you can't tell anyone why, not even him, until after we have our talk."

"You have it? How?" He sounded strained, his voice husky. "Never mind. Where, when?"

"We have a room set aside." She told him the arrangements,

then said, "And I repeat, you must not tell anyone why, not yet. Call it a gift from a grateful student or something. Can you arrange it?"

"Hell, yes! We'll be there!"

They talked another minute or two and when she disconnected, she breathed a sigh of relief.

Shelley had been gazing thoughtfully at the fire as Barbara talked. Now she said, "Do you think Lieutenant Hoggarth will follow up on Sam Norris? Ask him if he called anyone before the attack?"

Barbara shook her head. "He didn't say."

"It will depend on those over him," Frank said. "On his own, he would. He's a good investigator. But a lot of pressure is probably coming down on him to stay in his own jurisdiction, to leave it alone. And he subscribes to the chain-of-command theory. He follows orders. We wait and see."

"How long can we wait? You think Norris really knew someone was in that cabin?" Shelley asked, turning again to Barbara.

"He knows those woods, and he knows that's the only cabin up there. He glanced over that way when I told him about it, but it was raining and no smoke was visible. It would have been before the rain, the days before. I think he knew very well that someone was staying there and, as caretaker, I also think he would have called the family about it." She shrugged. "We'll have to find out, but I doubt he'd talk to Bailey or any of his crew. He's too close-mouthed. He's honest and probably would talk to the authorities, or counsel for the defense. That means after an arrest."

"He'd talk to me," Shelley said confidently. "People do, you know."

Almost in unison Barbara and Frank both said, "No!"

Frank leaned forward and said quietly, but with emphasis, "Shelley, you have to understand how big this is. Hundreds of millions of dollars are at stake, and someone's willing to spend whatever it takes to save it. No doubt a whole agency has been employed, and they must have been trying to find Elizabeth from the day she walked away with those papers. Now, believing she's dead, they have three issues to keep under control. One is to recover that research before it reaches Knowlton. If that fails, they'll probably have a case ready to convince a judge or others that Knowlton spent the last decade preparing those papers in order to present his case again. And the third and perhaps the biggest at this time is to keep the attack at the cabin a separate issue from the murder here. As long as Leonora Carnero is suspected of killing her lover, it's an airtight case, a case of jealousy or something of the sort. But if that first attack is seen as part and parcel of a larger conspiracy, that case falls apart. I have no doubt that after tonight, you'll become another target of a smear campaign and have your own followers, perhaps a tap on your telephone. The minute you set off in the direction of the cabin and Norris, you'll become a danger to them."

Shelley didn't flinch or draw back from his stern, steady gaze. Her mouth was set in what he could only think of as a stubborn line. He had seen that expression on Barbara too many times not to recognize it.

She said, "Certainly, I understand. We get deliveries all the time at the house. If Alan comes in a delivery van, brings flowers or something, I can leave with him and no one will suspect a thing. He'd have to drive around the back of the house, out of sight, to turn around. Our dog won't let anyone on the property without sounding the alarm, so there wouldn't be any way for anyone to see me duck inside the van." She looked from him to Barbara, and then back. "We're a team. In this together, and we all have a part to play. I can play my part."

After a moment of silence Barbara said, "She's right, Dad. We have to know, and it would work. We can set it up with Bailey when he comes back."

Wordlessly Frank stood and went to the doorway, where he paused. "Shelley, stay for dinner?"

"Thanks, but no. I told them I'd be back."

He still hesitated, then said, "How about if you bring Alex and the good doctor to dinner on Christmas Eve? No presents, just food, and maybe if people beg me, I'll sing a carol or two."

Shelley laughed. "I'll be here with my gang. We plan a quiet Christmas Day at home, our first one in our first house, but I'd love to come Christmas Eve. Alex and I will start begging the minute we get here."

He went on to the kitchen. They were right. They had to know if Norris had called someone and who that someone was and they couldn't wait until after an arrest. He knew very well that if Elizabeth was arrested, fingerprinted, a convicted murderer tagged with Leonora's name, she not only would go to prison, but she would be in a national data base the rest of her life, and would never get it straightened out again. They had to know.

Shelley looked like a lovely child, a delicate angel, but she was strong, and she was intelligent. It would work, and he had no doubt that Norris would talk to her. As she had said, people did. One dimpling smile was all it took.

* * *

After Shelley left, Barbara went out to the kitchen, where Frank had put wine on the table. "I wonder how Alex will take it," she said. "He'll know in a second that she's into something dangerous."

"Remember what she told us some time ago. He knows what she does, and he knew before they got together. And she said he'd never interfere with her work. He's proud of her."

That much was obvious, Alex couldn't hide it, Barbara thought. Just as she had been proud of her father, as her mother had been. They had known that at times he was making dangerous enemies, and they had been proud of him. She had forgotten that, she thought in wonder, how proud of him she had been all her life.

The doorbell rang and she went to admit Bailey. He joined them in the kitchen and helped himself to bourbon with just enough water to call it a mixed drink. When she told him Shelley's plan, he thought about it, then nodded.

"It would work. Alan will need a backup car, someone to tag along for a few miles, just to make sure no one caught on."

"If there's even a suspicion of a follower, call it off," Barbara said sharply.

"Sure, sure. Use your phone?" he asked Frank, who waved him away. Taking his drink with him, he ambled off to the study.

In a few minutes he was back. "All set. A florist will make a delivery day after tomorrow, around nine. She's to be ready at the back door. Backup car will be around."

Frank stopped whatever he was doing for a moment, then briskly put a casserole in the oven, without comment. Barbara drew in her breath. "They should be back in town by four or a little after."

"Got a minute?" Bailey asked Frank.

He nodded. "Dinner's in the oven. What else?"

"We checked out that old Kurtz house today," Bailey said. "Where Sarah Kurtz and Terry are staying. There's a guy with them, don't know who he is, a big one. Looks like a bouncer or wrestler. Anyway, the house is on University half a block from Eighteenth, by the Pioneer Cemetery, an alley behind it, and a lot of old-growth bushes and trees everywhere. I had my guy drive from there to the apartment on Eighteenth at a quarter after four this afternoon. Eleven minutes."

"The timing is perfect," Barbara said. "Everyone keeps saying the plane landed at three-thirty, without taking into account how long it takes to deplane, get to the terminal, get baggage. She couldn't have gotten to the apartment before four, and probably five or ten minutes after is more like it. Time enough to take a shower and shampoo her hair." She stopped, thinking of the next few minutes. In her mind's eye she saw Leonora putting on Elizabeth's robe, wrapping the towel around her wet hair, hearing a noise, thinking Elizabeth had come. Smiling a welcome...

A shot from across the room. Maybe she jerked on the floor, moaned. Another shot from above her. Then the killer went to the bedroom for a search. It wouldn't have taken long, just the one room, with nowhere else in the apartment to hide anything, just the one room.

"He thought he had plenty of time," she said aloud. "I said I wouldn't get there until a little after five, and he had no way of knowing that Elizabeth was coming. From start to finish it might not have taken more than half an hour."

Bailey saluted. "Thought you'd want to know. I'm going to go watch the news."

Barbara looked at Frank. "Whoever did it had the gun ready, knew exactly what to do and didn't waste a second thinking it over. Just waiting for an address. He must have shot her the instant she came from the bathroom." A shiver ran through her as if she had been touched by an icy hand. "An ex-husband, Jason's grandmother?" She shook her head. "The third person at that house?"

"We can't assume it was someone from that house," Frank said. "We can suspect it, but that's as far as we can go. It could have been the people tapping your phone, or someone we know nothing about. Tomorrow I'll get that corporate structure report, and a list of the heirs of the original investors."

"I can't help thinking how for so many weeks Elizabeth did everything exactly right. Then she called my office." Abruptly she turned and left the kitchen.

That night in the living room they planned the next day or two. "I'll have some names for you to look into," Frank said to Bailey. "I don't know yet how many or anything else about them."

"What we do know is that we want the dope on them as soon as possible," Barbara said. "And I have to go shopping," she added.

Both Frank and Bailey looked disbelieving.

"I need something to carry a stack of papers in. Not my briefcase, not to the Hult Center for a gala evening. And you can't carry them in your suit pocket," she said to Frank. "And later, I have to go home to dress for a night out."

"While you're doing that, I can go grocery shopping," Frank said, thinking about the dinner party shaping up.

"When Alan and Shelley get back to town, I'll meet them and transfer her to the SUV and deliver her somewhere. Her place? Here? Where?" Bailey asked.

"Here," Barbara said. "It's going to be another one of those days," she added, almost as gloomy as Bailey, dreading the mall three days before Christmas.

It took quite a while to work out their schedule for the next day, and as soon as they were finished with it, Bailey said he was going to bed. He would watch television in his room for another hour, Barbara knew; she had heard the TV the night before, and his low chuckle now and then.

"It's a mess, isn't it?" she murmured when Bailey left. "From the others' point of view Elizabeth has to be dead, and from ours she has to be alive and ready to testify about the source for that research. But if she's alive and they know it, would anyone be able to keep her safe? Whisk her away to a safe house somewhere? Then Jason's at risk, and if they manage to snatch him, she'll be their obedient servant."

"It's a mess," Frank agreed.

"The only out I can see," she went on, "is if we can come up with the killer. Not just a suspicion, but hard proof. And anyone who can shoot a woman in the face at close range isn't likely to break down and confess."

He nodded his agreement and they both were silent for a long time.

"Why do we do it, Dad?" she said in a low voice. "Play God

with someone else's life. You, Shelley, me. We're playing God again."

"Because we know there's a lot of time from when a bad law gets passed and when it gets repealed, if it ever does, and during that time real people get hurt by it, sometimes to the point of being put to death. Or," he continued, "because it's all we know how to do, that or flip hamburgers or wash dishes. Or become corporate attorneys. Same thing." He smiled faintly. "Or to get rich."

She laughed. "The phrase is filthy rich. Catch up, Dad. Get with it."

He laughed, too. He suspected that Barbara, with all the pro bono work she did, not only was not getting rich, but was playing it close to the edge much of the time. He sobered again quickly. "Or because we have to."

He stood. "It's going to be a busy day tomorrow. I'm going to take a bath and go to bed. When you go up, turn off the tree lights, and close the fireplace door." He kissed her cheek and walked out with both cats at his heels.

Because we have to, she thought, turning off the lamps. She sat down again with a lowering fire and Christmas tree lights the only illumination. No real choice at all, we just have to. She was thinking of the turning points that everyone can see clearly with hindsight. If she hadn't seen that sign for cabins, if she had not turned in on a whim, what? She had been pondering the offer to teach, she thought, almost in surprise. She had forgotten that she had considered it so recently. Too late now, she knew, but would she have accepted? She didn't know, and suspected that she never would be able to answer that question. If Elizabeth had not decided to go with Terry to look for that assignment, she would be editing her books, planning her Christmas with her best friend and child. Someone who might never have dreamed of killing anyone had become a murderer. Once you make that turn, she thought, you're swept up in a different current, unforeseen, unpredictable, unavoidable. Once you're in it, you have to go where it takes you.

She remembered what Elizabeth had said about her father, that he was such a presence when he was home. He worked, and had to travel several times a year, but when he was home, he was so completely there that neither she nor her mother had ever resented his absences or felt threatened by them. She might have been describing Frank, Barbara realized. His *travels* had been the times he had become immersed in a case, once or twice a year, no more than that. But the rest of the time, he had been completely there for her and her mother. How he had listened to her prattle as a kid, she thought, smiling, and then through her adolescent storms, and into the present. Always there for her. And she gave so little in return, she realized with regret. So little.

Yet he loved her without reservation, and he was proud of her. That thought surprised her, too. He had told her more than once that he was proud of her, but she never attached any particular importance to it. Parents said that to their kids. It wasn't like that, she understood that night, sitting by a dying fire. It was more than the dutiful parent encouraging a child. Alex was proud of Shelley in the same way that Frank was proud of her, the way she had been proud of him all her life. It was important, too important to dismiss without a thought.

The fire had burned down to no more than glowing embers by the time she got up to close the fire screen, turn off the tree lights and go upstairs.

Although San Francisco seemed a far distant past, almost another lifetime, the question the counselor said she had to answer had returned: What are you afraid of?

"Inadequacy," she said under her breath. Her own inadequacy.

20

At nine the next morning Bailey pulled to a stop before the Meier and Frank department store. The parking lot was already filled, with cars circling, drivers searching for a parking space. Barbara didn't look to see if her followers discharged a passenger; she took it for granted that she would be followed every step. She entered the store and headed for the accessories department.

That proved to be a popular shopping area, and the pretty evening bags much sought-after gifts. The forty percent off notices likely had an influence on potential buyers. She saw tiny silver or gold bags, beaded bags, crocheted, sequined. All of them big enough to hold a tissue or two, a small comb, a little makeup, maybe eyeglasses and not much more.

The regular handbags were no better for her purposes, none more suitable for carrying a half-inch stack of papers than the ones she already owned. There were school bags, day packs, backpacks, travel bags. She left the store and made her way to another one. The wide aisles were crowded, noisy, with incessant Christmas music. The next store was no better than the first, and the next…

Sometime during the two hours it took before she decided to sit down and rethink her plan, it occurred to her that she hated the "Little Drummer Boy." She had inspected every bag for sale in the mall, she thought morosely, and nothing. Although she found a coffee kiosk, there was no place to sit down with a cup of scalding hot coffee, and too many people jostling for space to try to manage it standing. Another child began to scream, and she could imagine the kid being put on Santa's lap and suffering a panic attack. Her sympathy was with the child.

A woman got up from a bench and Barbara hurried over in order to get there first, just to sit down and think for a few minutes. She should have called Shelley, who always had exactly the right garment or accessory. But she had to admit that what she was looking for was not exactly the right accessory for any occasion except this one. Could she carry the folder under her coat? Not unless she strapped it to her waist, like a money belt, she decided. Then her eyes narrowed and she thought again, like a money belt. She didn't have a coat that would work, not one that would flare out enough to conceal a package that big. She recalled the beautiful cape Mrs. Cortezar had been wearing when she showed up at the office. That would do it. The papers in a light pouch, around her waist, under a cape. Both hands free and visible, carrying a tiny decorative bag at most. She rose and headed back to a department store, this time aiming for the coat and outerwear department.

It was five minutes before twelve when she called Bailey to

come get her. Her feet were tired, her back was tired and she had a headache throbbing to the strains of the blasted drummer boy's *tum, de, tum tum.*

"See why guys don't like to go shopping with women?" Bailey said aggrievedly when she got into the SUV minutes later. "Three hours to buy one little thing."

"I couldn't find that one little thing," she said, just as aggrievedly. "They don't exist."

He eyed the bag at her feet. "So you killed some time anyway for the joy of shopping."

"The only reason I don't belt you is that I'm too tired to take over at the wheel. I hope the guy following me had as much fun as I did."

She suspected that Bailey's sympathy was for her follower.

"I'll show you," she said when Frank and Bailey looked at her purchases with incomprehension. There were two scarlet, velvet-covered cushions, yards of soft red roping and a hooded cape. "Where are those research papers?"

Frank had retrieved them along with the corporate structure report that morning before going grocery shopping. He went to his study to get them as she unzipped the cover of one of the cushions and removed it. She slipped the envelope of papers inside the cover and zipped it closed. "Pouch," she said. "Scissors? Where would I find them?"

"I'll get them," Frank said and went to the kitchen drawer to retrieve them.

Barbara made a hole through both sides of the pouch, just under the zipper, then worked the roping through the hole. After measuring it against her body, from the pouch over her shoulder, back down, she cut two lengths of the roping for straps. In a few minutes she had her enlarged money bag to wear around her waist, her own improvised version of a backpack. With the new cape on, the pouch was well hidden.

"Besides," she said, when done, "the cape is rather pretty, isn't it?" Dark blue with a red satin lining, it was lovely. "And practical," she added, although she suspected that it would get very little wear. Not her style. She walked around the kitchen with the cape and pouch in place. "I'll add a tie to keep it from moving around. That's why I got so much rope."

"Ingenious," Frank said.

Bailey was grinning. "Let those guys try to figure that one out. If it's reversible, you can be Little Red Riding Hood come Halloween." He looked at the other red cushion. "Why two?"

"Because you don't buy just one cushion," she said. Bailey and Frank exchanged puzzled looks.

After Barbara had taken off the cape and pouch, she took off her shoes and stretched out on the sofa with a book. Bailey left with copies of the corporate structure report and the list of heirs, and Frank went to his study to read the judge's decision regarding the first suit Knowlton had brought against the Diedricks Corporation.

Words blurred and ran together until Barbara realized that she was not reading anything and she closed the book. One of the cats came to help her rest, and later when Frank glanced in, both were sleeping.

When Bailey returned and, after a little arguing, she agreed to go to her apartment only long enough to pick up some clothes, then come back to Frank's house for another day or two. "But this can't go on indefinitely," she said, pulling on her jacket. "So they follow me, so what? Let them."

Bailey scowled and Frank frowned, and she added, "I said after another day or two, not tonight. Let's go."

The plan that night was for the Knowltons to arrive at the Hult Center at seven-thirty, mingle with the crowd in the lobby, then for Brice to escort his mother and his wife to their seats on the upper level, and leave them, ostensibly for him to collect his father, who had happened to come across an old friend. Afterward he and his father would say they had listened to the first part of the oratorio in a room set aside for that purpose with others who had failed to take their seats in time. Barbara and Frank would arrive close to eight. He would join the Knowltons first, and after the chimes sounded for attendees to be seated, she would.

All three were at a conference table when she entered the meeting room. The elder Dr. Knowlton was a tall, lean man with sharp features and a big bony nose. With thin gray hair a little too long and eyeglasses, he looked more like a college professor than Brice did. And he clearly was suspicious and wary of this unprecedented conference. Frank introduced Barbara, and the men watched with interest as she removed her cape and the pouch and placed it on the table.

"The young lady who showed me where the room is said we can hear the music in here," Frank said, as he turned a dial on a wall panel of dials and switches. Audience noise came in too loud and he adjusted it. The sound faded to little more than white noise. "I'll turn it up when they start," he said. "We'll want to know when the intermission comes."

"Now will you tell me what this is all about?" Dr. Knowlton said sharply. "Who are you two?"

Frank handed him his card, and Brice said, "Ms. Holloway is also an attorney."

Dr. Knowlton looked ready to leap up. He tossed the card on the conference table, but before he could rise, Barbara opened the pouch, withdrew the folder and handed it across the table. "Take a look, Dr. Knowlton. Do you recognize any of these papers?"

She shouldn't have done it that way, she thought in alarm when Dr. Knowlton opened the folder and looked at the first paper, then turned it over to see the next one. The color drained from his face, and he looked as if he might faint or have a heart attack. Sweat glistened on his upper lip and broke out in beads on his forehead.

"This is my work," he said in a hoarse whisper. "It's my work! Where did you get this? Why didn't you come forward twelve years ago? Why now?"

Brice put his hand on his father's arm, but his expression was no less demanding when he turned to Barbara.

"I had never heard of you or the Diedricks Corporation twelve years ago," she said. Then, looking at Brice, she added, "I didn't have any of that when I talked to you. I can't tell you how it came into our possession, but it's irrelevant in any event. Where we go from here is what we have to discuss."

"These are copies," Dr. Knowlton said, leafing through the papers. "Where are the originals?"

"In a safe place," Frank said. He cocked his head. Almost

below the threshold of audibility the opening strains of the *Messiah* floated in. He went to the wall panel and adjusted the sound, then resumed his seat. "We have until the intermission for this discussion," he said. "Dr. Knowlton, is that all of the work that you claimed vanished?"

Dr. Knowlton continued to examine the copies page by page. He stopped and made an inarticulate sound in his throat when he came to the sheet of practice initials. "I never did that," he said hoarsely. "That bastard did it!" Brice took the paper, set it aside after a glance. Finally Dr. Knowlton nodded. "It's the work we were doing that last year or two. Maybe three."

"I read the judge's decision in that lawsuit," Frank said. "He gave the only verdict possible at the time. There was no proof, no corroborating evidence, no other witnesses concerning the origin of that work. He had no choice. And your attorneys had no remaining options, Dr. Knowlton. You have to accept that. There were no options without some kind of evidentiary proof."

From his expression Barbara guessed that Knowlton would never accept that, but he made no comment.

"Why were there no witnesses?" Frank asked. "Coworkers or someone who knew what you were doing?"

Dr. Knowlton took off his glasses and rubbed his eyes, replaced them. "He was a loner all his life, Hank, I mean. He'd get his ideas alone and work out the preliminaries, then turn it over to R&D to follow through with. Nearly twenty years ago, he came across the work my team was doing with robots at Caltech, and he gave me a call. We met and he asked me to work with him. I was added to the research-and-development team in Portland, where Joe Kurtz was vice president, a joke, a title but no real input. I hardly ever worked there. Hank had a separate workplace on his property and that's where we did our joint work. Or sometimes at the cabin. I rarely went to the laboratory in town. Some of our work was doable fifteen years ago, some has been done and patented, is being used today and some was what the attorneys called visionary, Hollywood movie material. Visionary then, practical today. Microprocessors, nanotechnology were in their infancy, now they're a reality. I followed that field, and we both saw the role they could and would play in prosthetics."

He leaned forward as he talked, and seemed prepared to go into detail about the work they had done. Barbara glanced at Frank uneasily, and he interrupted Knowlton.

"All right, you two worked out of sight. At the house? Why didn't household help come forward to say so?"

"Not at the main house," Knowlton said. "There are three houses on the property—the main house, a guesthouse by a little lake and another fully furnished guesthouse close to the south entrance. Hank had bought that one when it came on the market, and he used it for a retreat. He had a workroom, his ham radio setup, television, everything he needed in the guesthouse, and that's where we worked. I was hardly ever in the main house."

"Hank is Henry Diedricks?" Frank asked. Knowlton nodded. "Why didn't he testify on your behalf? At least make a statement of support?"

Dr. Knowlton's face became twisted, with resentment, bitterness, grief, a combination of all of them? It was hard to read that expression. His tone was bleak when he answered.

"Thirteen years ago Hank crashed in his airplane. He nearly died. Head injury, broken bones, a shattered shoulder, punctured lung, other injuries. He was in intensive care, surgeries, back in intensive care. No visitors allowed for over a year. The guesthouse was locked up and I couldn't get in. I tried repeatedly to see him after he was sent home, but they always said he was too sick for company and wouldn't let me. I worked on some things we had nearly ready to turn over to the team during that period, but I wanted to get to my own work, and I finally consulted the attorneys about it. The family gave them a statement from Hank, signed by his doctor, that said his head injury had resulted in a loss of memory along with his vision, that he regretted that he had to refuse my request to talk to him, that there was nothing he could say to me. He rejected me, Mr. Holloway. Kicked me out. There wasn't a thing I could do about it. My attorneys got a court order to look over the work space in the guesthouse, but it was gone. Sarah and Joe Kurtz were living there, and swore they had lived in it for many years. An estate manager, a man named Lon Clampton, backed them up. There were no papers, no documents, nothing to show I'd ever set foot in the guesthouse."

When Frank asked him on what basis his former attorneys had accepted the case in the first place and had taken it as far as they had, he answered readily. "Because I was able to describe in exact detail the latest patent the company had taken out, my work, with Joe Kurtz's name on it. He couldn't have identified it in a pile of scrap tin. Their lawyers claimed I had looked up the patent and memorized the details, that anyone with my training could have done that and it was discounted."

Barbara was keeping an eye on her watch, and she tapped it a short time later. Frank nodded. "Dr. Knowlton, we have to wrap this up rather soon, I'm afraid. What we propose to do is contact your former attorneys, with your permission, and present them with the evidence they needed years ago in order for them to represent you again in a new lawsuit. They are best prepared to do this because they have done the pre-liminaries. You have to believe me, they did all they could with what they had before. I know some of the attorneys in that group and they're good men. They gave you good advice when they said not to try for an appeal, because they knew you would lose. Now they can press what I believe will prove to be an irrefutable case."

"They lost," Knowlton said bitterly. "And they gave up. How do you know who they are? I didn't tell you." His suspicions had surfaced again, narrowing his eyes, making his mouth look pinched.

"I read the court decision—their names are on the papers," Frank said.

Brice put his hand on his father's arm the way he had done before, and he said to Frank, "Can you give us a day or two to talk this over? It's pretty unexpected, I think Dad needs a little time."

Frank nodded and addressed his remarks to Brice. "There's another matter we have to discuss. Someone is desperately trying to locate that material, and they will do whatever it takes to prevent its surfacing again. You have to understand that Dr. Knowlton may be in extreme danger if it becomes known that he saw us and has an inkling of what we're proposing to do. We know there are people watching his house, and prob-

ably listening in on his phone calls. You saw the precautions
Barbara took in getting that material here tonight. I urge you
both not to discuss this meeting with anyone at all, and to take
every precaution in your phone conversations. There isn't a
thing you can do at this point except wait for attorneys to take
over the case and proceed with it. We may have to have an additional meeting in the future under strict secrecy, and as
soon as new attorneys accept the case, arrangements will have
to be made for meetings with that group."

Brice picked up Frank's card. "Can't you, your firm, represent Dad in this?"

"No. My firm doesn't handle criminal cases, and this one is
most certainly a criminal affair. Barbara doesn't have the staff
to manage this kind of case. You need a large firm willing to
commit as much time as it takes to seeing this through to a conclusion. I want to stress to both of you, until this case proceeds
to a legal status, there will be great danger if the other side
learns the research material is now available for a court to
examine."

"One more question," Brice said. "With that research material in hand why can't we simply call a press conference,
announce the fraud and go on from there? Publicity can be a
damn nuisance, but it can also be a shield."

Frank explained that they had to be able to produce the
person responsible for finding the papers, who would testify
as to where they had been located. "We can't do that at this
time."

"Elizabeth Kurtz," Brice said in a low voice. He turned a
searching look to Barbara. She remained silent.

Frank ignored his guess, also, and said, "The Diedricks Corporation's attorneys can claim that Dr. Knowlton has been working on those sketches and notes for years and is taking advantage of Joe Kurtz's death to make his claim again. We couldn't refute that at present."

"That's precisely what they would claim," Dr. Knowlton said angrily. "And they'd laugh at me for being an idiot with an idiotic story."

Applause sounded on the speakers. Barbara stood and reached for the papers to return to her pouch. "Time's up. Use your cell phone to call mine when you reach a decision," she said to Brice. "Make sure you're in a private place where we can talk. We'll go on from there." He wrote her cell phone number in a notebook, and she put the pouch back in place with the cape over it. One by one they left the meeting room to mingle with the crowd gathering in the lobby for an intermission.

21

"At ten after nine the florist delivered the flowers," Bailey said the next morning. "Shelley got in the back with Alan, and they went to the rendezvous point, switched cars and now Alan's driving her down to the cabin. Not a hitch, and no followers. An easy twenty bucks for the delivery man."

Barbara drew in a breath. They wouldn't get back before four, possibly a little after. It might prove to be a long day. Frank was ready to go to his office in Bailey's SUV, to replace the research papers in his safe. "I'll walk home," he said. "I have things to do here today." She felt almost jealous since she had nothing to do except wait for Shelley to get back.

He paused walking to the door when Barbara's cell phone rang. She switched it on and heard Elizabeth's voice.

"Have you seen the *Oregonian* newspaper?" Elizabeth asked. She sounded angry.

"No. What is it?"

"An article under the heading, Jason's Two Mommies. And it's exactly what the title suggests. There's a picture of me, curls and all. The reporter knows where I'm staying. There was a photographer outside here yesterday. I didn't see him, but that's a picture from yesterday, what I was wearing yesterday."

"Hold it, I'm coming over there," Barbara said. She disconnected, then repeated what Elizabeth had said. "There's no point in trying to hide her any longer. I'm going over to calm her down, and I'm driving. As far as anyone else is concerned she has nothing to do with the research, but it seems the general smear is in full swing." She pulled on her jacket. "And what's more natural than to call your lawyer's associate in a situation like this? See you later." Without waiting for any argument, she left, and was mildly surprised to see the clamshell still in the back of her car. She had forgotten all about it.

Elizabeth's flare-up of fury had subsided to a dull seething anger by the time Barbara arrived. "It's filthy!" she said. "Disgusting, what he's saying in that piece, and not a word of it's true! Jason called us both Mama from the time he could talk, then it was Mama One or Mama Two, whoever was there first, but not like that makes it sound. It was a joke for him. He called my mother Grandma One, and her cousin Grandma Two. A joke."

"Take it easy," Barbara said. "Where's the article?" She threw her jacket down on the sofa and went to the table in the dining space where Elizabeth had pointed and scanned the article quickly. It was every bit as bad as Elizabeth had said. Two lesbians fighting over a child they both wanted. Elizabeth's divorce shortly after she delivered, the two women sharing an apartment from then on. Leonora was made out to be a merciless money-grubbing bitch.

"Okay, so you know how the game's going to be played," Barbara said, tossing the paper down. "Your mother's sending me the divorce papers, so we'll have some ammunition to fire back, but not just yet. How are you, otherwise?"

"Caged. I was going to get a computer, but I realized how limited it would be. I can't use my own passwords for anything, and I don't know Leonora's. Start from scratch? Have a third identity? I'll have to, but if the police demand the computer later on, how would they interpret that? Besides, I'm afraid to spend my cash. Without a credit card I can't even buy a book at Amazon. And I'm going to run out of money. Mother's transferring money to Leonora's account, but I can't touch it. I don't know her mother's maiden name, for security, and if they fax a signature card, I'll mess that up, too." She spread her hands in a gesture of defeat. "Caged on all sides. I want to talk to Jason, wish him a Merry Christmas, but I'm afraid to do it on this phone. I'll have to find a place that sells international phone cards or something. I was looking at public pay phones yesterday, and they don't have real booths any more, just open stalls where anyone close enough can hear every word." She bit her lip, then said, "Sorry. It just seemed that suddenly everything was coming down on me at once. Everywhere I turned there was a new wall."

Barbara laughed. "Whoa! Let's take them one at a time. You're upset by that stupid article, but it's only the opening salvo. Ignore it for now. Got coffee?"

Sitting at the table with coffee, with the newspaper pushed aside, she asked, "Why can't you use Leonora's credit card?"

"Have you seen her signature? A scrawl that I can't come close to matching. I tried last night, and anyone could tell at a glance that it wasn't the same or even close."

"Would practice help?"

"Let me show you." She left and returned with the credit card and, as she had said, the signature was an impossible scrawl.

"I see what you mean," Barbara said. It would be nearly impossible to reproduce that scrawl easily, automatically, the way one signed for a credit card purchase.

"And I don't know what her limit is, or how close she was to the edge after buying her plane ticket here. I can't go on the Internet to find out since I don't have her password."

Barbara nodded. "Okay. Look, your mother gave me a check for ten thousand. It's in my safe at the office. I'll deposit it next week and today I'll take you to my bank and transfer that amount to you in order to open your own account, under Leonora's name, with the signature you provide. They'll give you temporary checks, and you won't have to wait for anything to clear. Forget the credit card. Then we'll go buy a laptop. Didn't Leonora have one with her?"

"She had a desktop computer at home. No laptop. Neither did I until I ran away."

"Well, you'll want something more portable from here on out. So that's wall number two down. Now about calling Jason. Is the time difference seven or eight hours?"

"Eight, I think. I have to call him by noon, before his bedtime."

"I think a call from you would be the perfect Christmas

present for him," Barbara said. "Tomorrow, come to Dad's house early and make the call from there. A safe phone, quiet, and you can talk as long as you like. Plan to spend the rest of the day. You can help me set up Dad's present, and play with his cats, or just nap, then have dinner. Would that work for you?"

Elizabeth's eyes were bright with tears, and she nodded. "Thanks," she said in a low voice. "That would work."

"Wall number three. Now down to business," Barbara said briskly. "Last night Dad and I met with Jefferson Knowlton." She described the meeting, and finished by saying, "I think Brice will talk him into agreeing to go back to the original firm. It's really the best way to proceed now. But while he was talking, he said some interesting things. He said they worked in a guesthouse. Do you know about that?"

"There are two," Elizabeth said. "Terry and I stayed in one by a little lake. That one doubles as a bathhouse. The bigger one was where his parents stayed. I just saw it from a distance. But Grandfather Diedricks couldn't get his wheelchair to either of them. The property's on a slope, with some terracing, the main house higher than the rest of it, and most of it's in woods. There are at least two sets of stairs going down to the lower levels. Not many steps, five or six, but still impassable for a wheelchair. There's a narrow gravel driveway connecting the two houses, and he couldn't manage that either. Sarah used a closed-in golf cart to go back and forth."

"He wasn't in a wheelchair when he worked with Dr. Knowlton," Barbara said. "Tell me about his injuries, what you know about them."

"Not much, I'm afraid. I didn't ask questions, but what I

could see was that his right arm was useless, paralyzed. And he must have hurt his hip, or his back, or something that put him in a wheelchair. And, of course, he's blind."

"But you said his mind's sharp and he uses a ham radio."

"Oh, yes. He's sharp. His mind's fine, it's his body that's a mess. He listens to audio books, history, biography, books on science and poetry for the most part. And Shakespeare. He can quote more Shakespeare than anyone else I ever met. And he likes opera, and Hoagy Carmichael. He has a complete collection of Hoagy Carmichael. Other jazz, too. He said it's music from the good old days. He listens to the news on the radio, BBC, NPR, a lot of different stations. He talks to people all over the world by ham radio."

"Where does he have the ham radio set up?"

"There's a little room off his bedroom. Maybe it used to be a dressing room, but now he uses it for the radio, and his music and books." She regarded Barbara with curiosity. "Why are you so interested in him?"

"I'm not sure. Would you say his memory had been impaired, from what you saw of him?"

"No way. He could recall things that I think of as ancient history—the dust bowl, when penicillin was introduced, names of jazz musicians I never heard of. All sorts of things."

"Okay. What about Lon Clampton? Where does he fit in that household?"

Elizabeth shook her head. "I couldn't quite figure him out. He acts as general manager, tells the cook what to make for dinner, bosses the gardener around and runs errands for the family, or did then. Terry hated him. I think at one time he was afraid of him because he's so big, over six feet and broad, strong and a little rough in his manner. Not the perfect English butler, although he does what a butler would do, I guess. I had very little to do with him, I just met him a couple of times. He lives in the main house. And he has his own assistant, a man who was in charge when Lon went to New York with Sarah and Joe. I didn't actually meet him, but they called him Bud."

"Anyone else up there?"

"The live-in cook, who's also the housekeeper, and she answers to Clampton. And a man named Gary Swarthmore, who goes in for a few hours every day to help Grandfather Diedricks. I guess to help him bathe, dress, whatever. I think he does physical therapy. Grandfather can stand up, he just can't walk, so he isn't totally helpless. Gary takes him out in the wheelchair around the upper part of the grounds, or out in the car for a drive. Grandfather Diedricks said he'd outlived everyone he ever knew, but he likes to get out of the house. I don't know if Gary is a nurse or what his official title would be. He seemed nice."

"If I called the house, who would answer the phone?"

"Either Lon or Bud, or you'd get voice mail."

"What did you mean that Sarah uses a golf cart to go back and forth? Does she actually live in the guesthouse?"

"Maybe *guesthouse* is exactly right. We were there for eight days and she and Joe had dinner at the main house every night that we did, and she had a bridge club meeting there that week. So I think she used the main house as if she lived there, but they slept in the guesthouse."

Barbara had a few more question about the living arrangements in the main house, and then they went out to her car to go to the bank and shop.

After Elizabeth got in the car and fastened her seat belt, she said, "You seem to have a giant clamshell in your backseat."

Barbara laughed and explained its purpose. "That's what I want to set up. It would really be neat if I could fill it with water and birds, but in the living room that could be a mistake. Anyway, birds are hard to catch. Don't you find it so?"

"I do," Elizabeth said. After a moment, she added, "If there's a craft store near any place we'll be, I'll catch you some birds." It sounded as though there was a catch in her throat as she continued. "Those weeks crossing the states with Jason we stopped in toy stores a lot, and several times in a craft store. You know, things to entertain him in the evenings before bedtime. Take me to a craft store and I'll fix your birdbath for you—my contribution to Christmas."

She turned her head away and gazed out the side window, and they both remained silent as Barbara drove to her bank. When they finished the chores on her list, she drove to Michaels craft shop, where the aisles were almost impassable with late shoppers. After a glance around, Elizabeth went to the art department and picked up a large sky-blue poster board and from there across the store to where there were tree decorations, decorations for flower arrangements, items Barbara couldn't even guess a use for. And there were life-sized faux birds on thin skewers. Elizabeth picked up two cardinals, a bluebird and a robin and said she was done.

"Lunch," Barbara said. A few minutes later, with salads in place, she asked, "Tell me something about the work you do. You're a book editor?"

Elizabeth talked about some of the books she had edited with evident pride and pleasure. "I didn't have to take a job, but I wanted to. I found that being a full-time stay-at-home mom wasn't quite enough, but I did a lot of the work at home. Since there were two of us to take turns, there was never a shortage of maternal care for Jason. It worked out well. Leonora had a sort of go-nowhere job with an auto insurance agency. She could take off pretty much whenever she wanted to and so could I. It was a good arrangement."

When she pulled up in front of the condo apartment, Barbara asked if Elizabeth wanted help getting the laptop up and running.

"No. It won't be a problem, and it gives me something to do. That's the hard part, not having anything to do. Maybe I can find Leonora's passwords. She isn't—she wasn't very computer savvy. Barbara, thanks. For today, for everything. I'll see you tomorrow before noon at your father's house."

She took her laptop into the apartment building and Barbara drove back to Frank's house. She had not looked for a follower a single time, and didn't now. She hoped the guy had followed them into the craft store, certain he would have loved it just about as much as she had.

She left the poster board and birds in the car in Frank's driveway a few minutes later, and thought that on the whole it had been a successful morning. It was two-thirty and the rest of the afternoon, waiting for Shelley's return, was not likely to be quite as successful. Inside the house, the fragrance of chocolate was intoxicating. Frank had made his Sacher torte. He always made Sacher torte for Christmas.

He came from his study before she had her jacket off. "Terry Kurtz is looking for you," he said. "He called the office and tried to get a cell phone number from Patsy first, then he called me. I told him I'd let you know."

"Now what? I'll have to see him, but where? Not the office. No one's there, heat's turned down and besides, I don't want to meet any of that crew alone. Not here. Shelley will come…" She thought, then said, "Martin's. I was going to drop in tomorrow with a gift for him and Binnie. I'll do it today."

She had found a pair of cloisonné peacocks, the cock in full magnificent display with a multicolored tail spread wide. The peahen at first glance was almost drab, but her colors, muted gold and silver, a faint peach hue, green-tinged in places, blue-gray, made her every bit as gorgeous as the male.

She called Terry's number. "I have from three until four," she said crisply. "Another appointment at four, I'm afraid. Or next week sometime."

"Where? I'll be there."

She gave him Martin's address. Then, blowing Frank a kiss, she left again, this time to go to her apartment, pick up the box and head for Martin's.

Martin and Binnie were as delighted with the gifts as she had known they would be. Martin threatened to break her ribs when he embraced her, and Binnie's eloquent expression made up for her silent thanks. Martin stroked the peacock and said, "Girl, you been watching me strut my stuff?"

"You've got it," she said, laughing. Binnie was stroking the peahen almost reverently, her beautiful smile heartbreaking.

Martin vanished into the kitchen and returned with his own box. "That Soave you like," he said. "Thought it might be nice for you to have now and then even if you don't come here to drink it."

"My God, Martin! Not six!"

"Just six. Ought to last a little while. Want me to put it in your car?"

She handed him the keys, and presently he came back in with a puzzled look. "You know you have a clamshell in the backseat of your car?"

"No! No way! Get out of here, I'm expecting company any minute. And that clamshell happens to be a birdbath," Barbara said, laughing.

"You want me to put up your In sign?"

"Nope. Just one customer and he's by appointment. I won't give him coffee or anything else, and when you let him in, make sure he's alone, will you?"

Martin's eyes narrowed and the merriment vanished. "I sure will," he said. He and Binnie picked up their birds and went to the kitchen. He came back seconds later when the doorbell rang.

Terry Kurtz was alone. He looked about the restaurant warily, as if to make certain he was in the right place, then took a chair opposite Barbara at her usual table and Martin vanished into the kitchen once more.

"Thanks for seeing me on such short notice," he said.

"What's on your mind?" She was studying him closely, not quite sure what had changed, but something had. Although he was not haggard, he did not look like a college boy now, and there were shadows under his eyes.

"I read that piece in the newspaper today," he said. "It's not true, Ms. Holloway. They weren't like that, what the article says. I don't know anything about Leonora Carnero, but I know Elizabeth wasn't like that. She was a fine, wonderful person without a mean bone in her and she adored Jason. Can I...can I tell you about her, about us?"

She nodded. "Please do."

"That year we had together, it was heaven. She loved me, Ms. Holloway. I know she did. That wasn't pretense or conniving to get pregnant. She really loved me, exactly the way I loved her. You can't pretend that, no one could pretend that. She was happy when she learned she was pregnant, but she was happy for both of us. And I blew it. Not Elizabeth. I was the one who blew it. I was jealous and afraid and I wanted us to go on the way we were forever. I blew it." He was looking at his hands on the table and clenched them both into fists. "I can't believe now how I did that. I didn't want a baby to come between us, and I thought she would choose the baby over me, freeze me out the way my own mother had always done. I ran away while she was pregnant."

His hands opened, clenched over and over. His fingers were long and shapely, like his mother's, but although he appeared to be looking at them, she thought he was not even aware of what they were doing. He was looking inward.

"When I went back, Jason cried and she picked him up to nurse him, and it hit me again, there was no room in her life for me. She had a child. Seeing him at her breast was like a knife stabbing me. Like a jealous boy."

He stood abruptly, looked around the restaurant, then sat down again. "Sorry. I should save it for a shrink. I keep looking at that picture of Jason, and I see her. He has her eyes, the same kind of teasing, mischief-making look about him. He looks so much like her. God! I was so goddamn dumb! So stupid!"

He stopped again and shook his head. "What I really wanted to say to you is that my mother can't have him. If Elizabeth said he's safe, he is. She wouldn't have left him with anyone who wasn't able to provide for him, to care for him. But whoever that is is under a lot of pressure, and it will get worse with the Amber Alert and the FBI, police everywhere watching for him. Whoever has him will hand him over, or they'll find him sooner or later and Mother will get him. She has that big reward out for information, his return. But she doesn't want him anymore than she wanted me. She'd farm him out to strangers, keep him out of sight. Please, Ms. Holloway, if you know who has him, please don't let that happen."

His voice had changed as he spoke, had become ragged, breaking in strange ways. It was almost as if he was having trouble breathing. "I'm begging you not to let that happen. I want my son. I want to be his father, take care of him, keep him with me. I want him to know he's loved very much." He shook his head. "He looks so much like her. Those beautiful eyes. Just like hers." It was little more than a whisper when he repeated it.

He stood again. "I guess that's what I really wanted to say. Just to beg you not to let my mother have my son."

Barbara stood, too. "Mr. Kurtz, are you staying here in town?"

"Mother and Lon left this morning. I'll stay here until they find him. You can call my cell phone any time, day or night, and I'll be here within minutes. Ms. Holloway—" He looked as if he wanted to make his plea again, to elaborate, explain, but he added nothing, perhaps realizing that he had said it all. He closed his eyes briefly. "Nothing. Thanks for seeing me."

"Mr. Kurtz, will you answer a question? You said you over-heard a conversation that convinced you that Elizabeth and Leonora were lovers. Did you hear anything like that?"

He shook his head. "Reading that newspaper today brought it home to me. I'm responsible for that. I said she had what she wanted and didn't need me anymore. Like a spoiled, jealous child, making excuses. Then I went along with it when Mother put her own interpretation on what I said. Spite, jealousy, a streak of meanness, I don't know what it was that made me say it, then go along with it."

"Thank you," Barbara said, and watched him as he walked to the door and out. She knew what was different, she thought. He looked like a man with a guilty conscience, but more like a man who had lost something irretrievable and re-gretted it bitterly. And she knew that he must never come face-to-face with Elizabeth, no matter what she called herself. Even with her eyelashes blunt and stubby, she still had those beautiful eyes that haunted her ex-husband.

22

Barbara was telling Frank about her time spent with Elizabeth when Bailey and Shelley arrived. She gave Shelley a big hug.

"I promised myself not to start worrying until four-thirty," she said. "You saved me from another gray hair." It was twenty after four.

Shelley laughed. "It was a picnic, sort of. Alan told me funny stories, and it's a beautiful drive. Mr. Norris was suspicious at first, but his wife said for me to come in and get warm and have a cup of hot chocolate, and I did."

Frank grinned. Everyone wanted to give her hot chocolate or candy or something. "Shelley, do you want coffee, wine, anything?"

She had coffee and Barbara wine. Bailey held out for his usual bourbon. They took their drinks to the living room where Frank poked the fire, and they arranged themselves on chairs and the sofa. Cats immediately chose laps.

Shelley drew in a breath, then said, "Not only did Norris see smoke on Tuesday that week, but someone from the village beyond the stacks at the beach saw Elizabeth and the child and congratulated him for landing some winter tenants." Shelley looked and sounded triumphant. "And sure enough he called the main house and left a message about them on the voice mail. No one called back about it, and he let it go at that. He had done his duty. On Thursday, the deputies dropped in and talked about the attack a little, asked a few more questions and after he ate Thanksgiving dinner, he called the house again and left another message, about the attack this time. This time a man named Lon Clampton called back within half an hour, he said. He had a lot of questions, none of which Mr. Norris could answer. What did she look like? Was she alone? Things like that. And since he hadn't seen her himself and he just had your description, he told Clampton about you, who you were and told him what you had said about Elizabeth."

"Well, it appears that Mr. Norris can talk after all," Barbara said dryly. "Did he also tell you what the deputies had to say when they dropped in?"

"He didn't, but Mrs. Norris did. She said they thought they had it all figured out. They gave up the idea of a cougar attack early on, then they gave up the passing vagrant idea." She shook her head. "Alan and I drove over there after we left the Norrises, and to have considered a passing vagrant in the first place was more than a little insane. Anyway, they gave it up. What they settled on was that Elizabeth had a man with her all along. He beat her up, and left her in the rain to teach her a lesson while he started to load the car. Mrs. Norris said one of the deputies told her *they* do things like that to their women."

Barbara made a rude sound and Shelley said, "I second that. Anyway, he heard you coming and hid, and as soon as you were gone, he finished loading the car and they all took off."

"Did they mention the child? What he was up to, running down to the beach for help?"

"They said that kids like that are afraid of the men their mothers pick up, and of course he tried to run away from him. It's natural."

"All neat and done with," Barbara said. "Now it can be shelved and forgotten. Assholes!"

She thought for a few seconds, then asked, "Did they tell you anything about Lon Clampton, why he was he one who called back?"

"Not Mr. Norris. He remembered that he had things do to somewhere else, but his wife talked a lot," Shelley said. "It seems that all decisions come from Clampton. For instance, some years back, after Dr. Diedricks had the accident, Mr. Norris didn't know what to do about the cabin. Turn off the electricity, keep firewood stacked, just general caretaker kinds of things. He couldn't get through to anyone but Clampton, who gave him orders to keep the electricity turned on, keep brush cut back, firewood and so on. Clampton said they'd get in touch if the orders were changed. No one ever called back to change anything, so he went on doing what he had always done, and every month a check came along. Not much, Mrs. Norris said, but a little and it helped out."

She sipped her coffee, then said, "Mrs. Norris said it seemed funny to her that they never laid eyes on Lon Clampton, yet he seemed to be in charge, and even signed the checks. It seemed a terrible waste to her to keep up a cabin that no one

ever used. She's convinced that Dr. Diedricks intends to come
back some day, maybe to die there. And they keep it up exactly
as if they expect that to happen."

Barbara thought of a sick cat crawling off to die in a secret
place. Quickly then she recounted her day, the newspaper
article, shopping with Elizabeth. "She brought up Lon Clampton's name, too. Apparently he's a majordomo up there and
runs things generally. But the most interesting part of my day
was later when I met with Terry Kurtz." She told them about
that meeting. "I don't know what to make of him yet. Two different stories about his relationship with Elizabeth and each
time he appeared sincere. Back burner for now. Elizabeth said
he hated Lon Clampton and used to be afraid of him."

Frank turned to Bailey to ask, "Do you have the information about the original financial backers of the corporation,
possible heirs?"

"Three investors in the beginning," Bailey said. "Five percent
of the company each. One sold his share back years ago, and
there are five living heirs of the other two. One in Austin,
Texas, one in Tucson, one a rancher in Harney County, a li-
brarian at Oregon State University, and a doctor in Vancouver,
Washington. None of them has a thing to do with the company
except collect their share of profits. Full report," he said,
reaching into his duffel bag to retrieve a folder. "It will take
more digging to find out where they all were on the days of
the attacks."

"Well, there haven't been any profits for the past seven
years until recently," Frank said. "They bought a building to
remodel for corporate headquarters in Manhattan, and built
a production plant in New Jersey, and went into debt to do

it. Since the Iraq war they've landed a big government contract and business has picked up, but it was a dry spell for quite a while."

"They seem to live pretty high for a profitless corporation," Barbara commented.

"Good salaries," Frank said. "One of the reasons profits are scant."

"Isn't that interesting?" Barbara said. "Sarah isn't employed by the company and never was. Joe was the money earner in the family. And her father keeps hanging in there, so she doesn't inherit, either. How will she keep up her expensive habits? Insurance? A company death benefit plan? I think if I were Dr. Diedricks along about now I'd want a food taster."

Frank frowned at her and Bailey looked shocked. She grinned.

"One more thing," Frank said. "We've been thinking of a sale in the hundreds of millions of dollars, but that's perhaps too modest. Think instead of a billion dollars. Apparently futurists foresee a growing need for prosthetics."

"Bionic man and woman, here we come," Barbara said after a moment. She found that she could not comprehend what was really meant by a billion dollars. She turned to Shelley. "One last bit to impart. Our meeting with the Knowltons, father and son."

"You think he'll go back with the first attorneys?" Shelley asked when Barbara finished describing the meeting.

"I hope so. It would simplify things just a little." Then, looking at Bailey, she added, "I also think that sooner or later we're going to have another security problem, as soon as, or if, anyone realizes how far we've gone with that research material, and that Dr. Knowlton is now engaged in it."

He scowled. "He needs a safe house. No way to keep him secure in that retirement community."

"Maybe it will come to that."

"Well," Frank said getting to his feet, "if that concludes this impromptu briefing, I'll go start some dinner. Shelley, join us?"

She dimpled and shook her head. "It's been a long day. I'd better get on home. Alex has been acting so mysterious, hiding something and I want to catch him at it before whatever it is gets all wrapped up."

"She," Frank said, jabbing a finger toward Barbara, "never waited for Christmas until she was grown up. Guess you haven't reached that point yet."

Shelley laughed. "Guess not. It's big, whatever it is, and not a pony. He wouldn't try to keep a pony in the house." She did not sound certain about it.

She left with Bailey soon after that and Frank went to the kitchen. Barbara continued to sit by the fire and in her mind's eye she was again seeing that haunted look in Terry Kurtz's eyes. A guilty conscience could account for it, she brooded, especially if he had shot his ex-wife in the face. Or he could have come to know too late that he still loved her, that he had thrown her away and now she was gone forever. Or he could be thinking of an unimaginable fortune slipping out of his grasp.

However that turned out, what his visit implied was that he continued to believe that she and Elizabeth had in fact talked and that she knew where Jason was. And now, believing Elizabeth was dead, he and his bunch might also believe that Barbara was the only active player. They knew she had flown to Las Vegas and mailed something from there. Possibly they were puzzled about her intentions and they must wonder if she knew the real significance of those papers.

If they believed she and Elizabeth had met and talked, that she had taken Elizabeth as a client, then they also believed that she had lied about it to them and to the police. Such a talk would have had to have taken place at the cabin, or during the period after Elizabeth fled and vanished for more than a week following the first attack. Barbara assumed that they knew whatever the police did, that Elizabeth had spent five days at the shelter, but that still left several days when she and Barbara could have met before Barbara returned to Eugene. There had not been any time when their spies were not on the job after her return. And if they believed she had lied about that, they were no doubt considering that she might be holding out for an offer, that she might resort to extortion or might be investigating the actual worth of what she had in order to cut a deal.

They were as much in the dark about what she knew, what she had, where the research material was, as she was about putting a name on that unknown *they.* She nodded to herself. It was something to keep in mind.

She went upstairs to her makeshift office and using her laptop she went into Google Maps and located the Diedricks property, then made a printout of the map. Taking it and an Oregon road map she entered the dining room to spread them both on the table, but she stopped moving when she saw the flowers on the table.

Inexplicably the image of Terry Kurtz's haunted eyes came to mind as she gazed at the flowers, and her thought that he had thrown Elizabeth away and she was lost forever. Darren's e-mail rose in her mind.

"I haven't thrown him away," she said under her breath. "I haven't." Abruptly she left the dining room, still carrying her maps.

"Want to see something interesting?" she said to Frank after dinner. "A Google map of the Diedricks property. People kept saying it's up in Portland, but it really isn't. It's twenty-five miles southwest of the city in the hills, and the R&D section is in town."

She put the two maps on the kitchen table and pointed. "This is the guesthouse where Knowlton said they worked and that Sarah said she and her husband had lived in for years."

The map was excellent, all three residences very clear, the driveway to the guesthouse, the lake and bathhouse with walkways leading to them and the main house, all well separated, landscaped around each building, and the rest of the property covered with trees.

"The interesting part," Barbara said then, indicating the road map, "is that it would take only a few minutes to get to I-5, and from there to Eugene and points south is freeway driving and fast. An hour and a half at most to get to Eugene, probably less when traffic's light." She traced the highway with her finger as she said, "And then another three hours to get to the cabin. Elizabeth was attacked between one and one-thirty, I think. It was about two when I got there."

Slowly Frank nodded. He knew it could be a mistake, but they were both assuming that someone from the Diedricks house had taken that drive in November.

He also assumed that whoever had shot Leonora to death thinking she was Elizabeth would not hesitate to kill anyone else who might stand in the way of a billion dollar deal.

23

Elizabeth arrived before noon the following day, looking anxious and nervous. Barbara took her raincoat and led her straight to Frank's office. "All yours," she said, pointing to the telephone on his desk. "Take as long as you want."

Elizabeth emerged forty minutes later with traces of tears on her cheeks. But she was smiling. "They'll spoil him to death," she said softly. "He said Grandpa Ferdy let him ride a horse, but it wouldn't run. And Grandpa said he would buy him a pony, and he intends to teach it how to run." She laughed. "He asked me when I was going to come home and I said I had to finish some work first, and he said okay. I was afraid he'd be upset. Mother and Fernando will see to it that he doesn't get upset over anything. I should have known better."

She looked at Frank and asked, "Is there anything I can do to help out? Earn my dinner?"

He shook his head. "Both of you, out of the kitchen. Why don't you go somewhere and have lunch?"

"He knows I'm a kitchen klutz," Barbara said, "and I think he believes most females are at heart. I want to pick up a centerpiece for the table. Let's head to the Fifth Street Market."

"What's the matter with those flowers on the table?" Frank asked. "I thought we'd use them."

"Too big, too much, too high. We wouldn't be able to see one another."

"Can I have a look?" Elizabeth asked. "Maybe I can arrange something smaller with them."

Barbara showed her to the dining room and she nodded. "Okay. Is there a florist at the market you mentioned? I want a piece of OASIS."

Barbara didn't have a clue about what she meant, but she said there was a florist and they left. Although the market was crowded, the food court was spacious and they found a table, inspected the various small eateries and had lunch, then visited the florist where Elizabeth bought what looked like a green brick and a spool of green tape.

"You have some evergreens in the yard, don't you?" she asked. "A spruce tree or pine or something."

"Several."

"Then we're all set."

Back at the house Elizabeth said they should soak the OASIS in the bathroom sink and keep out of Frank's way. All she needed was a saucepan. She put the green brick in the sink with warm water, added the saucepan filled with water on top of it to weigh it down and then went outside to cut some greenery.

It was like magic watching her work with the flowers and greenery a short time later. The OASIS had become dark green after soaking up most of the water, and had softened. She put it in a low bowl, tied it in place, clipped stems, poked greenery into the OASIS, added flowers and it seemed in no time she had a beautiful low centerpiece. She arranged the remaining flowers in a slightly smaller vase, where they looked untouched, as beautiful and luxuriant as ever.

"How many languages do you speak?" Barbara asked when they drew back to admire her handiwork.

"Several," Elizabeth said. "Mother entertained a lot of people from the UN. She thought I should learn to speak with them in their own language."

"And I bet you can cook, too," Barbara said morosely.

"Some. Why?"

"If you can also sing, I might have to kill you," Barbara said.

Elizabeth laughed. "Saved by a voice like a frog and a tin ear."

Bailey wandered in and, while not actually smiling, he had a pleased expression. "Guess what?" he said. "Just talked to Hannah. One rainstorm after another down there in sunny California. No golfing, no fishing, just sitting around yapping and fighting. She said it's just as well that I'm not in the middle of it, and she wishes she could leave. I promised a trip to Hawaii next month if I could just meet her in Portland instead of flying down for a day or two, and she thinks that's more than a good deal. Never thought I'd be grateful for rain." He grinned. "Bet they don't close down fishing in Hawaii. And they invented sunshine."

"Keep thinking of sunshine and come help bring in stuff from my car," Barbara said.

They brought in the clamshell, poster board and birds, the pedestal and the box of wine from Martin. "That goes on the back porch to chill," Barbara said, and Bailey took it out. After Barbara and Elizabeth set up the birdbath, Elizabeth cut out a circle of the blue poster board to fit in it, and worked the skewers with the birds through it, then put it in place.

"Presto, water and birds."

"It's wonderful!" Barbara said. "Perfect. Now we'll pretend we haven't done a thing and let Dad discover it when he will."

"If it lasts that long," Elizabeth said, watching the two cats who appeared extremely interested. "You might end up with feathers all over your house."

Barbara shooed them away from the birdbath, and sat with Elizabeth chatting by the fire. Before long Frank joined them with wine, cheese and crackers. He stopped in midstride. "Well, I'll be damned." He set down the tray and went closer to the birdbath to examine it, chased one of the cats away and then said, "Just what the garden's been needing for a long time. Thank you."

He walked back to the sofa and kissed Barbara on her forehead. "Pity we don't have cardinals here," he said. "But you fixed that."

"She did it," Barbara said. "We don't have fireflies, either," she added to Elizabeth. "Strange, isn't it? Seems a perfect climate for them."

Nibbling cheese and chatting about inconsequentials, she thought this was how life was probably supposed to be, not one crisis after another. Life in utopia, she added, not in her own here and now. Her cell phone rang minutes later, and her caller ID showed that it was Brice Knowlton calling.

"Excuse me," she said, and left the living room. So much for peace and quiet, she thought derisively in the kitchen. "Okay. Alone. What's up?"

"Dad will go along with whatever you and your father decide is best," he said. "He knows he bungled things last time around."

"Good. Nothing's going to happen until Tuesday. Monday's a holiday and probably no one will be available. When we get something set up, can I reach you at this number?"

"Day or night."

"Good. One more thing. We're going to have to get your father and mother to a safe place where we can meet with him, and where the other attorneys can, too. On Monday, get him to call up and down the coast to get a reservation for at least four days, a week would be better. It doesn't matter where it is, anywhere from Brookings to Astoria, because they won't actually go there."

"On his land phone?"

"Yes, indeed. We want them to listen in and know your folks are off for a few days at the coast. And meanwhile I'll want to see you again to fill in some details. I'll call you back on Monday to arrange it."

When she disconnected, she was thinking furiously. Where could they hide Dr. Knowlton and his wife for days, possibly a week or longer, and how to manage another meeting with Brice and not have it known? Later, she told herself. Deal with it later.

"I'll set the table, and then I have to go wash my face and change into something besides jeans and walking shoes," she said minutes later, back in the living room. "Seven of us, right?"

"Eight," Frank said, rising. "I invited Darren. As I said, no one should be alone on Christmas Eve." He left the room quickly without waiting for a response from her.

"That's what he told me, too," Elizabeth said. "He's pretty terrific, isn't he?"

Barbara nodded. He was. But Darren? She didn't want him to come near her, not now. Not until this was all over. They would take notice, look him up. She remembered how immobilized she had been when she had come across him at her apartment, as if caught in a frozen moment of time. *Don't make an issue of it,* she told herself sharply. He's an old family friend, like Dr. Minnick. That's all. Just a family friend. She closed her eyes hard.

There were hugs and kisses with Shelley, Alex and Dr. Minnick, more a father figure to Alex than just a friend and mentor, but she didn't dare touch Darren, and he was just as careful. She introduced Elizabeth as Leonora and that was that. She had told Elizabeth about Alex's disfiguring birth defect, but no one was ever really prepared for the reality of his grotesque appearance. Elizabeth caught her breath, made a quick recovery and didn't avert her gaze, which was always embarrassing. She accepted him exactly the way he had accepted her, a woman under suspicion of murder.

Frank had prepared an especially scrumptious meal, Barbara thought at the table across from Darren, but avoiding looking at him—ducks with a brandied apricot glaze; sweet potato puffs, crisp and brown on the outside, and melting inside with a touch of ginger and honey; asparagus, a lovely salad. The Soave helped, she knew, as she refilled glasses, but she was acutely aware of Darren every second.

The talk drifted from topic to topic until movies were mentioned, and Frank said, "They just don't make them the way they used to."

"No," Barbara said. "Now people talk, and there's color, and music, not just an out-of-tune piano. Not at all like they used to."

"Scoff all you want," he said agreeably. "Now it's car chases and explosions and near naked women running for their lives, and monsters."

"What's your favorite old-time movie?" Alex asked.

"Let's narrow it down to a favorite scene," Frank said, standing. "Scene—a cabin in the wilderness, a snowstorm raging, the pretty young thing holding an infant and the villain leering and twirling his mustache. Villain, 'You must pay the rent.' Pretty young thing, 'I can't pay the rent!'"

He was doing the voices, one falsetto and tremulous, the other deeply villainous, and Barbara was suddenly plunged back into a memory of sitting up in bed while he read the Pooh books. Lugubrious Eeyore, perky Tigger...

She blinked rapidly, then glanced across the table and caught Darren's gaze on her. She looked away quickly.

Frank was finishing, "Hero, 'I'll pay the rent!'" Everyone laughed and applauded. He bowed deeply and sat down, grinning.

Laughing, Dr. Minnick stood. "Remember the Saturday serials? Wonderful stuff! Scene, The bad guys have caught Dick Tracy and he's handcuffed to a water pipe in the bottom of a pool. The villain is leering in this one too—in the good old days villains always leered and sneered—"

Watching him, paying little attention to the ridiculous story line, Barbara thought what a wise old man he was. He had taken in Alex, a suicidal, tormented adolescent and saved him. How many others had he salvaged during his long years as a juvenile psychiatrist in Manhattan? How painful it must have been when he failed, and finally now he had a family that loved him and one he loved without reservation. Golden years. That was what the phrase meant, she realized, having a family you loved who loved you in return.

Dick Tracy saved himself and was free to fight crime another day. Barbara laughed and clapped along with the others and watched and listened to Shelley ham it up about the pretty young thing in a sheer nightgown investigating a noise in that dark cellar. If she had ever had a sister, Barbara thought, watching, she would have wanted her to be Shelley. Beautiful, rich, unspoiled, brave, all the things one would want in a sister. Then Alex did the dying composer who struggles to stay alive long enough to finish a great symphony. He fell over dead, in a final bit of histrionics, to laughter from those at the table. Shelley had said once that when she looked at him, she saw a beautiful shining man. Barbara had come to know what she meant.

When Darren stood, Barbara felt every muscle go tense. She kept her eyes downcast, listening. He was doing a Harold Lloyd bit, a clueless hero who, oblivious, avoids several murderous attempts on his life.

His voice, always musical and low, seemed especially so in the retelling, evoking both amusement and suspense. He had a magical voice, Barbara thought, and remembered the magic of his large warm hands massaging tension from her shoulders. His hands were always warm. Magical healing hands, a magical healing voice. He was a good actor. He had mimed the parts beautifully.

Elizabeth stood. Barbara hadn't known how much she would go along with the game, but apparently Elizabeth had felt the trust in the group, the acceptance and even love they all shared. She described a western village where everyone is huddled inside in terror. "In one house the hero is taking a revolver from a closet shelf. He loads it as the pretty young thing watches eyes wide. 'What are you doing? You mustn't go out there. It's dangerous. You can't go out there!' She runs to stand in front of the door. He straps on his gun belt and holsters the gun." In a bass voice Elizabeth said, "'A man's gotta do what a man's gotta do. Get out of the way.' She moves aside, wringing her pretty little hands helplessly. 'I love you. Be careful,' she whispers. He exits. And she bites her knuckle." She received especially enthusiastic applause.

Barbara did a roomful of scientists at computers, all trying to arrive at the right combination to detonate explosive devices in a mammoth meteorite hurtling toward earth. "One by one computers flash big red messages—Error, and go black. A woman scientist is keying in code as fast as she can, working feverishly. Sweat is on her forehead as she works. Another computer goes black. Someone is praying. Another computer goes black. The man at it rises and leaves the room with slumping shoulders, his head bowed. There is the sound of a shot. For a second the woman stops all motion, then resumes even faster. Hers is the only computer still working.

A young male scientist is standing over her shoulder watching. Suddenly she gasps and clutches at her chest, then slumps, unconscious. Reaching past her the young scientist finishes the last bit of code, and in space there is a tremendous explosion, then another and another. And everyone is hugging the young male scientist and laughing hysterically, or crying, as the woman falls to the floor."

"Come on, Bailey, don't be a holdout," Barbara said, after taking a bow. She didn't look across the table toward Darren, but she knew he was watching her, smiling, as he had been doing all evening, every time she happened to glance his way. Watching, smiling.

Bailey scowled at her. Reluctantly he stood. "Okay. This guy and his girlfriend kiss good-night." It was about a werewolf, who escapes the strong room his servant locks him in, and is last seen loping with red eyes toward the pretty young thing with the dewy eyes walking by the moonlit lake. He told it exactly the same way he gave one of his abbreviated reports.

Barbara wanted to hug him. He should have been down in San Diego with his family, his wife's family but, instead, here he was with this family, as much a part of it as anyone else at the table.

They all applauded, and he scowled even more, and sat down.

"Enough of this frivolity," Frank said. "No time for Oscars. It's time to clear the table and get down to the serious business of dessert."

They cleared the table, then ate Sacher torte, had coffee and some brandy. Afterward they all helped wash the silverware and crystal, load the dishwasher, do the pots and pans. When Frank tried to participate, he was chased away.

"It's been a lovely party," Shelley said later, pulling on her coat. "Mr. Holloway, you outdid yourself with dinner tonight. It was wonderful, everything was wonderful. I love your movie game."

They left, and Barbara turned from the door to see Darren watching her, still smiling. "It was wonderful," he said softly. "I'll be taking off, too. Thanks, Frank. One of the best Christmas Eves I ever had." He said it to Frank, but his gaze remained on Barbara. When he left, she realized that they had not touched all evening. They didn't dare touch each other.

Elizabeth nodded. "For me, too. I was dreading tonight, but it was lovely. Thank you."

Then, when all the guests were gone, and Bailey had gone up to his room, Frank sat down by the fire. "A good evening."

Barbara nodded. "A good evening. You throw a mean party, Dad."

After Frank went to bed, she continued to sit by the fire, but now her thoughts revolved about the new issues to be settled. What to do about the senior Knowltons to keep them safe, how and where to meet with Brice and how to manage a secret meeting with the attorneys who had handled the Knowlton business originally? Then, she found herself thinking again of Darren's big warm hands and his magical, musical voice, and the way he had watched her, smiling all evening.

24

On Christmas morning when Barbara went downstairs, there was a box at her place at the breakfast table. Not a wrapped box, but a cherrywood, elaborately-carved box that she hadn't seen in twenty years. Frank was already seated with the newspaper, coffee in the carafe.

"Merry Christmas," he said.

She wished him a Merry Christmas, sat down and touched the box with her fingertips. As a girl she had loved to sit on her parents' bed, waiting for her mother to open it on the rare occasions when they brought it home from the safe-deposit box. How she had held her breath waiting for her mother to open it and take out a necklace, or a ring, or something else that was exquisite. The box had held the little gold and sapphire tiara her mother had worn at her wedding and the diamond ring she wore on very special occasions. For the past few years Barbara's annual gift had been a treasure from that box.

"Open it," Frank said gruffly.

It was compartmentalized, and some of the compartments still held treasures from the past. The tiara was there, the diamond ring and a jade and emerald necklace. She looked up at Frank and to her surprise felt tears in her eyes.

"She wanted you to have it all," he said. "She told me it was all for you, however I wanted to give it to you. Whenever."

"I don't know what to say. It's too much. Dad, are you sure? It's so much."

"It's yours."

"Thank you," she whispered. "Thank you." She went to him and put her arms around him. "Thank you. You and Mother always gave me so much, and I gave you both so little."

"Christ on a mountain," he said, disengaging her, drawing back. "Haven't you learned yet that some things aren't about quid pro quo? Sit down and have some coffee while I finish the waffles." He stood and crossed the kitchen to turn on the waffle iron. "Later you can vacuum up feathers in the living room while I set up the birdbath in the garden. Those damn fool cats had a party of their own overnight."

Late that afternoon, in the study with Frank and Bailey, Barbara said, "We have little more than a week before Hoggarth will have to make a move, probably an arrest. Our first priority is to get the Knowltons somewhere they'll be accessible for the Portland group of attorneys, and where they'll be safe. I've been thinking. What if we have a couple of ringers drive off to the coast in the Knowltons' car, with the tails following, and after an hour or so, to make sure the coast is clear, have the Knowltons driven up to Portland to a hotel apart-ment, or something like that?"

"Sylvia," Bailey said promptly. "She'd love it. She's on the phone at least once a week begging for a new job. And I can find someone to go with her."

Sylvia Fenton was one of the state's most flamboyant women, married to one of its wealthiest men. She had been an actress in off-Broadway shows when Joe Fenton saw her and was smitten, decades ago, and despite family objections he had married her. Sylvia loved to play cops and robbers, and had proven extremely good at it more than once.

Barbara and Frank both nodded. She would be ideal. Given a picture of Mrs. Knowlton, with her own skill at makeup and disguise, Sylvia would play the part flawlessly. Barbara said she would ask Brice to furnish a picture.

"She wouldn't have to stay on the coast more than a day," she said. "They change their minds and head back home, and take a detour to meet old friends—the Fentons. And Sylvia's back where she belongs. Think she'd do it?"

"Are you kidding? She wants to partner with me, set up a real agency, with offices and staff and get a license to pack a gun. A few details to work out and I'll give her a call," Bailey said.

"Not today," Frank protested. "It's Christmas."

"Tomorrow," Bailey said.

"Once that's taken care of, with any luck by Wednesday I'll breathe easier," Barbara said. "Tomorrow I want to take Eliz-abeth to the Gateway Mall, shop a little and go to a movie at the multiplex there. I've been looking over times and what's playing, and if Brice Knowlton takes his two kids, plus a couple of their friends, to see a film, and Elizabeth and I go to a different movie a little later, Brice and I can duck out and meet in a third one, a dog with few people, where we can talk. We have to let him know exactly what's at stake here, and get his cooperation to get his folks out of town. How does that sound?"

After some discussion they all agreed the plan should work. The mall would be a madhouse the day after Christmas, and the kids' movie would be packed. Many parents would leave their children to watch movies while they hit the sales and returns. And four young kids, aged eight to ten, would be more than enough cover for Brice.

Barbara went to call Elizabeth, and to go online to buy movie tickets. Then, using her cell phone, she called Brice on his.

"All set," she said afterward. But she was apprehensive, with just one week to go before Elizabeth might be arrested, or have to reveal her identity and face other consequences, and most assuredly be at grave risk. Not enough time, she kept thinking. There simply wasn't enough time to stop the inevitable. Without something real, something concrete to give to Hoggarth, it was going to happen. She narrowed her eyes, thinking, then went upstairs. There was a light under Bailey's door, and a faint sound from the television. She tapped lightly.

"Let's talk," she said when he opened the door. Indicating the little office she used in Frank's house, she led the way and Bailey followed.

He scowled at the only chair besides the one at her desk, but he slouched down into it. "So, talk."

"I've been thinking about something you said, something about Alan and dope, and the three stooges holed up in an apartment."

"It went like clockwork," she said the next evening. She had brought Elizabeth back to Frank's with her, and they were at the kitchen table as he did mysterious things to a salmon. "The mall was even worse than I had thought it could be. Hardly space to move. I hope my followers had fun. They must think I'm a shopping freak by now."

She had met Brice in the back row of a nearly deserted showing of some kind of space adventure. He had been stunned when he learned the truth about the Diedricks Corporation buyout and how much money could be involved. And he had provided a good picture of his parents for Bailey to pass on to Sylvia. He would be waiting for Bailey's call to give him the details about getting them out of town.

"The Knowltons have a bed-and-breakfast lined up for four days starting Tuesday, in Waldport. New Year's weekend was hopeless. We'll have to work with that. Can we get the rest set for tomorrow?" she asked Bailey.

He nodded. "It's all set. Sylvia is gung ho, and she said Joe would play a role this time. We'll make the switch at Freddie's on West Eleventh, big crowded store with dressing rooms. They'll stay on the coast until early on New Year's Eve, then head for home. Big party planned for Saturday. Posing as the Knowltons they'll look like just another couple going to a weekend party." He looked at Frank. "She said she invited you and you told her you stopped leaving the house on New Year's Eve. She said to tell you she'll get you yet."

Frank laughed. Sylvia's constant threat, or possibly regarded by her as a promise, was to snare Frank after Joe passed away.

Elizabeth looked from one to another in bewilderment, and Barbara explained what they intended to do. "After you, Jefferson Knowlton is most at risk. We want him on ice until things are under control."

Elizabeth regarded her for a moment, then said, "And you're right up there with us, aren't you?"

Across the kitchen, Frank stopped squeezing limes abruptly, then began again more vigorously than before. No one answered Elizabeth's question.

Breaking the silence that had fallen over them, Bailey said, "Tomorrow morning I'll take that picture out to Sylvia and we'll plan exactly how to make the switch. I have to be in Portland at four to pick up Hannah, and I'll take the Knowltons up and see that they get in the hotel apartment. Tonight I'll go home to turn on the heat and make sure everything's okay. I think I left some dirty dishes, and that's a no-no as far as Hannah's concerned. She'd blister me for that. Are you going to hang out here?" he asked Barbara.

She nodded.

The next morning when Barbara sat down at the breakfast table, she saw a newspaper article circled with a magic marker. Three Seattle men had been arrested in a drug raid for possession of an unspecified amount of methamphetamine. The article had little more information than that, but it was enough, she thought in satisfaction. It was enough.

She drove Frank to his office after breakfast, and listened as he placed a call to Kevin Lorenz, the attorney he knew on the team that had represented Jefferson Knowlton years before.

After Frank explained what they had and what it meant, he said, "Seems it could go a couple of ways. He could press for criminal charges of fraud, grand larceny, whatever, and no doubt win a hefty settlement. Or he could insist on reestablishing his rights to the material, having the patents in his name and hold out for a percentage of the company. Keep it quiet, let the sale go through, retain some authority in the research and development department, and complete some very important work, if he chooses, collect a more modest settlement or back pay or something."

Barbara nodded her approval. She had made the same suggestions to Brice, who had seemed doubtful that his father would cooperate to that extent. He really wanted to destroy everything in his path, Brice had said. But if an attorney pointed out the real benefits of doing it that way, he might be swayed, he had acknowledged.

"I know," Frank was saying. "We'll be able to establish provenance in a week or two. But it's enough to start with." He listened again, then said, "Good enough. I'll fax the material, and you can let us know after you consult your partners. I understand that he can be a difficult client, but there's an awful lot at stake here. If you agree to take him and his case again, I'll get the original material to you."

"What do you think?" Barbara asked after he hung up.

"They'll take him back. Just being cautious. He brought up the same question I did, where did the material come from. But they'll take it. I'll get Patsy started on the faxes. And then call Milt Hoggarth."

* * *

Hoggarth didn't keep them waiting for his lunch hour that day. Minutes after the faxes had been sent and the research material put back in the safe, he arrived. His cheeks and nose were fiery from the walk over in the cold and he said yes promptly when Frank offered coffee. He held the cup with both hands, warming them. "Your dime," he said, eyeing Barbara with suspicion, as if he knew it was her show.

"I want to tell you a story," she said. "I'll keep it short, just a plot outline, I think they'd call it in school. But first, to repeat, every word in my statement was the absolute, literal truth. We'll go on from there. I've talked to a number of people and learned a lot of things I didn't know when you and Janowsky first came around asking questions. I feel it's my civic duty to let you, the authority in the case, have access to the same information, to facilitate your investigation."

Hoggarth's suspicions increased and he made no effort to hide the fact. "Just an innocent bystander, as usual," he muttered. "Go on."

"Right. Let's start back in October. Suppose Elizabeth Kurtz came across some papers that were very damaging to the Diedricks Corporation, papers that indicated a serious crime had taken place. Now suppose she took the papers and fled in order to have a chance to read through them all and consider what to do about them. But she recognized her danger and, accordingly, took her small child with her, and managed to keep out of sight for weeks as she gradually made her way to the west coast. For whatever reason she returned to the cabin she had visited in the past with her ex, and since she had the cables and connections for a laptop and printer, we'll assume that she had made copies of the documents she had taken. Now we don't have to assume or suppose, but accept as fact that the caretaker of the cabin knew a woman and child were in the cabin from the day she arrived, and he conscientiously called the Kurtz house in Portland to report this. He left a message on the voice mail. The caretaker told Shelley that was the case," she added. "I told you someone had to check that out. Anyway, back to our story. Two days later Elizabeth was brutally attacked and left to die. Her laptop and printer and every scrap of paper vanished."

She paused and sipped her coffee. "Fast forward," she said then. "You know about the next days at the shelter, but nothing real after that until I received a call from her. But we know there was a tap on my phone, and we know that between the time of the call and the time I got to the apartment to keep our appointment someone entered the apartment and shot as a woman walked out of the shower and into the living room, then shot her again just to make sure. That person searched, possibly looking for the originals of the copies that had been taken during the first attack. Now, wouldn't you say that if we knew who had a tap on my phone, and who was called that day, it might be a significant lead to follow in investigating who fired those shots?"

Hoggarth had not said a word, and didn't say anything when she paused again. He helped himself to more coffee and leaned back, waiting.

She smiled slightly. "I know you and Janowsky doubted my story, that I had not met with Elizabeth, and Sarah Kurtz and her son Terry were equally disbelieving. So much for a reputation of truth-telling. But it seems that Bailey got it in his head that if someone had put a tap on my phone, that same person might want to know if I met with anyone about certain papers, and even hired some people to keep an eye on me, follow me around to note to whom I talked. You know how Bailey is once he gets an idea. He can't let it go and, lo and behold, he proved his point. I had a constant shadow, and he set out to find out where they holed up, and if possible who had hired them. He found out where they were and told me the address. Then, to my surprise, I read in the morning newspaper that three men at that same address, men from Seattle apparently, had been involved in a drug bust. What a strange coincidence, I thought."

Hoggarth turned a deep red and set his cup down hard. "By all that's holy! Jesus Christ, you set them up! And now you're telling me about it!"

"Lieutenant," she said in protest, "come on. I'm just pointing out a remarkable coincidence. Of course, if those men are private investigators, and if they truly are involved in dealing in meth, that could be a very serious offense, one that would cost them their licenses and put them in prison. Isn't that so? I wonder, if they knew anything about the phone tap would they be willing to talk about it? Just wondering, you understand. They might not know a thing about it, of course, and just take their chances with the law."

"You're framing those guys, and you expect me to go along with it! I'll have *your* license, Holloway."

She spread her hands and shook her head. "For what? For wondering out loud? That's all I'm doing, just wondering. Of course, if it turned out they had a green van filled with electronic gear, that might move idle wondering more to the speculation department."

Bull's-eye, she thought in satisfaction when his eyes narrowed. "I don't imagine that guys from Seattle have a local attorney ready to spring them instantly, post bail bond and such. But on the other hand, depending on who hired them, it might not take very long for someone to rush to their rescue. It would be nice if someone had a chat with them before that happened."

She poured more coffee and held the carafe up in an inquiring way. He shook his head. Musingly she said, "If I were leading the investigation into that shooting, I'd wonder if a gun dealer in Sacramento had inherited a small fortune from a long lost uncle recently."

"That guy gave a sworn statement. Made a positive ID, said there was a man with her, Hispanic, giving her advice about what to buy. They left together."

Barbara shrugged. "The newly deceased uncle might have been quite wealthy. Anyway, I'd also wonder if old Dr. Diedricks, who was a field surgeon in Germany in World War II, brought home any souvenirs, possibly a Luger. I understand many soldiers did. And I guess I'd like to find out if he still has it stashed away in a box somewhere."

"You're accusing the Kurtz family of homicide," Hoggarth said heavily. "They cover each other. In the old Kurtz house all that evening."

"It takes eleven minutes to drive from there to the apartment at that time of day," she said. "And Elizabeth gave me very good directions on the phone. BiMart across the street, Albertson's on the corner. Hard to miss that intersection. She even told me about the drive behind the apartment where there's parking with a back entrance to an alley. Whoever had that tap had the same information."

"You have the statement from the caretaker?" Hoggarth asked.

"I'll have Patsy make a copy for you," she said, taking it from her briefcase. She handed it to him to read first.

He handed it back after examining it carefully. "Don't bother making a copy," he said. He ran his hand over his scalp.

She wondered if he missed his hair, and felt the need to check now and then, to verify that it really was almost all gone.

"You don't have anything," he said. "Speculation, nothing there I can take to the D.A. He thinks he already has all the case he needs to convince a jury, and he thinks you're trying to squirm out of taking the stand and testifying under oath. He intends to call you as a hostile prosecution witness and ask hard questions. That week they were having a funeral, then a memorial service; the house was full of people, business meetings, conferences. There were probably dozens of calls, that's just one more call on voice mail, maybe never even listened to." He stood. "He's ready to take the case he has to the jury right now and doesn't want any complications."

"He'll get them, Lieutenant," Barbara said softly. "I promise you, he'll get them, and they start the day he orders the arrest of Leonora Carnero."

25

Barbara had been sitting in her office gazing at the calendar, brooding. Three working days, she kept thinking, no more than that. Then another long holiday weekend and the following Tuesday back to regular work schedules, and no doubt the police would move in on Elizabeth. It mattered little how dissatisfied Milt Hoggarth was with his case; he would follow orders. She had to admit that if the district attorney dismissed the attack at the cabin as the first of two aimed at Elizabeth, he had an airtight case. A case he would win. And she, Barbara, would be his key witness. Insane, she thought again and again. Arrested, tried and convicted for the murder of oneself. Insane. As Leonora, she would be convicted of murder. As Elizabeth, she'd end up another murder victim, if not immediately, soon. Too much money was at stake to let her stay alive. They would find her, no matter where she was hidden. And no defense was possible without the truth coming out.

Recognizing the futility of going over this same scenario yet again, Barbara finally got up, put on her jacket and told Maria that she would not be back that day. She drove to Elizabeth's condo apartment building.

"I don't know what I'm after," she said to Elizabeth. "We have to do something, and at this particular point in time, I don't have a clue about what that something is. Let's just talk. Let me ask questions, try to fill in some blanks. Game?"

"Sure, Barbara, whatever it takes. I understand the situation. I even considered hightailing it out of here, but I'm done running. All out of hiding skills, I guess. I just want to get it over with." She spoke with hopelessness, verging on despair, and looked like someone already defeated.

Barbara began asking questions, sometimes randomly, sometimes following up on something already said, and after two hours, she didn't know if she had gained anything worth the effort or not. "Let's back up a little. Gary Swarthmore. You think he's a physical therapist or a nurse?"

"Probably a therapist. Grandfather Diedricks didn't really need a nurse as such. He needed help with his bath, and someone to take him outside in the wheelchair and in the car now and then. And to help exercise. Gary was there only a few hours a day. Grandfather isn't totally helpless. He ate dinner with the family and was very good with one hand, despite being blind. The cook cuts up anything that needs it in the kitchen. He's proud and doesn't want anyone fussing over him. Gary didn't. He seemed matter of fact, but apparently was very fond of Grandfather. I don't think he had anything to do with anyone else in the family, and seemed to deliberately avoid Lon Clampton."

She drew a house plan and pointed out various areas—the kitchen, Grandfather's rooms, a den, a spacious dining room, an office. "It's not a mansion in the usual sense of the word," she said. "It's a big rambling house, two-story, old-fashioned and very comfortable. A good house, with the entire main floor accessible for the wheelchair."

Barbara studied the house plan. "Dr. Diedricks's rooms are pretty well separated from the rest of the downstairs. Could he hear much of the activity in the other rooms?"

"Probably not. When I was in there helping out with his French I couldn't hear a thing."

"And no one could hear him, either, I guess," Barbara said thoughtfully.

"Well, he wasn't much of a noisemaker, you know. But you're right. When he was out of sight it was as if he didn't even live there," Elizabeth replied.

Barbara's phone buzzed and she saw that it was Frank calling. "Hold it," she said to Elizabeth. "Latest from the second front, or something." On the phone she said hi, and then listened.

"Bailey checked in. Everything's taken care of and he's on his way home. And Kevin Lorenz is dropping in tomorrow to renew old acquaintances. Thought you'd like to know. Are you coming home for dinner? And where are you?"

"Good news on both accounts," she said. "I'm chatting with your client, and is it okay if I bring company? If things are underway and that's inconvenient, we'll pick up a bite first and then come over. There's something I want to do there with her."

"You know there's always plenty. Bring her."

She disconnected, then said, "Well, we're invited to dinner. How about that?"

Elizabeth laughed. "That was brazen, getting me invited that way! I'd better not."

"I think you sort of have to, in order to finish up something. Dad's used to cooking for me, he does it all the time and he loves company. Anyway, his message was that the Knowltons are safely stowed away, no longer our responsibility. And the law firm that handled Knowlton's case years ago are taking him on again, now that he'll have the original research to back up his claim. Good news."

Elizabeth regarded her curiously. "Why were they your responsibility in the first place? And, as far as that goes, why do you think my welfare is your responsibility? Isn't that a bit above and beyond the call of duty?"

Barbara shrugged. "Damned if I know why. Just how it works, I guess."

Elizabeth shook her head. "It's a good question, evasive answer."

"Okay, back up a bit. Jefferson Knowlton and his claim have nothing to do with the murder that the D.A. is pursuing, granted. But those papers are at the center of it, as you know. We had to tend to that and get it off our plates if possible. Done. Next, you can't be arrested and tagged as Leonora, entered in the database that way, or it will be a lifelong struggle to get out of it again. One you might lose. You can't be tried for your own murder, because they'd convict you. Twenty-five years to life. Who knows? The judge might hate your curly hair or something and go for the limit in his instructions to

the jury. Finally, you can't be identified as Elizabeth until they
have the killer pegged and put away. You're the missing link,
the only one who can swear to the origin of that research, and
frankly your chances of staying alive as Elizabeth are pretty
dim." She smiled faintly. "Both Dad and I have lost cases now
and then, but never a client, and we don't intend to start
now."

"You think there could still be doubt raised about the
research, in spite of all the papers, the notes, drawings, all of
it?"

"Most assuredly doubts would be raised. They'd claim that
Jefferson Knowlton spent the last ten years producing them,
and now sees a chance to present his case again."

"So I lose, no matter what," Elizabeth said wearily after a
moment. She ran her hand through her hair and added in a low
voice, "And no judge could hate these damn curls more than
I do. What's my role in whatever you're planning? I've already
told you everything I can."

"Let's go eat Dad's good cheese and drink my excellent Soave,
and let me think a bit longer. But whatever the play is you're
the central character. You'll have the starring role. Let's go."

"Now what are you up to?" Frank asked when he admitted
Barbara and Elizabeth.

"I need to think it through," Barbara said, taking off her
jacket. "And I want Elizabeth to start making a written statement of everything she did after finding those papers in Joe
Kurtz's safe. We'll go on from there." She took Elizabeth's
jacket and hung it in the closet along with her own. "Are you
up to that?" she asked her.

"Sure. Why here?"

"I don't want it to be on your computer, just in case." She didn't want it on her own laptop for the same reason—either or both could be taken by the police through a court order. "You can use Dad's desk computer." Belatedly she glanced at him. "Is that okay with you?"

"Of course," he said. "First, come on out and have a bite to eat." He suspected that Barbara had not had a thing since breakfast. She often forgot that real people ate lunch in the middle of the day, and Elizabeth looked as if she was suffering from sleepless nights, and she was probably skipping food unless and until someone told her to eat. "Come on out to the kitchen. I have a few things you can nibble on until dinner's ready, sevenish."

He had cheeses and a pâté, crackers and bread, olives. Barbara grinned and said to Elizabeth, "See? I told you he'd feed us."

Then, as they ate, she said, "Start with the day Terry went to your office, and take it up to when you left the women's shelter and headed north. Take your time with it, make it as long or as short as you need, just so it's complete to that point, including some explanation of why you did this or that, how you were feeling. Everything you can think of. Okay?"

Elizabeth nodded. She finished the bit of cheese she held and spread pâté on a piece of bread.

"One more thing," Barbara said. "At one time you said you planned to go to Dr. Diedricks and tell him the whole story and let him decide what to do. Address this report to him directly, will you? Just as if you planned to mail it to him, something like that."

"Okay, but there's no point in mailing it. Lon Clampton scans his mail and decides what to pass on for Gary to read to Grandfather."

"I'll keep that in mind," Barbara said.

Later, after leaving Elizabeth at Frank's computer, Barbara Googled Gary Swarthmore under physical therapists in Portland, and found his name associated with a group there. Deep in thought she returned to the kitchen, where Frank was still busy with dinner preparations. She refilled her wineglass and sat down, waiting for him to pause. The kitchen was fragrant with the combined smells of lamb, garlic, roasted chilies, tomatoes and olive oil. She had another cracker with cheese.

Frank put a covered bowl into the oven, and joined her at the table. "Give," he said. He knew that look in her eyes, he thought, pouring himself a glass of wine. What it sometimes meant was frequently just short of being illegal.

"First, a favor, something I feel a little awkward about," she said, avoiding his gaze. "It seems that Gary Swarthmore is a physical therapist, and is quite fond of old Dr. Diedricks and tends to him every day. I wonder if Darren knows him, and knows him well enough to give me a reference or something. You know, an introduction by phone, something of that sort." Her expression was bland, and to all appearances she was fascinated by the wine swirling in her glass.

"For God's sake!" His first impulse was to tell her to do it herself, but he suspected she wouldn't. She was too damn stubborn. She'd find a different way to the same end. "What do you want him to tell Swarthmore?"

"Oh, just something like I can be trusted. I don't mean any

harm to Dr. Diedricks, enough to let him know that I'm more or less okay. That he, Darren, trusts me, maybe. And I need to talk to him in the next day or two, not in person, just by phone."

They both knew that it mattered little if Darren knew Swarthmore, because he most certainly would know who Darren was. He was one of the most respected physical therapists in the country. The interns he trained were guaranteed the best jobs, and the rehabilitation clinic he headed was considered the best on the west coast. Frank placed the call on the kitchen phone. Barbara stopped playing with her wine.

After he had explained what was wanted, Frank answered a question or two, listened, then shook his head. "No, don't call me, call her. I'm done being middleman as of now. Thanks, Darren."

He frowned at Barbara. "He'll get in touch with Swarthmore. He does know him, and he'll call you back after they talk."

She murmured her thanks and returned to wine gazing. "I plan to get into that house and make a deal with Sarah Kurtz, and I need Swarthmore to know ahead of time. Still working on the minor details."

"No, you won't," he said flatly. "They might shoot you on sight."

She shook her head. "No, *they* won't. You see, I have something Sarah wants. I have the research papers. Just a few details to think through first. You know what they say about where you can find the devil—in the details." She stood. "I need to think about this. Is Bailey going to check in tonight?"

"He'll call. He said if you plan to stay here overnight and not be out wandering about, with the three stooges locked up for the time being, it should be safe enough. He'll stay home."

"When he calls, tell him I want him first thing in the morning, will you? Make it over here. And how about if I make up the bed in the guest room for Elizabeth? What she's doing is going to take a long time, I'm afraid."

He nodded, and she walked out. He knew she would pace the upstairs hallway until dinner, and he knew she was not likely to say a bit more about what her intentions were until she was good and ready.

Elizabeth praised the casserole highly, then asked, "How did you keep the green beans so crisp? When I add them to a casserole they get overcooked and limp."

"Blanch them first, and add them toward the end," Frank said. "Works every time."

Barbara had a fleeting image of shouting "Boo!" at beans on the counter and watching them blanch. She felt confident that it was not what Frank meant.

"How far along are you with your report?" she asked Elizabeth.

"On my way to the shelter, with the woman driving my car. It shouldn't take much longer. I find it much harder and slower to write the material than to edit it. I had no idea how long it would take."

"No problem," Barbara said. "Why don't you go bring it up to the next stopping point and I'll shove dishes into the dishwasher. We might both be done at the same time and go on to phase two. Oh, would you mind staying over tonight? I have

·nightshirts, gowns, a robe, new toothbrush, everything you'd need. It could be late before we finish."

Elizabeth hesitated, then nodded. "If you want me to."

Barbara was in the living room making notes when Elizabeth came out the next time. She looked very tired.

"Take a break and let's just talk a minute," Barbara said. "Coffee? You look as if you could use some."

"Good old lifesaving caffeine," Elizabeth said, sinking down into a chair. "Yes, please."

The carafe and cups were on the low table. Barbara poured, and passed the cup across the table, then refilled her own cup. "The next part gets a little tricky," she said. "I don't want to get your mother involved, for openers."

"God, no!" Elizabeth said. "I was going to tell you I wouldn't add a word about her."

"We're still on the same page," Barbara said, smiling. "Okay, try this. You called your mother and told her what happened. She put you in touch with a relative who lives in Canada, and the relative agreed to come collect Jason and let him visit her awhile. Leave out all names and locations in Canada and references to Spain. Does that work for you?"

Elizabeth considered it a moment, then nodded. "It's not quite right, but pretty much how it happened. That's okay."

"Then on to what you were planning, what you were deciding to do. Like come back to Eugene, rent an apartment, call Leonora to bring the passports, get in touch with me, things like that. Not a thing yet about taking out the stitches or the perm. Just what you were thinking when you knew Jason was going to be safe."

She reached across the table and patted Elizabeth's hand. "See, I warned you it would be a late night. Think you can finish it?"

"As long as the coffee holds out. It's like an editorial deadline, or even more like grad school with a paper due at the crack of dawn. You're a demanding teacher."

"And you're passing with flying colors," Barbara said. "I'll make sure the carafe is kept full at all times until we're both ready to tuck it in. Can you keep drinking it right up to bedtime? I can. It's a true addiction, I guess."

"Me, too," Elizabeth said. "Maybe that's one of the things we all learned in grad school, how to develop a caffeine tolerance, whether we learned anything else or not."

Elizabeth didn't linger long, but returned to the study and the second half of her story. Frank came from it carrying two of the recent books he had been reading. He was eager to finish the book he was writing on case law, and get on to what he had come to see as the most exciting of the three he intended to have published. The first one had been published, the second was nearly complete and the third was clamoring to get out of his head. It would be the most fun of them all, he had decided—closing statements, and how each side presented and interpreted the same evidence according to the needs of either the defense or the prosecution.

He put his books down on an end table and regarded Barbara. "The coast is clear for now. So what are you up to?"

"We agree that next Tuesday the boys in blue will come around with an arrest warrant for Elizabeth. Right?" She didn't wait for his affirmative response. "I don't intend to let that happen. And we agree that Elizabeth has to stop this charade of being Leonora Carnero. Right? I do intend to let that happen. In fact, I intend to orchestrate it myself." Her phone buzzed and she held it up, not quite apologetically. "Excuse me."

When she heard Darren's low, musical voice, she felt the same kind of frozen-in-motion sensation she had felt both times before when first seeing him. She walked from the living room.

"Hi, Darren," she said. "Did you call him?"

"It's all set. He said it would be best for you to call tonight because he's hard to reach during working hours. He's a busy man. He'll cooperate, if he can without harming Dr. Diedricks. Got a pencil? I have his cell phone number for you."

"One second," she said, going to the notepad by the kitchen phone. "Okay." She jotted it down, then said, "Thanks, Darren. I really appreciate that."

"One other thing," he said quickly. "Don't hang up yet. I asked you a question a while ago. Forget it, scrub it, consider it unasked. Too much, too soon. A different question. I don't expect an answer now, just whenever you're ready. I'll be waiting. Barbara, will you give us a trial run? Move in with me? Give us a try at making a go of it? If it doesn't work, leave. I love you very much." He hung up before she could think of a thing to say.

She became aware that she had not moved for a long time only when her hand began to ache, and she realized how hard she was gripping her cell phone. Carefully she put it down on the table and flexed her fingers. She crossed the kitchen and got a glass of water, then returned and sat down. Gary Swarthmore, she thought, remembering she was to call him that night. She shook her head impatiently, picked up her phone and dialed the number Darren had provided.

When she reentered the living room minutes later, Frank put down the book he had been reading, tented his fingers and said, "Well?"

"Gary Swarthmore says there's nothing wrong with Dr. Diedricks's head, his memory, his heart or his nerves. It's the rest of him that's wearing out. He's eighty-nine. I asked him to find out if Diedricks brought a Luger home from Germany and if it's still where it should be. He'll do that and call me tomorrow. We'll go on from there. One of the details I'm working with. Then I need for Hoggarth to tell us if my eavesdroppers called someone at the Kurtz house in Eugene the day I got the call from Elizabeth. If that's a yes, and if Gary's answer fits, I'm ready to go. I'm pretty sure I already know the answer to both questions."

"Pretty sure isn't good enough to go off half-cocked," he said darkly. "A suspicion won't make it, and you know that."

"But if I'm right, I have to be ready because time's running out fast, Dad. And you know that."

"So tell me the rest of it, and I'll tell you why it's a rotten idea."

"Probably you will," she murmured. She was telling him minutes later when Elizabeth came in. She helped herself to coffee this time.

"Break," she said tiredly. "I'm almost done, but I keep thinking of things I should have included earlier. I can't imagine how people did it before computers."

Frank laughed. "I don't know. You get used to a quill pen

and think it's pretty super, compared to the chisel and slab of stone your grandparents used."

"I rather liked the rice paper and paintbrush method, myself," Barbara said.

Elizabeth grinned. "How about alphabet soup letters on a paper plate. Now that's a real challenge."

"One you tried, I bet," Barbara said, laughing.

"You win."

"You know, I don't expect a literary masterpiece," Barbara said after a moment.

"I can assure you that you won't be disappointed. I can meet low expectations every time."

Elizabeth finished her coffee, stood and stretched and went back to work.

"She'll do," Frank said approvingly.

"I know. Well, back to my game plan…"

They were still talking when Elizabeth finished. "I saved it in the file name Elizabeth," she said.

"Great. I'll burn it onto a CD and make a printout. But now, you're off to bed. I'll show you where," Barbara said.

Frank stood. "Let's sleep on it all and talk in the morning. I'm going to bed, too."

Upstairs, Barbara showed Elizabeth to the guest room, pointed out the bathroom and a drawer of toothbrushes, clean towels, and then led the way to her own room.

"This is great," Elizabeth said, gazing about. "He keeps it for you?"

"Ready year round," Barbara admitted. "Nightshirt or gown? Robes in the closet. You pick. Mine's here on the bed."

She chose a loose nightshirt, the kind Barbara preferred, and a robe, then paused at the door. "You're so lucky. So many people love you, it must make you feel very special."

Barbara looked at her in surprise. "You mean Dad? Isn't that pretty normal for a lot of us?"

"Not just him. Obviously you're the center of his life, but Shelley and Alex both worship you, and Dr. Minnick looks at you in that special way. Darren adores you. Even Bailey, for all his dour looks, is really focused on you. I watched them all at dinner the other night, and I thought how lucky you are to have so much love in your life. I don't think that's normal at all. Most of us have very few, mostly family, we can claim truly love us. Good night, Barbara." She left, closing the door behind her.

26

The picture of Jason Kurtz was on the front page of the newspaper again the next morning. The reward for information had been raised to fifty thousand dollars. Another statement from Sarah Kurtz was prominently displayed, complete with pleas for the ones holding her beloved grandchild to release him, and for the authorities to serve Barbara Holloway with notice of arrest if she didn't reveal what she knew about the abduction.

Barbara scanned the article and tossed it aside without comment. Elizabeth was watching her curiously.

"After breakfast, we'll go into the study and look at that printout," Barbara said. "There are two places where I think you should elaborate on what you were thinking and feeling. Just a line or two. Then on to part two, taking out the stitches, the perm, what happened after you came to Eugene up to the present."

Elizabeth moistened her lips. "Why do I have the feeling that this is in preparation for a time when I might not be around to tell it in person?"

Taken aback, Barbara realized that Elizabeth had summed it up perfectly. It sounded exactly like that. "Not my intention," she said. "I promise you that is not in the game plan. Think of this as bait, no more than that. Remember when I asked you why Sarah Kurtz was coming on like a worried grandmother thinking only of her missing grandchild? You said she was playing her role, but I think it goes beyond that. She has prepared the ground for if and when the police determine that whoever had a tap on my phone called someone in the old Kurtz house the evening of the murder. I believe she will claim that, of course, she hired detectives to locate you and her grandchild. I don't want to underestimate her."

Elizabeth put down her fork. "You really think it was one of them? Sarah, Terry or Lon Clampton? You really believe that?"

Barbara nodded. "That's what I believe. And I'm preparing my own ground with your statement as bait."

Elizabeth pushed her plate back, to Frank's regret. At least, she had eaten part of the omelette he had prepared. The doorbell sounded. "That's probably Bailey. I'll get it." He left the table.

"Tell him I'll be out in a minute or two," Barbara said, getting up, with most of her breakfast still on her plate. "Come on," she said to Elizabeth. "If you're done, let's get at it again. Back to the salt mines for you, my girl."

She showed Elizabeth the two places where she thought it

needed another line or two, and then said, "Label the next section Part Two, new page, and finish it. So far you have four pages. When you're done, we'll paginate it and make a new printout. At the very end, I'd like for you to include today's date, and copy a few headlines from today's newspapers, to prove the point. A couple from page one, then skip to an inside page and copy a couple more headlines along with that page number. Okay?"

"Are you going to tell me what you intend to do with all this? I mean specifically."

"Yes," Barbara said. "Later today I'll tell you. Good enough? I have to give Bailey some instructions right now."

Elizabeth hesitated a moment before pulling out the chair at Frank's desk and Barbara left to tell Bailey what she needed from him.

"How big are those rooms?" Bailey asked later, looking over the house plan Elizabeth had drawn.

"She said the den is about eighteen by twenty-four. She thinks they're more or less to scale with that. But it was six years ago that she was in the house. Allow for that."

"Sure," he said. "You can't go in there wired. And neither can I, so forget that."

"I already did," she said. "That's why I want you and your genius helper to come up with something."

"Okeydokey." He folded the paper with the house plan and put it in his duffel bag. "Where will you be later on?"

"Here and there. Give me a call when you're ready. I'll be back here later today."

He saluted and ambled out in a way that always appeared

too leisurely to be serious, but she well knew that that was deceptive. Bailey always delivered.

Frank looked at his watch after showing Bailey out. "I should go," he said. "Lorenz said he'd come around ten, and I'll have Patsy make another copy of those papers before he gets here."

"And a copy of the disk Elizabeth made," Barbara reminded him.

"I know that," he said irritably. They had not yet had the talk he knew was necessary, but there would be time. He would see to it that she stopped moving long enough for a talk.

"After we wrap things up here, I'll take Elizabeth back to her apartment. Maybe we'll both be done in time for lunch. I'll let you know."

He thought of the wasted breakfast and hoped for lunch. He was putting on his raincoat when she pulled her cell phone from her pocket. He waited at the door to see if it was something he should know about.

"Thanks," she said on the phone. "I really appreciate that." She looked dangerously angry when she replaced the phone in her pocket. "That goddamn pissant D.A. intends to subpoena me and get a sworn deposition! That was Brice Knowlton. His sister dates a guy at city hall, and that's the buzz this morning."

"After you take Elizabeth home, come directly to the office," Frank said in his lawyerly voice. "It won't happen immediately, but it won't take long, either. And don't answer the doorbell here. We'll see about this."

"I'll ask Elizabeth to come to the office and have Patsy notarize her signature on that statement she's making," Barbara said almost defiantly. After a moment Frank nodded, and she knew he had come around to seeing that what she intended to do needed doing her way.

Infuriated, Barbara stood still, thinking. If they issued a subpoena, they could demand her laptop as well as her presence. And they would have access to everything on it; no one could stop them once they had it. Her jaw was clenched nearly as hard as her fists. She'd drop it into the river first, she thought then. They couldn't have it. And if losing it, or claiming she had lost it, or that it had been stolen, cinched whatever they were thinking, so be it. Better that than to have Darren raked through the muck. The thought of his son's friends making life a horror for Todd, coworkers and patients at the clinic whispering, turning away when Darren approached, hiding knowing looks and smiles... *"They can't have it!"* she said under her breath.

"You said you'd tell me what you're up to," Elizabeth said in Barbara's car, as she pulled up to the apartment building later.

"When you come in this afternoon, I will," Barbara said. "There are too many things happening all at once, but there will be time this afternoon. Try to get a little rest, take a nap or something. I promise, this afternoon around three, when you come in to the office."

"Okay, but, Barbara, I have to say this. I won't sign that statement until I know what you're going to do with it. I'm sorry, but that's how it has to be." Her voice was firm and her gaze unwavering as she said this.

"I wouldn't have it any other way. That's precisely the stand you should be taking. As Dad said, you'll do. High praise from him. See you at three or thereabout."

* * *

When Barbara parked behind her father's office building, she sat quietly for a few minutes, watching passersby. They were scurrying for the most part, not eager to spend much time out in a cold drizzle. Satisfied that no one was lurking near the door of the building, she left the car and walked swiftly to the entrance, went inside and up the stairs, not willing to wait for the elevator.

"Made it," she said to Frank when he admitted her to his office.

"So did Lorenz," he said. "We had a nice chat. He'll give me a call when those papers are locked up in his safe. Seems he has a travel companion, a big fellow who didn't have much to say and seemed content to sit out in the reception room and read magazines."

"Good. A companion is good." Her phone buzzed again and she sat on the sofa and put her feet on his coffee table, then answered. It was Gary Swarthmore this time. She listened, then said, "Thank you, Mr. Swarthmore. I know how busy you are during the day, but may I call you back tonight?" She thanked him again and disconnected. "We have to haul Hoggarth in," she said. "Feed him lunch again or something. Diedricks brought a souvenir Luger home from Germany, and it's not where he used to keep it."

Frank grunted and sat opposite her. "You're right about Hoggarth. That's how I see it," he agreed. "How much to tell him is the question."

"Enough to satisfy him, at least. And a promise that we'll all come in voluntarily on Tuesday, the first working day of next week, you and your two clients."

"That just leaves two working days of this week," Frank said. "Can we really count on putting things in order in two days?"

"What choice do we have? You want to read Elizabeth's statement while I call Terry Kurtz?"

He did. She handed him the folder with the statement and went to his desk to use his phone. Terry Kurtz answered almost immediately.

"Barbara Holloway," she said crisply. "Mr. Kurtz, I want to arrange a meeting with you and your mother for Friday, and I don't want to call her house and go through voice mail. Will you set it up?"

"Have you found him? Is it about Jason?"

"No discussion yet, Mr. Kurtz. Let's have the meeting with both of you present."

"My uncle is at the house. Do you want him present also?"

"Of course, if he's available. It's a family affair. Please tell your mother it concerns certain papers she is interested in. I'll be at this number for the next two hours, awaiting your return call." She gave him Frank's number.

"Ms. Holloway, if it's about Jason, I beg of you, don't include her in a discussion. Let me meet with you first."

"This is about papers, Mr. Kurtz. You might tell her that I expect to be served with a subpoena, and will be required to testify in a sworn deposition about everything I know of the situation, including what I know about those papers. It would be best if we have our meeting before that happens."

She disconnected while he was still talking.

Frank finished reading and said, "Good statement, clear and concise, exactly what it should be. After she signs it, we'll have

Patsy run off some copies. Now for Milt." He took her place at his desk and placed the call.

Milt Hoggarth was noncommittal when Frank said he would bring both of his clients to the district attorney's office on Tuesday. "You'll surrender Carnero at that time?"

"Let's leave it at that. We'll all three be there, and we can sort out the pieces together," Frank said smoothly. "What time do you suggest?"

"I'll let you know." He turned his suspicious gaze to Barbara. "Someone alerted you about a possible subpoena, is that it? Jesus, that office is like working in a fishbowl."

He had varied his diet. He had ordered ham and cheese on rye bread, and he attacked it with fury. Between bites he said, "Those guys were hired by Lon Clampton, and that's who they called. The DA had a chat with Mrs. Kurtz, and she said of course she had her assistant hire detectives to find her grandchild. She intended to see Elizabeth Kurtz the next day, after getting the address. End of chapter."

Barbara nodded. "I figured as much. Lieutenant, remember the hypothetical I posed the last time we lunched together? Something to do with important stolen papers? It's not a hypothetical, Hoggarth. I know you're not interested in corporate fraud, and neither am I, but in this instance it plays a part. It seems that a certain Swiss corporation is negotiating the buyout of the Diedricks Corporation, and the money they're talking about involves many hundreds of millions of dollars, possibly a billion dollars. The old man, Dr. Diedricks, owns fifty-five percent of the company, outsiders own ten percent, and between them Sarah Kurtz and her brother own the rest.

But when the old man kicks, the two of them will own ninety percent—and if that sale goes through, we're talking about real big money. Those papers could scotch the deal. It's that simple."

"How much of that do you know and how much is guesswork?" To all appearances he had forgotten the sandwich he was holding.

"I'm not guessing, Lieutenant," she said quietly.

"I ought to haul you in right now for obstruction of justice," he snapped.

She looked at Frank. "Am I obstructing? I've been trying to steer him in the right direction from day one and kept getting the brush-off."

Hoggarth looked as if he might toss his sandwich down and whip out handcuffs.

"Easy, Milt," Frank said mildly. "This case is like most. You start out knowing nothing of the situation and gradually pieces fall into place here, then there, and you put them together as best you can. I can assure you that my client," he nodded toward Barbara, "has not obstructed your investigation. We're all just looking at different parts of the same puzzle. Like blind men describing the elephant. Your department got stuck looking in one direction while we were looking in another and we kept finding more odd pieces. If you had been looking where we were, you would have seen them, too."

"So this little meeting was just to get me to call off the subpoena, because you're going to stroll on over voluntarily at your convenience," Hoggarth said bitterly. "Corporate fraud! You're right, I'm not interested. Let the Securities and Exchange Commission take it on. I'm in homicide."

"Well, I admit I had a little more on my mind," Barbara said.

"I'm just waiting for a phone call to confirm a date with the Kurtz family. I want to make a deal with them. In exchange for what I know about the stolen papers, they hand over a killer. I think they'll deal."

For a moment she thought the lieutenant would choke. He sputtered—enraged—and turned fiery red.

"Jesus Christ! You're accusing them of murder and expect them to cooperate! You're out of your mind!"

The phone rang and Frank got up to answer it. He had told Patsy to put through a call from Kevin Lorenz or from Terry Kurtz, no one else. It was Terry Kurtz on the line. He beckoned Barbara.

"She wants to see you up here, on Friday," Terry said. "Can you make it at two?"

"That's a good time," she said. "I'll be there. Thank you."

Returning to the sofa, she said, "That's my confirmation, Hoggarth. Would you like to join our party?"

"Not his jurisdiction," Frank pointed out.

"The murder was in my town," Hoggarth said. "I go where the leads take me."

"With autonomy?" Barbara asked in a musing way.

"It's always been my understanding," Frank said, facing Barbara, "that as long as there's an ongoing investigation, the lead investigator to a large extent has autonomy. Once there's an arrest, the district attorney's office directs further investigation. Has that system changed while I was paying little attention, Milt?"

"Goddamn it to hell!" Hoggarth said, glowering first at Barbara, then at Frank. "Cut the crap. You both know damn well that I'm in charge."

"Good enough," Barbara said. "Are you going to finish that sandwich? I have a satellite photo of the Diedricks spread I'd like to show you. Pretty interesting, what they can do."

He finished the last few bites and wiped his hands. "So what's the map supposed to prove?"

"Well," she said putting it on the table, "it's just interesting. The original property, bought back in the early fifties, then the additions when they came on the market. A guesthouse here, and the lake and another building, a bathhouse now, both with access to the county road, here." She pointed as she mentioned them. "And a lot of trees, an awful lot of trees. After our chat on Friday, it wouldn't surprise me at all if someone took a stroll and tossed a gun somewhere, I'd guess into the lake, but maybe just into the woods."

"What gun? We know Elizabeth Kurtz bought a handgun in Sacramento, and there was never a gun in the Diedricks house. The old man wouldn't allow them. We asked."

"How strange," Barbara murmured. "Maybe you asked the wrong people. I asked Dr. Diedricks's therapist to find out if the doctor brought one home from Germany after World War II, and he did, a Luger. It's gone missing. But that was so long ago, maybe they just forgot about it."

"That old man is senile, with dementia. He admitted years ago that he had a loss of memory when his head was practically caved in. I saw his letter, signed by his doctor, with Diedricks's signature on it."

"How interesting. His therapist says his mind is sharp, no loss of mental functions at all. Again, maybe you asked the wrong people." Barbara leaned forward and said emphatically, "They thought he'd die from that accident, and they stole work he and another man had done, but Diedricks didn't die. And the other man sued for the return of his work. They came up with that statement, signed by a bogus doctor, no doubt, and since Diedricks was blind, whatever they said they were reading to him for his signature was not what was on that paper."

Hoggarth ran his hand over his florid scalp, with its scant covering of thinning hair. He poured himself more coffee. "It's empty," he said, jerking his thumb toward the carafe.

"We'll get it refilled," Frank said. "Milt, it's a no-brainer. You know as well as we do that those two attacks are related, and committed by the same person. There have been too many spoons in this pot. You want the killer and so do we, and it's not my client."

"It's not just a matter of our convenience when we appear at the D.A.'s office," Barbara said. "We have to have a little time to arrange a party, a private conversation with the Kurtz bunch. And I don't want to have to dodge a process server for the next several days. I don't have time for that."

Hoggarth's eyes narrowed, and he said, "What are you planning?"

"There's a condition," Barbara said. "You have to agree that the one who throws the party gets to call the tune."

After another long pause Hoggarth nodded, and Frank went to tell Patsy they could use more coffee.

27

Hoggarth had been gone only a few minutes when Elizabeth arrived. She shook her head at the offer of coffee. "I'm caffeined out for now," she said.

Then, with all three seated around the low table Barbara said, "I learned that I was going to be subpoenaed, forced to give a deposition under oath and of course I can't do that at this time. We can stall on that for a short time, but we have to make our move fast, now. On Friday, I intend to take your statement, and a taped version for Dr. Diedricks, and offer to trade my silence concerning it for the murderer of Leonora Carnero."

"If it was one of that group, it had to be Lon Clampton," Elizabeth said. "Terry couldn't have done that, deliberately fired at her face. I saw her face, Barbara." A long shudder rippled through her and she looked away. Then she said in a lower voice, "I'll never believe Terry would have done that, or could have done that. Besides, he would have known it wasn't me."

Barbara had made that same argument with herself, but she had taken it one step further. Whoever fired that first shot had to make certain the victim was dead, since she might have identified the shooter if she survived. And Terry might have had less hesitation to shoot Leonora in the face than he would have felt about his ex-wife. She said none of this, but waited for Elizabeth to continue.

"And I can't believe Sarah—or any other woman—would have left her grandchild to die in the wilderness. They had to know Jason was with me. It must have been Clampton. He's Sarah's agent, her gofer, whatever. If he knew she wanted me gone, he was capable of getting rid of me."

"Well," Barbara said, "I'll play the tape of you reading part one of the statement, show them that I have it in hard copy and see where it leads. They know very well that if I go public with that, their potential sale is dead."

"And part two? What's that for?"

"After the police have the killer, Elizabeth, we have to come clean about your identity. You can't continue as Leonora and expect to leave the country using her passport, and we can't have you listed among the dead a day longer than the killer is at large. We have to straighten it all out, wipe the slate and let you get your own life in order with your child. And you have to affirm where those research papers came from."

"What will they do to me? For making false statements? Lying." She was very pale.

Silently Frank got up and went to his bookcase where, behind the *T's,* there was a concealed bar. He opened it and brought out a bottle of cabernet sauvignon and glasses. After returning to the table he uncorked the wine, poured a glass and handed it to Elizabeth, all without a word.

"You're our client," Barbara said, accepting her own glass. "Your mother retained me to look after your interests, and you retained Dad to do the same thing. Between us, we'll protect you. There will be a gigantic eruption when it comes out, but after the dust settles, we'll work things out, and they'll go along. What choice do they have? Shown to have believed a woman committed her own murder? I don't think they'll want to become fodder for late-night comics." Saying this, Barbara left unsaid a fervent hope that she was right—they would work things out.

Elizabeth sipped her wine, then put the glass down. "You said a tape for Grandfather Diedricks, and that you'd trade your silence for the killer. What does that mean? We forget the fraud, or let Grandfather do whatever he wants about it?"

Barbara nodded. "That's it. Let him decide. Gary Swarthmore says his mind is as sharp as ever, but he doesn't know what's been going on. He should make the decision."

"That's what I decided," Elizabeth said after a moment. "His choice." She sipped the wine, then said, "You want me to read the statement into a tape recorder? Do you have the tape recorder here?"

Frank had an excellent tape recorder, one he used illicitly in court whenever Barbara was defending a capital case. He brought it out from his desk and placed it on the table. "It's got a new tape ready to go," he said.

"When you get to the end of part one, stop and let me put in a few words," Barbara said. "Okay?"

Elizabeth nodded. Barbara handed her the statement, and in a clear, steady voice she began to read it.

An hour later it was all done, the statement signed and notarized, copies made. As Elizabeth pulled on her jacket Barbara said, "On Friday I'd like Shelley to meet you and take you out to her place. It's a lovely house in the foothills of the Coast Range, lots of hills and forest, and you'll get to see some of Alex's artwork. He's very good."

"Why?" Elizabeth asked sharply. "What do you think might happen Friday?"

"Probably nothing, but I also like insurance. They might decide to get cute and make a premature arrest while Dad and I are busy somewhere else. I'm just being cautious. It's my nature."

"You said she'll meet me. You don't even want anyone to know I'm with her, do you?"

"You've got it. I don't want them to suspect a thing. So you're taking the day off to shop or something. That's all they need to know if it comes up, but as I said, I don't think it will."

"All right," Elizabeth said. "It really doesn't matter much to me where I spend the days. Killing time, waiting, that's all I do anymore. Should I call her, or will she get in touch with me?"

"She'll call before noon. You can get lunch on the way."

Elizabeth shrugged as if to say food was the last thing on her mind. After she was gone, Barbara sank down onto the sofa. "The trouble with having a sharp client is that they know when to ask questions, and they want real answers."

She was still slouched there when Frank answered his phone and spoke with Kevin Lorenz briefly. "No problem," he said to Barbara afterward. "He and the partners are quite eager to take on the Kurtz legal team again, now that they have a real case. They had a preliminary discussion with Jefferson Knowlton and smoothed the waters, apparently, and they'll be set to move the minute they get proof of origin for the research papers."

Barbara drank her wine, thankful for a few minutes of relaxation, wishing she could turn her brain off and let it relax as well as her body. Her phone buzzed and reluctantly she pulled it out to see who was calling this time. It was Maria.

"Hi," she said. "What's up?"

"I hate to interrupt," Maria said, "but I didn't know what to do about Terry Kurtz. He called to make an appointment and I put him off, no appointments until next week, but he came anyway. He's out in the hall waiting for you. When I told him you might not even be in today, he said he'll wait, and he'll be back tomorrow and wait all day if necessary."

"Shit," Barbara said. It was ten minutes before five. "I'll come around and see what's on his mind."

She told Frank where she was going.

"Come to the house after you see the fellow. Let's go to Martin's for dinner later. I'll call to reserve a booth."

"I told Gary Swarthmore I'd call around seven."

"We'll make it after that."

When she arrived at her office building, Terry Kurtz was sitting on the floor by her door with his back against the wall. He jumped to his feet, and she motioned him to follow, waved to Maria in passing and led the way to her office.

"I've had a long day, Mr. Kurtz, and I'm tired. What do you want?"

He looked different again, she thought, taking off her jacket. She tossed it onto a chair and sat behind her desk. He looked determined, and the shadows under his eyes made him appear older, almost formidable.

"I want to make a deal with you," he said, as brusquely as she had spoken. "Did Elizabeth tell you what we were looking for in my father's files? Never mind, I forgot, you don't give out anything. Well, it was a share assignment, a cut in the company. I found it, and she found something else. I don't know what it was, but it sent her running. Anyway, I have that assignment, and it's legal as hell. Here, today, I want to sign it over to you, in exchange for my son. My mother's offer of fifty grand is peanuts compared to what that assignment's worth. It's yours if you'll swear you won't let her get her hands on Jason, but turn him over to me."

"Mr. Kurtz, I don't know the laws of New York, but here a father's wishes would prevail, not a grandmother's. Legally you have far more right to gain custody of your child than she does."

"You don't understand. She'd put him somewhere out of reach and play it out in court for the next five years, and meanwhile he'd be in hell." He took an envelope from his pocket and tossed it down on her desk. "The assignment. Look it over. We can transfer it on the spot."

"Why would she do that, Mr. Kurtz? You seem to believe she has no interest in him. Why would she fight for custody?"

"Christ, I don't know why. That's what she intends to do if Elizabeth's mother tries to gain custody, and she was appointed by Elizabeth as his legal guardian in the event of her death or incapacitation. Maybe my mother's just playing out her act. I don't know why, I just know she would do it."

She pushed the envelope toward him and stood up. "I'll think about what you said, Mr. Kurtz."

He put the envelope back in his pocket and regarded her for a moment. "Ms. Holloway, if you intend to make a deal with my mother that includes letting her get her hands on my son, you'll regret it. I swear to you, you will regret it." He wheeled about and left.

She waited a moment, then went to the outer office. "Is he gone?"

"Yes, indeed," Maria said. "Slammed the door on his way out."

Shelley came from her own office and looked about as if checking. "Whew. He was one furious guy."

"Come on back," Barbara said to her. "A few things to go over, but it shouldn't take long." She looked at Maria and said sternly, "And you can knock off trying to look busy and go home. It's past time for you." She knew it was a futile effort.

28

Bailey pulled up to the deep porch of Henry Diedricks's house at five minutes before two on Friday. Earlier it had rained, now a fine mist hung in the air, and fog was forming in the shrubs and trees, rising wraithlike from the driveway. At one side of four or five stairs, a ramp led down from the porch to a well-groomed walkway that curved out of sight among the fog-shrouded trees. With Bailey right behind her, Barbara mounted the stairs and rang the doorbell. She pulled her jacket closer against the cold misty air.

A very large, tall man opened the door and looked her over, then turned the same close scrutiny to Bailey.

"Barbara Holloway," she said, "and this is Bailey Novell, my driver and a private investigator."

"*You* can come in," the man said, opening the door wider. "*He* waits outside."

"Don't be ridiculous. No one can be expected to wait outside in this weather for over an hour. Come along, Bailey." She pushed past the man and Bailey entered with her. "Tell Mrs. Kurtz I'm here," she said.

"Wait here," the man said, and walked down the wide entrance hall toward the rear of the house.

She assumed he was Lon Clampton, six feet plus an inch or two, heavy and muscular, light brown hair, pale blue eyes, and clearly quite angry with her but not willing to heave her out bodily. At least not without direct orders to do so.

Sarah Kurtz returned with him, and again Barbara was struck by her size, five nine or ten, and at least two hundred twenty pounds. That day she was wearing a floor-length, long-sleeved gray silk dress with a black tunic. The outfit did nothing to slim her appearance. She moved easily for one her size. She nodded curtly to Barbara and looked Bailey over. "Your man can wait in the kitchen with the cook," she said coldly.

"No. Have *your man* bring a chair out and let him wait here where he can keep an eye on his van. He's paranoid about it." Her voice was as cold as Sarah's, and at her side Bailey nodded with a bland expression.

For a moment no one moved, then Sarah Kurtz motioned to Clampton. "Bring two chairs. Stay with him. Have a look at the van first."

Clampton went out, and Bailey went with him to watch him look over the van. Barbara took off her jacket. They waited silently for the men to return, and again for Clampton to leave and come back with two straight chairs. Barbara hung her jacket on the back of one of them, and Bailey sat down on it, very close to one of the tall glass panes that flanked the entry door.

Sarah Kurtz motioned to Barbara and led the way through the hall. As Elizabeth had said, the house was old-fashioned and gracious, with wide halls, wainscoting in pale polished wood, wide plank floors, high ceilings. Sarah opened a door and they entered an office. There was a conference table, a computer desk and chair and two upholstered chairs. Terry Kurtz was standing near tall sash windows, and seated at the table was another man, who rose when they entered. Terry nodded without speaking.

"My brother Lawrence Diedricks," Sarah said. "This is Barbara Holloway. I'd like to look inside your purse," she said to Barbara. Lawrence looked hesitant, as if he didn't know if he should offer to shake her hand or not. She nodded in his direction and he sat down again. He was tall and heavy, like Sarah, but not as overweight as she was. Barbara put her purse down on the table and opened it for Sarah to have a look, then picked up her briefcase and put it on the table.

The briefcase looked old, a little beat-up, well used, although Bailey had insisted it was new. He had left it in the rain, run over it with his old car, cleaned it up and there it was, fixed. The top was finished with a brass plate with her monogram in raised brass letters. And as soon as she undid the clasp and opened it, an electronic transmitter was activated, or so Bailey had assured her. It would pick up any sound within twenty feet, he had said, and transmit it to receivers within a hundred feet. He also said he had tested it thoroughly, and she had taken his word for it.

She undid the clasp and turned back the opening.

Sarah looked inside, and pulled out the tape recorder. "What's this for?"

"I have a tape to play for you," Barbara said. She took the tape recorder and opened it to demonstrate that it contained no tape yet. She reached inside the briefcase and brought out the tape, inserted it. "Why don't you sit down and let's get on with it."

Sarah's mouth tightened, but she walked around the table and pulled out a chair where the windows would be behind her. The drapes had been drawn all the way open. Barbara did not comment. She had no need to watch Sarah's expression. She took a chair, and Terry sat down, choosing a chair well-separated from the others.

"Ms. Holloway, I did not appreciate your peremptory call for this meeting—" Sarah said.

"Mrs. Kurtz, please sit down. I want to get through this as quickly as possible, and there's no need for talk at this point. I have something you want, and you have something I want. Now let's get started." She turned on the tape player. Sarah Kurtz sat down, as stiff and upright as a person could be. The tape player made the usual whirring sounds, and then Elizabeth's voice could be heard clearly.

Terry gave a start, half rose from his chair, sank back down again, staring at the tape player as if hypnotized by it.

There was not a sound in the room except that of Elizabeth's voice for the next several minutes. No one moved.

"I decided what I had to do," Elizabeth said on the tape, "was to enlist the help of someone, and I thought of Barbara Holloway. She had saved my life and the life of my son at the cabin, and I had looked her up on the Internet and felt I could trust her. I planned to go to Eugene, call Leonora to bring our passports and take her and Jason to go stay with my mother in Spain, and to entrust the papers, and the decision concerning what to do about them to Barbara Holloway."

Then Barbara's voice was on the tape. "What you have just heard was read from the written text provided by Elizabeth Kurtz in my presence, and that of others. The written text is signed and notarized."

Barbara turned off the tape recorder and removed the tape.

"Where is that relative who has Jason?" Terry said hoarsely. "Where is he?"

"As she said, he is safe and being cared for," Barbara said. "You all know what happened when Elizabeth reached Eugene. And you know that I flew to Las Vegas and recovered those papers from the storage locker. I put them in a prepared envelope and took them directly to the post office and mailed them. They are now in the hands of a law firm in Portland. There are about a hundred papers involved—drawings, pages of practice initials, notes, computer codes and schematics of various prosthetic devices, some signed by Jefferson Knowlton, some with his initials only, and some with Henry Diedricks's notes included, or more often notes with Hank Diedricks's name."

Lawrence Diedricks was leaning forward with his elbow on the table, his hand covering his face. In a harsh whisper Sarah Kurtz said, "You don't have anything! Anyone could have made such a statement, any cheap actress could have read it. Knowlton's had years of insane rage driving him. He could have made a million copies of anything he came across on the Internet, through the journals. It doesn't prove a thing!"

"Mrs. Kurtz, I can assure you that a court of law takes a notarized statement very seriously. That document will withstand any scrutiny anyone directs at it. And I possess the original."

"What do you want?" Sarah said in the same harsh voice. "What's your price?"

"I want the murderer. When Elizabeth went to that cabin, Sam Norris called this house to inform you that a woman and a child were there. I have no idea what conversation followed that call, of course. But two days later, on Thanksgiving, someone went to the cabin and attacked her with murderous ferocity and stole her computer, every scrap of paper and certain disks. She was left to die in the rain, and Jason was left to die in the wilderness. After the attacker realized the stolen papers were not the originals, I was followed, spied upon and my telephone was tapped. When Elizabeth called and gave me her address, her attacker immediately went to the apartment and committed murder. The persons tapping my line called the Kurtz house in Eugene that evening, and three of you were in that house. One of you left and committed murder. I want that killer. That's my price."

"Leonora Carnero killed her," Sarah said. "The police know that. Leonora Carnero did it."

"No, Mrs. Kurtz, she did not. And I don't intend to let her suffer for that murder. We deal, or I will hold a press conference and play that tape. We deal now, today. On Tuesday I will be required to submit to a deposition, testify under oath. What we decide here and now will determine exactly what I say at that time."

She looked at Terry. He was so pale he looked bloodless. "Who left the house on Thanksgiving? Did you?"

Without uncovering his face, Lawrence Diedricks said in an anguished voice, "We played cards for awhile. Terry, my kids, I... Lon found cards for us, and set up the card table."

"I was in bed with a migraine," Sarah cried. "Don't you remember? I was ill from Wednesday until you called, Lawrence. Don't you remember? You called to say dinner was ready on Thursday. I told you I was lying down. I had a severe migraine."

"Who left the Kurtz house the evening of the murder?" Barbara demanded. "I want a name and some proof."

Sarah Kurtz drew herself up even more stiffly, her face hidden in shadows, her voice almost guttural in its harshness. "Do you think you can come into my home and threaten us with impunity? Do you believe we'll let you get away with this outrage? How much is your own life worth to you?"

"You're wasting time," Barbara said, unperturbed. "You've looked me up, had me investigated. You know I'm not stupid. You know I have insurance, with explicit orders for others to follow if I happen to have an accident."

"What's your real price?" Sarah cried. "How much? A hundred thousand? Two hundred thousand? Name your price! One percent of the company? Do you realize one percent of a billion dollars is ten million? What's your real price?"

"I told you what I want, the name of a killer and sufficient proof to insure an arrest and trial for murder. And I don't intend to dicker about it." She pushed her chair back slightly, preparing to stand.

"Lon," Sarah whispered. "He hired them. I told him to hire

detectives to find my grandson. They called him and he came to where I was sorting through pictures and said he had to go out for a few minutes, he'd be right back."

Terry jumped up, staring at his mother in horror, his face ashen.

"Why didn't you say something to the police?" Lawrence cried. "You let them think that woman did it when you knew. Why didn't you say something?"

"Because it doesn't matter! One piece of trash getting rid of another piece of trash—let her rot in prison, what difference will it make? Do you know where we stand with the sale? Eight hundred fifty million! And it will go up. We can't let our names be dragged through the mud!"

"She would have died in the rain, and Jason alone, miles from anyone, the tide coming in…" Terry's voice was tremulous, and he was shaking. "What kind of monster are you?" he whispered. He turned and, staggering, walked out.

Sarah leaned forward and cried, "What more do you want? I gave him to you. I demand the original of that statement. I taped this whole meeting, I have your word."

"I said proof," Barbara said coldly. "You gave me a name. That's not enough. I need proof."

"I'll make a statement, sign it, whatever they need."

"And no doubt he'll do the same."

Barbara put the tape recorder back in the briefcase, the tape in her purse. "Are we finished here?"

"I saw him throw something in the lake," Sarah whispered. "He didn't know I was watching. When we came home for Christmas, he threw it away. I'll tell them where he threw it, where he stood. I watched."

"When?"

"Tomorrow. I'll call the police and tell them I saw him. I was afraid. He threatened me, and I was afraid, but I'll tell them. Tomorrow. Not now. I feel ill. Tomorrow."

"Call me afterward and I'll come back," Barbara said, rising from her chair. She glanced at Lawrence, who had put his arms on the table, his face pressed into them. She thought he might be weeping. "Good day, Mrs. Kurtz," she said. "I can let myself out." She closed her briefcase.

Sarah Kurtz and her brother Lawrence were both still sitting there when she walked from the room.

29

When she opened the door of the van, she barely glanced in the rear seat where Frank and Hoggarth were huddled in wool blankets. They both held tape recorders. Bailey got behind the wheel, and turned on the engine. "It warms up fast," he said.

Without looking behind her, Barbara asked, "Did it come through okay?"

"Loud and clear," Frank said, and no one spoke again as Bailey drove out to the road, the same place he had stopped on the way in to let Frank and Hoggarth out. They had walked the rest of the way concealed by the trees and shrubs, then waited until the van had been checked out, as they all had suspected it would be. The road Bailey entered fed into the access road to I-5. He turned off that one a short distance later onto a county road and slowed down. A man standing by the side of the road waved, and he stopped to let Hoggarth leave to join his men.

"You have some explaining to do," the lieutenant said heavily to Barbara, opening the sliding door.

"Tuesday," she said. "As agreed."

"Maybe you can stop by tonight, when you get through here," Frank said.

"Yeah," Hoggarth said. "Yeah, I'll stop by." It sounded more like a threat than a promise. He got out of the van and Frank moved to the middle seat behind Barbara.

Sarah Kurtz passed Lon Clampton in the hall on her way out. He was carrying the chairs back to the kitchen. "They're gone," he said.

She did not reply. Outside, she got into the golf cart and took it down the drive to the guesthouse, where she went straight upstairs, then up a second flight of narrow stairs to the attic. The light was dim, and she knew there was no electricity, but the small dormer windows were enough. Passing one facing south and the county road out front, she paused, then caught in her breath as a van stopped, a man got out, and the vehicle turned and went back the way it had come. The man had vanished among the shrubs and trees below her line of vision.

"A trap!" she whispered harshly. "That bitch was setting a trap!" She glanced at the floorboard she had come to remove, then backed away from the window and retraced her steps downstairs, where she stood in the kitchen, shaking, her lips a tight grim line. After a moment she sank down to a chair and willed herself to calm down, to think.

When Bailey shifted and started to drive again, Frank put his hand on Barbara's shoulder. "That was good work," he said quietly.

She patted his hand but made no response. Filthy work, she thought, and immediately another voice in her head replied, it would be filthier if Sarah got away with it. There was no answer to her counter argument. It would be filthier if she got away with it.

Bailey didn't linger when he took Frank and Barbara home. "I'll get another copy of that tape," he said. Frank handed him a small black box and he put it in his duffel bag. Barbara removed her tape player and tape, and left the briefcase on the passenger seat. Bailey saluted and drove off as Frank and Barbara entered the house.

"Step two," she said in the kitchen a minute later, pouring wine. "One to go. I'll call Shelley and tell them the coast is clear. But maybe I should wait. If I don't call before nine, they plan to put Elizabeth up overnight. What do you think?"

"Let's wait and see what Milt has to say."

She nodded. "Sarah might still squirm out of it, one way or another. We'll wait."

At nine that night, Barbara gave up pacing and going up and down the stairs long enough to sit in the living room and frown ferociously at Frank. "He isn't coming, that bastard. It must have fizzled on the vine, and he's empty-handed and sore as a boil."

"Maybe," Frank said. "He probably stopped long enough to eat. Let's give him time."

"Right." She got up and headed for the stairs again.

Frank picked up the book he had been trying to read without much success. Half an hour later the doorbell rang and he got up to admit Hoggarth.

"Come in, Milt. Come sit by the fire. Nasty night out there."

"Cold, wet and fog, what more needs saying?"

He took off his heavy jacket and Frank hung it in the closet, and motioned toward the living room. A tray on the low table held a bottle of scotch, an ice bucket, pinot noir and the coffee carafe. "Are you off duty yet?" Frank asked.

"Yeah. As of right now."

"Well, help yourself. Fix it the way you like it," Frank said, motioning toward the scotch.

Barbara entered a moment later and was surprised to see the lieutenant sipping what looked like straight scotch with a single ice cube. She never had seen him drink anything but coffee.

His nod to her was curt and perfunctory. Then he ignored her and spoke to Frank. "One of my men stopped her just short of the lake, she had a paper bag. He asked what was in it, and she handed it to him. Half a loaf of bread. She was on her way to feed the ducks." He drank again.

Barbara poured herself a glass of wine and sat down without a word.

"She made me go in with her so she could get my full name, rank, supervisor's name. Wanted to know what we were doing on her property." He poured another drink.

"She said," he went on in an almost toneless voice, "she intended to report me, bring charges. That I was acting in collusion with an extortionist, in a plot to force her to pay millions for the return of her late husband's stolen research papers. She said she told you whatever you seemed to want to hear just to get rid of you, stall long enough to contact her attorneys for advice. She accused you of concealing evidence

of an abduction, possession of stolen property, attempted extortion, conspiracy to commit extortion."

"The best defense, attack first," Barbara said scornfully. "She
has that gun! She smelled a trap. Get a search warrant before
she has a chance to get rid of it!"

"It's the district attorney, isn't it?" Frank said. "He likes the
case he has and doesn't want trouble."

"He's going to ask me why I was there without a search
warrant, who tipped me off, and when I tell him, he's going
to blow." He was speaking as if Barbara were not even in the
room. His expression was grim and hard. "He wants that
deposition, and he intends to charge her with obstruction,
misleading and false statements and withholding evidence in
a capital case. And she did all of that. She's lied to us from
the start. A tip from someone involved, with a possible
criminal charge pending, would be tossed out, and whatever
it led to would be tossed with it. That's how the game is
played. If Sarah Kurtz had had the gun, if she had confessed
when we stopped her, it would be different, but she stone-
walled and her story is better than hers." He barely glanced
at Barbara as he said this.

"I told you I haven't lied!" Barbara said hotly. "I haven't!"

Before she could continue, Hoggarth finally looked directly
at her, wrathful and hostile, all but quivering in his anger. "You
spent time with Elizabeth Kurtz. That tape proves it or else it's
as phony as everything else you've been telling us. Who's going
to trust your word about anything else you have to say, or any
evidence you claim is valid? Not the DA, and frankly not me,
either. Your name is mud, and your word is shit."

"Lieutenant, are you really off duty?" Barbara asked. "I

assume you are, but the real question is if you learn something when you're off duty, what is your responsibility regarding it?"

His eyes narrowed even further and he shook his head. "That's a goddamn dumb question, and you know it."

"It's a pity," she said. "It means I can't tell you what I know and it will have to wait for the DA. I'd rather have it out with you first."

"Jesus Christ! You want to make a deal with me? You're out of your mind! I wouldn't trust you to hold my coat at this point."

"Let's try a different question," Frank said. "Tomorrow, Saturday, is New Year's Eve, and of course Sunday is a holiday, and so is Monday. I imagine the district attorney's office will be closed until Tuesday, isn't that right?"

"Yeah. You know it. So?"

Frank and Barbara exchanged a look and she nodded. "Excuse me a second," she said. She went upstairs and retrieved her tape player and the tape, which she had not rewound yet. When she returned with it, she said, "You heard the first of two parts, Hoggarth. Let me play the second part for you."

It picked up where it had left off, and Elizabeth's voice was clear and firm as she continued. "After my hair was cut, and with a permanent, my eyelashes trimmed short, I thought no one looking for a woman with long dark hair, traveling with a small child would give me a glance. I came to Eugene and rented the apartment on Eighteenth. I called Leonora…"

After listening for a minute or two, Hoggarth carefully put his glass on the table. He was leaning forward, both hands now clasping the arms of his chair in a white-knuckled grip as Elizabeth voiced her fears, and the reasons for her deception, and her first meeting with Barbara.

After she told the date, and read the newspaper headlines, the tape was finished. Barbara turned it off.

"I don't believe a word of it," Hoggarth said in a strangled voice.

"Believe, Hoggarth. Believe," Barbara said fiercely. "She was terrified. She had every reason to believe that if it were known she was still alive that she would not live for twenty-four hours. And she saw Leonora's face. She fell apart. Her hysteria was real and by the time she was rational again, she was convinced that her only chance was to play it out as Leonora, never imagining that as Leonora she would be the prime suspect for murder."

"Jesus Christ!" he muttered. He reached for the carafe and poured coffee, added sugar, then apparently forgot it. "How long have you been sitting on that?"

"I met her last week," Barbara said, "after she gave her signed statement, and I've been running at a dead heat ever since." Swiftly she went through her reasoning about Elizabeth's identity. Then she said, "A paid assassin would have had no reason to destroy her face like that. A clean shot in the head would have been plenty. Whoever fired that second shot did it out of hatred, pure, blind, irrational hatred. When it began to make sense I went over to talk to her. And I left with the key to that storage locker in Las Vegas."

She told the rest of it and Hoggarth's expression gradually changed from hostility and disbelief to doubt, and finally to acceptance and anger.

"Her mother went along with it! Misidentified the body! Jesus!"

"Neither of them even considered that she, as Leonora, would be suspected of murder. They both thought it was the only way to keep her safe."

"And you let her go on with the lie."

"How many resources does it take to safeguard a witness? Do you have those resources? She wouldn't have lasted a day, that's the reality. Not with so much money at stake. Sarah brought it home. One percent of a billion dollars is ten million! Maybe Sarah's insane, maybe not. I think she is, but maybe she's just driven by hated and greed, but whatever it is, she's fearless and ruthless, and determined to get that sale. You heard them. Her brother and Terry played cards with the brother's kids. Clampton set up the table and found the cards on Thanksgiving, and she claimed she was alone in the guesthouse from Wednesday until called to dinner on Thursday. She's intelligent. That was a good recovery tonight, fast thinking, enough to send you packing. Anyway, we are all agreed that before an arrest, Elizabeth will have to tell the truth."

"Where is she?"

"In safekeeping. We'll bring her with us on Tuesday. Until Sarah's in custody, or Tuesday, whichever comes first, Elizabeth's under wraps. We don't want a premature arrest. God knows it's complicated enough without that."

"I told you I wouldn't move on her until next week," he said roughly.

"And I believe you," Frank put in. "We both do, but there are others over you, and a lot of persuasion going on, a lot of pressure being applied. We have no reason to trust those others."

"You know what's going to happen," Hoggarth said. "Kurtz will bring in a flock of lawyers who know every dodge invented by man to keep their client out of jail. It could be years, or never, before there's a trial, even if we did have any evidence, and we don't. It's going to be a whole new investigation, maybe even an accusation against Elizabeth Kurtz, the only one who knew Carnero was in town. Maybe they really were fighting over the kid, jealousy, even those research papers. It's a goddamn fucking mess! You'll come clean on Tuesday, then what?"

"Maybe things will move a little faster than that," Barbara said, leveling a steady gaze at him. "I had a long talk with Gary Swarthmore last night. More insurance, you might say. I wanted to know what shape Henry Diedricks is really in. And he told me. This morning Alan McCagno delivered one of those receivers to Swarthmore and he and Diedricks heard every word said in that conference room. I asked him to make sure Dr. Diedricks remained in his room throughout, and he did."

"Jesus, he's old. Senile, demented. Kurtz has power of attorney concerning him. What was that for?"

"He's old, but not demented, and maybe senile in body, but not in his mind or his spirit, according to Swarthmore. Sarah never had power of attorney. As a vice president of the company, Joseph Kurtz had it in order to make corporate decisions when Diedricks was thought to be on his deathbed, but it died along with Joseph Kurtz."

Hoggarth ran his hand over his scalp and turned to Frank.

"At his age, if he goes to sleep and doesn't wake up, who's going to ask questions? Do you realize what she's done?"

"I know what I've done," Barbara said. "Starting today Swarthmore is training an assistant to replace him in order to take a little vacation in a couple of weeks. Alan will make a good assistant, and he'll be there overnight for a while."

"What are you expecting to happen?" Hoggarth demanded, getting to his feet, glaring at her.

"Maybe nothing. Maybe the last act of an ongoing drama. Maybe a final nudge to someone teetering on the edge."

30

"Happy New Year's Eve," Frank said when Barbara joined him for breakfast the next morning.

"And to you, Happy New Year. I made a resolution already. And since I don't believe it gets zapped if you say what it is, I'll tell you. I resolve to lead a calm, quiet, sane life for all of next year, maybe take up knitting, although that's still in the possibility column, not in the must do one."

Frank laughed. "And I intend to wrap up that book and be done with it." He turned to the stove. "The difference is that I'll keep mine."

"Oh, ye of little faith. After breakfast I guess I'd better take a run out to Shelley's house and collect Elizabeth. Let's not leave her alone tonight, okay?"

"Absolutely. I'll put a bottle of champagne in the fridge."

When she called Shelley, however, a different plan was

proposed. It sounded suspiciously rehearsed. "What we thought we might do," Shelley said, "is ask you and your dad to come out for dinner, have a teeny party here, and put you up for the night. Alex found a wonderful surprise up in the woods. I'm dying to show you. And we want to keep Elizabeth."

Frank shook his head at the idea. "As I said, I stopped leaving the house on New Year's Eve. You go."

When Barbara relayed this to Shelley, her script had an answer prepared. "Okay, but he has to come to dinner tomorrow. A good-luck dinner with black-eyed peas, collards and pork. I guess ham qualifies. Alex wants to show off his newest skill—bread making. He makes champion breads!"

It was a perfect day, she thought later. Shelley and Alex's house was a sprawling ranch house with wings going off this way and that, a mammoth fireplace in the living room with a good fire, Alex's art everywhere and books on every table. The watchdog sprawled in front of the fire, pretending to sleep, but his ears twitched now and then, making it clear that he was working. Periodically he stood, stretched and padded out his dog door. All he needed was a time clock, and a card to punch to prove he was on the job. When he returned, he rolled on his own rug by the fire, then sprawled again. A drenching rain precluded the walk in the woods, but the following day promised to be clear and not too cold. Today, Shelley had said, she and Elizabeth were making dinner, and the next day Dr. Minnick and Alex would take over.

"And I'll happily keep out of the way and watch," Barbara said. As she unwound late that afternoon, she thought this was the kind of life real people should lead—peaceful, calm, good company.

Almost as if echoing her thoughts, Elizabeth said, "Mother's house was always like this. No one ever rushed, or raised a voice. Leonora and I would take Jason and go stay for weeks at a time in the summer, to Spain, I mean, and just sort of fall apart, we'd relax so completely. You get into a different kind of pattern living in New York City. You forget how it can be."

Dr. Minnick was eyeing Elizabeth curiously, and Alex started to say something, glanced at Shelley as if questioning her, and remained quiet.

Barbara sighed and said, "You heard it right. This is Elizabeth Kurtz, not Leonora."

Elizabeth looked stricken. "It's all right," Barbara said. "Family secrets are safe here. But I guess a little explanation is due."

She explained, and when she finished, Dr. Minnick said thoughtfully to Elizabeth, "Your reaction was classic, what you called turning to ice, when you became dissociated. That's a shock reaction, followed by hysteria. Your survival instinct was in charge. Possibly nothing else you could have done or said would have kept you from blurting the truth of the matter and, as you know, you would have been at extreme risk. Interesting. That survival instinct is a poorly understood mechanism. What part of your brain knew that was your most expedient behavior?" He shook his head. "So many mysteries, so very many mysteries."

"What happened at that meeting up there yesterday?" Elizabeth asked.

Barbara hesitated only a moment, then told about playing

Elizabeth's tape and her own demands and Sarah's reaction afterward. She finished by reporting what Hoggarth had said later.

"But they've gone to trial with a lot less than that," Shelley said in near disbelief.

"It's political," Barbara said. "Money, politics, influence, they're all being brought to bear. All the DA knows, remember, is the case against Leonora, and that's pretty solid, even airtight." She looked at Dr. Minnick. "I keep wondering if Sarah Kurtz is insane, or lapses into insanity now and then. Can people do that? Go in and out of insanity?"

"There's little about behavior you could suggest that people can't do," he said. "From what you said, it sounds as if the possible loss of that much money may be overwhelming. But clinically insane? That requires tests, evaluations, observation. There are certain criteria we use, you understand, and she may or may not meet them. Enraged, certainly, and determined to do everything within her power to prevent that financial loss. Her survival skills seem to be working to allow her to avoid the trap you set, and the private investigators, her reason for hiring them, and so on. That kind of quick thinking, seemingly rational explanations, sometimes go with insanity, of course, but can she tell right from wrong? Can she control her impulses? That would determine insanity, not just acting out of greed. Our mental institutions would be overflowing if that were the sole criterion."

Dinner was a cassoulet with duck and small white beans, salad that had artichoke hearts, avocados, scallions and dried cranberries, topped with a sprinkling of roasted sunflower seeds. Alex proved Shelley's claim—he provided a warm, coarse dark bread that was perfect for the meal. Barbara didn't even try to guess how Shelley and Elizabeth had managed to prepare a meal when it had seemed they were never in the kitchen for more than a few minutes at a time. She had stopped questioning kitchen magic a long time ago, and had no intention of starting again.

They played Scrabble and Elizabeth won. "Not fair," Shelley said. "You're an editor. You know words that haven't even been invented. Again."

Dr. Minnick won the next game.

They watched the ball fall, and drank a toast to the New Year, and soon afterward Barbara was in a small guest room standing at the window watching rain streak down the windowpane.

Where was Darren this night? Alone in his house? Out with friends? Hosting a party for Todd and his pals? She hugged her arms hard about her and tried to shake the thoughts away, but they persisted and were accompanied by a sharp pang of desire.

The woods were dripping and, with shafts of intermittent sunshine illuminating them, vividly green with brilliant moss. The fragrance of fir hung in the air. The trail was spongy, covered by a thick carpet of fir needles, muddy in spots, and the air was fresh and sharply clean smelling. Mammoth ferns waved in the breeze, dark green and tough, and very beautiful in their unchoreographed graceful dance.

Alex led the way up into the woods, stopping now and again to point out mushrooms, a downed tree serving as nurse to a number of seedling trees, or a rock encrusted with pink lichen. Elizabeth appeared entranced.

Barbara heard the surprise Shelley had promised before it came into sight. Water splashing. As they rounded a curve in the trail, it appeared, a flashing, tumbling, noisy waterfall, sending diamond-like sprays of droplets high into the air. It had a plunge of no more than ten or twelve feet, but the recent snow, now melting, and the heavy rains of the past days had turned a tiny freshet into a white-water stream of furious energy. No one spoke as they drew nearer.

When they finally turned to start back down, Alex said, "Last summer that was barely a trickle, hardly enough to keep the rocks wet."

"You have a piece of Eden here," Elizabeth said. "It's all so perfect."

Not Eden with the implications of evil to come, but rather an enchanted forest, Barbara thought, as she finally forced herself away from the newly created waterfall.

They stopped once more, and Barbara had a sharp memory of stopping at the same place a year before with Darren. It had been raining. The scene below, the rambling house, a small stream off to the side, mist rising. He had said, "You're a creature of the woods." And they had said, almost in unison, the scene was like a Japanese painting. She closed her eyes willing the memory away. Not now, she told herself. Not now.

When they reached the house they found Frank in the kitchen talking to Dr. Minnick, comparing different ways to prepare a smoked Virginia ham. "I soak it a couple of days in water, change it every few hours, then a day in apple cider," Dr. Minnick was saying.

"My mother used to add a little vinegar to the first soak waters," Frank said. "It seems to draw out the salt just fine."

Barbara shook her head. A retired psychiatrist, and a semi-retired criminal defense attorney coming on like two house-wives.

She went up to change her wet clothes. They got wet whether or not it rained, she knew, and she had come pre-pared. Her phone rang as she was pulling on dry pants.

"Ms. Holloway, Gary Swarthmore here. Look, we know this is highly irregular, since tomorrow is a holiday, but Dr. Diedricks is determined to have a meeting tomorrow, and he specifically wants you to attend if at all possible."

She sat down on the side of her bed for what proved to be a long conversation.

When she returned to the living room Shelley was speaking earnestly to Elizabeth. "I have anything you'd need, but if you really wanted to go to your place first, we could do that."

"It's just such an imposition. I feel like the man who came to dinner."

"I'm talking her into staying over until Tuesday, and let me deliver her to the DA's office," Shelley said to Barbara. "Tell her it's a good idea."

"It's a good idea," Barbara said obediently. It was a great idea, she was thinking. She hadn't looked forward to telling Eliza-beth that she would be on her own the coming day, alone in her apartment, worrying about the session with the district attorney, no doubt. "You've relaxed so much out here, another day is a really good idea."

"See? So it's settled. The boss said so," Shelley said.

Barbara had already decided not to mention her conversation with Gary Swarthmore, not to bring the reality of murder and corporate fraud into what was turning out to be a good break for all of them. Later, she told herself. Later, back in Frank's house, she would tell him, but not here, not now.

"It isn't as if I don't have enough clothes to share," Shelley was continuing to Elizabeth, "and just about everything I have fits you to a *T.*"

"Okay. You win." Elizabeth looked at Barbara, and added, "She could open her own boutique."

Alex joined them. "They kicked me out," he said. "They told me to get lost, that the pros would take care of dinner. And it's to be served at six, because Mr. Holloway doesn't want to be on our good country roads late at night with fog rolling in."

"Me, too," Barbara said. Even that was working out, she thought, exactly what she wanted, an early night, time to talk things over with her father.

At ten minutes after nine she pulled into the driveway behind Frank, and ten minutes later they were in his study. When she said impatiently that there was no point in messing with a fire, he had raised his eyebrows the way he often did instead of coming right out and asking what she had on her mind.

"I had an interesting phone call from Gary Swarthmore," she said, seated in a leather-covered wing chair. He was in the old brown chair that he prized and she thought was ready for the junk heap. Each of them had a cat.

"Diedricks heard every word. Nothing wrong with his hearing, apparently. He wanted to join us, but Gary talked him out of it. And he began to ask pointed questions about what he had heard. Of course, Gary doesn't know all the answers, but he told him what he could, and Diedricks had him call Jefferson Knowlton. I left that number for him, just in case. They had a long talk and, Dad, yesterday Diedricks had Gary take him out for a drive. He does that now and then and apparently no one thought a thing of it. But he met Knowlton and they talked again. Gary said he never heard two old men use language like that."

She drew in her breath, then continued in the same abbreviated way telling the rest of it. "Anyway, believing their father was not going to make it, Sarah and her brother told Diedricks years ago that Knowlton had absconded with the work and had taken it to a competitor on the east coast. Diedricks had no idea they were screening his calls and his mail, no idea Knowlton had tried repeatedly to get in touch with him and no idea about that original lawsuit. He tried twice to call Knowlton, and both times Sarah dialed a number and he heard the message that the phone was no longer in service. He had to accept what they said. He said he never signed anything that said he didn't remember Knowlton or the work they did together. And Gary knew nothing about any of that. He was there for just a few hours each day, and he started eight years ago, not back when all that was happening. He didn't know what was going on. So they straightened that out. And Diedricks and Knowlton are working on some kind of deal. I don't know what it is, but maybe tomorrow I'll find out." She stroked the cat she was holding. Its purr sounded like a motor. "If Diedricks backs Knowlton now, that means that Elizabeth's home free, as far as that bunch is concerned."

Frank nodded. "I'm glad that Alan's up there. It may well be that the danger zone has shifted somewhat." He was thinking of an old blind man in a wheelchair.

"I told Gary not to lie to Diedricks about Alan," she said slowly. "No more lies. He knows who Alan is and why he's there. I'd like to know what's going on in Diedricks's head now. Did he connect the dots? Can he really accept that his daughter is most likely a murderer? That she could represent a threat to him?"

Frank rubbed his eyes, trying to put himself in that position. It was impossible. "I imagine that back when he was beginning to recover, he had no reason to believe his daughter and son would lie to him. There's something to that old canard, Blood's thicker than water. Until proven wrong, we tend to trust our family. And all too often the proof of betrayal isn't accepted. The clan instinct prevails even then."

Barbara tried to imagine the way life must have been for Diedricks for a decade, after he had recovered enough to know what he had lost. First the long slow painful recovery, hearing and believing that his one ally, his creative equal had abandoned him, no longer able to draw his visions, to see his visions realized first on paper, then in the necessary metals and plastic, no longer able to sketch his ideas for others to complete. No one to discuss ideas with, no one who really understood the way Jefferson Knowlton had understood. What had sustained him for so many years?

"I think Henry Diedricks must be a very strong man, no matter what shape his body's in," she said. "I'm looking forward to meeting him."

"Let's talk about that," Frank said. "Has Diedricks told the family what he knows?"

"Gary said he hasn't. Apparently he plays his cards in close, and always has. A born loner. Maybe that's what the meeting's to be about."

"I want to go with you."

She shook her head. "It's Diedricks's show and you're not invited. He's calling the shots right now."

"If not me, we'll call Milt and let him know it's going on."

She shook her head again. "Dad, Alan will be there. And Gary Swarthmore said he'll be there. No one's going to do anything out in the open, in public, so to speak, or at least not before witnesses. And I'll come straight home afterward. I think I can move faster than Sarah." She smiled faintly. "In fact, I'd like to take her on and beat the shit out of her. But I'll restrain myself."

"It isn't *your* self-restraint that concerns me," Frank said soberly.

31

Terry Kurtz opened the door promptly at three that afternoon. He nodded to Barbara, and took her coat. "They're waiting for you in the office," he said.

He looked like an escapee from Shangri-La, she thought as they walked down the hall. He had aged again in the past few days, and the haunted look was more pronounced than it had been before. He escorted her to the office, then said, "I'll tell Grandfather you're here."

There was a group of people in the office. Jefferson Knowlton stood with a small wiry-looking man with a shock of gray, unruly hair, the kind of hair that could be tamed only by letting it grow long and capturing it in a ponytail, or else cutting it in a burr. He had done neither. It looked like a winter bush. He came forward with his hand extended. "Kevin Lorenz," he said in a surprisingly deep baritone. "I'm very happy to meet you."

Jefferson Knowlton had lost the ten years that Terry had gained, she thought, as he greeted her with a smile. Not a wide smile or expansive in any way, but she assumed that his thin face had forgotten how to express pleasure in a more visible manner.

"This is Robert Crais," Lorenz said, as a third man came to meet her. In his sixties, thin, harried and flustered in his appearance, in a crumpled suit, he looked like a man who seldom glanced in a mirror. His briefcase was like an ID badge—another attorney.

Neither Sarah Kurtz nor her brother Lawrence acknowledged Barbara beyond glancing up to see who had entered. They were all still standing when the door opened again, and this time Terry held it open for his grandfather in his wheelchair, being pushed by a muscular man she guessed was Gary Swarthmore. He grinned at her and said his name, confirming her guess.

"Dr. Diedricks," he said, "this is Barbara Holloway."

The old man held out his left hand for her. It was covered with age spots, wrinkled skin, with prominent blue veins; nevertheless, he still had long and shapely fingers, like Sarah's. His grip was surprisingly firm. He was wearing sunglasses and looked shrunken, with a deeply lined face and very little white hair, a lap robe over what appeared to be sweatpants. Of course, she thought. No zippers for a man with the use of one hand only. His paralyzed hand was under the lap robe.

"How do you do," he said in a wheezy voice. "I'm greatly indebted to you, and I wanted you to witness the fruits of your efforts. Please sit here at my left."

Sarah had been walking toward that chair, and veered to take the middle chair across from the windows.

"Everyone, sit down, please," Dr. Diedricks said. "Robert, on my right, if you will. Jeff, at the other end of the table."

They all seated themselves, with Sarah and her brother side by side across from Barbara, and Terry in the middle between her and Kevin Lorenz. Gary Swarthmore pulled a chair close to Dr. Diedricks and sat down.

"The purpose of this meeting," Dr. Diedricks said when the sound of chairs scraping and rustling ceased, "is to announce the results of our conference of many hours. Robert, please."

Sarah looked bored, and examined her fingernails, and Lawrence Diedricks had a strained expression, his mouth tight, his eyes blinking rapidly, darting a glance here, there, nowhere.

Robert Crais cleared his throat, opened his briefcase and brought out a legal pad and a sheaf of papers. "Yes," he said, "of course. Dr. Diedricks and Dr. Knowlton have come to an agreement about certain arrangements, and a press statement has been prepared for immediate release. Before I read it to you, a few other matters have been settled to the satisfaction of Dr. Diedricks. First, there is the matter of corporate profits. Dr. Diedricks is setting up a nonprofit foundation to insure the continuation of research into prosthetic devices into the future, and to assist the rehabilitation of indigent patients who lack the necessary funds to seek proper medical care for their own recovery from serious accidents and the wounds of war. Dr. Diedricks's share of the corporate profits, that is, fifty-two and one half percent, will establish the foundation in an irrevocable trust, to be established with all due speed. Accordingly, he has also changed his will to reflect this trust fund. A draft codicil has been written and witnessed by a number of people, signed and duly notarized by my secretary.

"In a mutually acceptable agreement, Dr. Knowlton has been appointed vice president of the Diedricks Corporation in charge of the research and development department. He will assume his duties immediately. His compensation package takes into account the many years he has been deprived of his livelihood, plus a salary commensurate with his duties, and also a two-and-one-half percent share of the company."

Sarah had forgotten her fingernails apparently. Her face was undergoing a rapid change, becoming mottled with red blotches against white. Her eyes were narrowed and her mouth a tight, hard line. She started to speak and her brother put his hand on her arm.

"Let's hear the rest of it," Lawrence said in an undertone.

"There are a few other details, but at this time I'll go to the press release," Crais said. "I have a copy for everyone present at this meeting."

He read from a printout,

"The Diedricks Corporation announces a reorganization plan to take effect immediately. Mr. Lawrence Diedricks wishes to announce his retirement as of this date and Dr. Jefferson Knowlton will assume the vice presidency left vacant following the death of Joseph Kurtz. A talent search is underway for other positions that will become open in the near future—"

"This is nonsense!" Sarah cried. "It's a meaningless fiasco. My father is incompetent, demented. He no longer controls the company! I have power of attorney to make any and all corporate decisions, and Mr. Crais is not associated with the company in any way! *That's* the press release! Not your twaddle!"

"Mrs. Kurtz," Crais said, "I'm afraid that isn't quite correct. Your late husband was granted power of attorney, but that is not a heritable asset. It ceased with his demise."

"That's a lie! It's a damned lie and you know it! My company lawyers will show you who's in charge of my company!"

"Sarah, you have no position in the Diedricks Corporation, and no voice in company decisions," Dr. Diedricks said, cutting through her tirade. "Your presence at this meeting is not required. If you can't be quiet, leave."

"Father, there's no need to go to such extremes," Lawrence said soothingly. "That sale was a proposal only, just something to be considered, not a done deal by any means."

"You're damn right it isn't a done deal," his father said. "My company is not for sale."

"You don't understand!" Sarah shouted. "You don't understand how much money is involved. You'll be rich as Croesus. You don't need the company anymore. You've done your bit, paid your dues."

"Read the whole story," Diedricks said fiercely. "Read the ending, not just the dazzling parts. I don't want to be as rich as Croesus. What for? I have everything I need. You'll still have your share of whatever profits are left. You don't need any more than that. And, Lawrence, I suggest you accept your resignation, or face being fired outright. Do you understand? I'm still the president of this company and I make the rules. *Do you understand?*"

Although his voice was reedy and without the power to roar, he spoke with the authority of many decades of success, and Lawrence mutely nodded and mumbled, "Yes." He seemed to shrink back into his chair.

Sarah gave him a contemptuous look and leaned forward with both hands on the table. "We won't let you get away with this. They've fed you a pack of lies. We *are* selling the company and you can't stop us," she said hoarsely, glaring at her sightless father. "We'll fight you through every court in the country! You can throw out Lawrence, but not me! I'll fight you. You're just a crazy old man! A dead man!" Her hands were opening and clenching spasmodically, and she was breathing in open-mouthed gasps, as if she had been running and couldn't catch her breath. She looked at Barbara with hatred. "You did this, you bitch! He's a sick, dying old man and you brought your filthy lies here. Get out of my house! Get out! Or I'll have you thrown out!"

Gary Swarthmore moved in a little closer to Dr. Diedricks, watching Sarah warily.

"Dr. Diedricks," Barbara said, "you heard the first of two parts of the tape Elizabeth Kurtz made. At this time I'd like to play the second part, if you agree."

He nodded. "If there's more, I want to hear it," he said.

Barbara retrieved the tape player from her purse and set it on the table. She had rewound it the night before, and it was ready to pick up again where it had stopped previously.

Elizabeth's firm, clear voice came on, and it and Sarah's labored breathing were the only sounds in the room. Then Terry Kurtz made an inarticulate noise, and leaned in toward Barbara, staring at the tape player.

"I looked at her face—blood and shattered bones—and I thought that was supposed to be me. It was meant for me—"

Terry grabbed Barbara's arm. "She's alive? Elizabeth's alive?"

Across the table, Sarah jumped to her feet, swaying, shaking her head. "She's dead! I know she's dead. She's dead!" she screamed.

Elizabeth's voice was continuing, and Sarah screamed again and shoved her chair back, knocking it over. No one else moved as she ran from the room. Barbara turned off the tape player. A stunned silence followed.

"This meeting is over," Dr. Diedricks said in a faint voice. "Gary, take me back to my room." No one else moved as Gary wheeled him out. Then Lawrence lurched to his feet and followed them, as pale as death.

Where had Sarah gone? Barbara wondered, glancing uneasily at the window. To get the gun and come back with it? Use it on herself? Get in her car and speed away? And where was Alan?

"She's alive," Terry whispered, breaking the silence. "Elizabeth's alive."

"Someone should see to Mrs. Kurtz," Crais said nervously. He was watching the windows, also.

"Terry! Go take care of your mother," Barbara said.

"What? Yes, yes. I'll see to her." He went to the door, but it was flung open before he touched it, and Sarah walked into the room.

She was not hurrying, apparently oblivious of everyone but Barbara, her eyes narrowed to slits. And she was carrying a butcher knife. She was moving deliberately, almost slowly, the knife at waist level, close in to her body. "I killed her twice,"

, she began to
oned himself
trying to pull
em.
o looked like

speaking into

rson Knowl-
out of here,"
ut to the hall,
to a chair. He
ter them and

d as someone

had glimpsed
onger scream-
terward Alan

said.
arthmore was

eard that first
nk God. He's

s. Terry stood

gnizable. "Twice! And
lut twice! You should-
ve to take her place."
im. He looked frozen.
She jerked and pushed
ir, sending it spinning,
of it. Barbara scram-
t of Sarah, backed up,
rah knocked Barbara's
ot taking her eyes off

nd ducked as the knife
face. Barbara pushed
ked again as the knife
Hoggarth right behind
e had done Terry. He
he neck from behind,
ted. She screamed and
forcing it down and
d he kicked it away.

Hoggarth and Alan,
om carrying a sheet.
f Sarah, dodging her
ught to restrain her.
o be almost in slow
Sarah's arms secured
he sheet to Alan, who
d the other arm and
he sheet around her.
men to control her

violent jerks and then, with her arms restrained
kick. Gary forced her into a chair and posit
behind it holding her as she kept kicking and
away. She screamed obscenities as she fought tl

"Go get another sheet," Gary said to Terry, w
a waxen statue. "Now! And a pillow."

Terry ran from the room.

Hoggarth already had his phone out, and wa:
it. Barbara heard only "...violent, insane..."

She was shaking hard, and realized that Jeff
ton's arm was around her shoulders. "Let's ge
he said, drawing her around the table with him
across it to the dining room, where she sank ir
sat down, and both Crais and Lorenz came a
pulled out chairs. No one spoke.

Sarah's harsh voice screaming obscenities fad
closed the office door.

An ambulance had come and gone. Barbara
Sarah trussed in sheets, held fast to a chair, no l
ing, as she was carried out that way. Soon a
came to the dining room.

"The lieutenant wants you all in the den," he

Dr. Diedricks was not in the den, but Gary S
there.

"Is he all right?" Barbara asked.

"He's okay. I think he's known ever since he
tape. He couldn't hear much of it tonight, th
resting."

They began to arrange themselves on chai

she said, her voice so harsh it was unrecognizable. "Twice! And you kept bringing her back. I killed the slut twice! You should-n't have brought her back. Now you have to take her place." She stepped past Terry as if unaware of him. He looked frozen.

Then he roused and grabbed her arm. She jerked and pushed him away as if he were a child. He hit a chair, sending it spinning, and caught himself before he fell on top of it. Barbara scram-bled from her chair and shoved it in front of Sarah, backed up, groping behind her for the next chair. Sarah knocked Barbara's chair away and kept moving forward, not taking her eyes off Barbara.

Barbara backed up into Terry's chair, and ducked as the knife slashed through the air, inches from her face. Barbara pushed Terry's chair in front of Sarah, and ducked again as the knife flashed at her. Suddenly Alan ran in with Hoggarth right behind him. Sarah shoved Alan aside the way she had done Terry. He straightened, and grabbed her around the neck from behind, and Hoggarth grabbed her wrist and twisted. She screamed and tried to slash him. He twisted her arm, forcing it down and back. The knife dropped to the floor and he kicked it away.

As she struggled violently with both Hoggarth and Alan, Gary Swarthmore hurried into the room carrying a sheet. Moving with purpose he got in front of Sarah, dodging her flailing arms while Alan and Hoggarth fought to restrain her. Gary's deliberate motions appeared to be almost in slow motion as he managed to get one of Sarah's arms secured under the sheet, and passed the end of the sheet to Alan, who yanked it, pulling it tight. Gary secured the other arm and moved in close as he and Alan wound the sheet around her. Alan held it in back. It took all three men to control her violent jerks and then, with her arms restrained, she began to kick. Gary forced her into a chair and positioned himself behind it holding her as she kept kicking and trying to pull away. She screamed obscenities as she fought them.

"Go get another sheet," Gary said to Terry, who looked like a waxen statue. "Now! And a pillow."

Terry ran from the room.

Hoggarth already had his phone out, and was speaking into it. Barbara heard only "...violent, insane..."

She was shaking hard, and realized that Jefferson Knowlton's arm was around her shoulders. "Let's get out of here," he said, drawing her around the table with him out to the hall, across it to the dining room, where she sank into a chair. He sat down, and both Crais and Lorenz came after them and pulled out chairs. No one spoke.

Sarah's harsh voice screaming obscenities faded as someone closed the office door.

An ambulance had come and gone. Barbara had glimpsed Sarah trussed in sheets, held fast to a chair, no longer screaming, as she was carried out that way. Soon afterward Alan came to the dining room.

"The lieutenant wants you all in the den," he said.

Dr. Diedricks was not in the den, but Gary Swarthmore was there.

"Is he all right?" Barbara asked.

"He's okay. I think he's known ever since he heard that first tape. He couldn't hear much of it tonight, thank God. He's resting."

They began to arrange themselves on chairs. Terry stood

by the bar; he was white-faced and looked ill. Lawrence Diedricks was already seated in the corner of the room. He appeared to be in worse shape than Terry, shaking now and then with a whole body tremor. He kept his head lowered, his face concealed. When they were all seated Hoggarth introduced himself, then said, "What happened in that room?"

No one spoke for a moment, then Crais said, "I was explaining what we discussed in meetings earlier. Then Ms. Holloway played a tape…"

"I'll tell it," Lorenz said brusquely, and he did in great detail. Apparently he remembered every word that had been uttered.

Hoggarth listened attentively but asked very few questions. "I understand there's another man in the household, a Mr. Lon Clampton. Where is he?"

"Dr. Diedricks booted him out," Alan said. "Day before yesterday he told him to pack his bags and beat it. Mrs. Kurtz said he didn't have to go because he worked for her and Dr. Diedricks told him to get his ass out of here, to go to her house if he worked for her. He gave him five minutes. Then Gary was supposed to call the police and have him arrested for trespass. He packed up and took off."

Crais cleared his throat. He glanced uneasily at Lawrence, who had not stirred or looked up. "Lieutenant, perhaps we could arrange a meeting for tomorrow with your district attorney to discuss this unfortunate incident. Of course, certain facts will have to be made public, but perhaps we can limit the damage to a fine old man and his esteemed company which has always enjoyed the highest possible reputation."

Hoggarth nodded. "That can probably be arranged," he said.

"If there is such a meeting, my father, who represents Elizabeth Kurtz, should be present," Barbara said quickly. "After all, she is a very interested party."

"And I should be present, as well," Lorenz said. "Mr. Knowlton is one of the most seriously damaged parties in this affair."

Hoggarth looked resigned. "I'll bring up your concerns," he said. He knew as well as Barbara that the district attorney would seize any opportunity to come out of this whole affair looking good. *Turn the spinmeisters loose,* she thought cynically. Poor Mrs. Kurtz suffering from grief, had become deranged and was under medical care.

Hoggarth noted their names, addresses, where he could reach them, and soon afterward, he stood. "We'll want statements from all of you. For now, Mrs. Kurtz will remain in custody to undergo a psychiatric examination," he said. He looked at Lawrence, then had to say his name in order to get his attention. "I'd like a few words with you," he said. "The rest of you are free to leave." He glanced at Barbara and added, "I'll drive you back to Eugene when we're done here. I'll have someone bring your car back tomorrow. Mr. Diedricks, if you will come this way."

No one lingered very long after that. Before leaving, Jefferson Knowlton came to Barbara and for a moment looked as if he wanted to embrace her but didn't quite know how. He settled for a handshake and a muttered thank-you. Crais spoke briefly to Gary and left and then Gary Swarthmore and Alan talked in low voices for a minute or two. Gary said he would be on his way after checking in on Dr. Diedricks. They walked out together.

Still standing by the bar, Terry asked in a low voice, "Do you think she'd see me?"

Barbara shrugged. "I'll tell her you asked. It's up to her."

"And let me see Jason?"

"I'll tell her."

"I understand," he said. "Thank you." He walked out.

She went to the bar and poured herself a rather strong drink of bourbon and water, then called Frank as she sipped it. He made strangled noises when she recounted the scene in the office. "Sit down, Dad. Deep breaths. It's okay. Over. I thought you might call Elizabeth and tell her. She could call her mother and arrange for her to bring Jason home. I guess Elizabeth will be required to stay here long enough to straighten things out. But they can be together while that's going on." She told him Hoggarth would bring her home, and he said he'd have something for them to eat when they got there. She shook her head. Good food to vanquish bad memories? She didn't think it would work this time.

Hoggarth spent nearly an hour with Lawrence Diedricks and looked disgusted when he joined her in the den. "Are you off duty?" she asked.

"All day," he said heavily. "It's a holiday, remember?"

"Why don't you have a little something then? One for the road."

He went behind the bar and began to examine the bottles. With his back to her, he said, "You knew she'd break if she heard Elizabeth Kurtz's voice, knew she was alive. You gave her the nudge to send her over that goddamn edge."

It wasn't a question and she didn't respond. She took a longer drink, this time draining her glass.

32

"You sent him, didn't you?" Barbara asked Frank at the dinette table where they had eaten.

He nodded. "I didn't trust her," he said, "but Lord knows I wasn't expecting her to turn homicidal before witnesses."

"And I just thought she might say something incriminating," Hoggarth said. "I wanted to get statements if that happened before the memory wipes got to work." He rubbed his scalp. "It's a damn good thing Swarthmore was there. If Alan had been able to get a hand free, he would have shot her. Or I would have. Jesus, what a mess that would have been."

Barbara pushed her plate back. "Dad, I'll put things in the dishwasher, and then I'll collect my gear and head for home."

His gaze was searching as he examined her. "Are you all right? Not angry that I let Milt in on what you were up to?"

"God, no! Alan would have had to kill her. He had no

choice. She was like an enraged giantess. I'm just tired. I want a long hot bath and early bed."

"Leave this stuff. I have all night. We're due at the district attorney's office in the morning. I'll pick you up at a quarter to nine."

"I'll run you over when you're ready," Hoggarth said. He looked awkward for a moment, then added to Frank, "Thanks for supper."

Her sleep was troubled that night, inhabited by a giant mad woman chasing her with a knife dripping blood. So much for her New Year's resolution, she thought, making coffee the next morning. Her first day out, and blooey.

Frank picked her up and they arrived early at the district attorney's office. Shelley and Elizabeth were already waiting in the corridor. Elizabeth was radiant, and Shelley could not have smiled wider, or shown more dimples.

"They're coming on Thursday," Elizabeth said. "Mother's bringing Jason on Thursday, to Portland. I'll go up and meet them."

"And she's much too high to drive, so I'll be chauffeur," Shelley added.

Barbara glanced around to make sure no one else was close enough to hear, then said in a low voice, "Elizabeth, do you care what story they put out? What fairy tale they spin as long as you're out of it?"

"I couldn't care less," Elizabeth said. "Why?"

"Something I think will work," Barbara said. Then she spoke in a normal voice. "So how are you going to spend the next couple of days?"

Hoggarth had drawn close.

"Shopping," Elizabeth said. "I want a Christmas tree, and a million presents to go under it."

"You may have to settle for a fake tree, but half price on everything," Barbara said with a smile. "Best time to shop, the week after Christmas. Good morning, Lieutenant. Are we ready?"

"Yeah. I sent a crew to get statements from that bunch at Diedricks's place. You'll get your car back this afternoon. And I called him this morning and gave him the highlights," Hoggarth said, motioning toward the district attorney's door. "He has a lot of questions."

"I'm sure he does," Barbara said. "Let's do it."

The district attorney, Ted Lansdown, was a portly man with heavy jowls, handsomely dressed in a good gray flannel jacket and black slacks, and he was not a happy man that morning. He greeted them soberly and motioned toward chairs. Already seated, Lieutenant Janowsky scowled and barely nodded to the entering group. Still wearing tweed, he looked hot, and impatient, as if he had a lot of questions, too.

"You gentlemen have met my client, Elizabeth Kurtz," Frank said smoothly. "In order to expedite things here, I thought I might play a tape that Ms. Kurtz recorded for us, and no doubt afterward there will be a few questions."

Neither the district attorney nor Janowsky showed surprise and Frank put the tape player on the desk and started it. Elizabeth looked at her hands as her voice sounded, and Janowsky leaned in closer. Lansdown maintained a thoughtful expression as if he were listening to a supreme court justice explain a point of law.

Frank played the entire tape, and when it finished and he turned it off, there were questions for Elizabeth. Lansdown was respectful, Janowsky furious.

"You let us conduct that hunt, issue an Amber Alert, and all the time you knew exactly where he was! That's a criminal offense!"

"Gentlemen," Barbara said, "let me be the first to congratulate you all for a stunningly successful sting. Due to the brilliant detective work of Lieutenant Hoggarth, in full cooperation with the district attorney and the state investigator, Lieutenant Janowsky, and also with Ms. Kurtz's aid, you captured one of the most heinous and devious murderers this city has ever seen."

She turned her gaze to Janowsky, who was unappeased, and said, "Lieutenant, Ms. Kurtz tried to reassure you that Jason was safe and being cared for. Mrs. Cortezar said the same thing, and neither of them showed any concern about his well being, but you chose to believe the lies of a homicidal maniac. It's one story or the other, I'm afraid."

He scowled at her, then at Elizabeth, but he had no more questions.

There was a lengthy discussion, and more questions for Elizabeth, then a statement for her to sign, and finally Lansdown said, "Ms. Kurtz, you are free to leave at this time. Thank you for your cooperation." Shelley left with her.

Her mother had not been mentioned, and she had not elaborated on the distant relative said to be caring for Jason.

They kept Barbara for another hour. When she got up to leave, Lansdown said in his thoughtful way, "Ms. Holloway, if I may make a suggestion, I think it would be wise if no one makes a statement to the media until one is issued by this office. I'll have a copy forwarded to you and Mr. Holloway beforehand, of course."

She nodded gravely. "I think that is very wise." She suspected that Hoggarth had bitten his cheek until it was bleeding to keep from smiling.

"Mr. Crais and Kevin Lorenz are coming at noon," Frank said, going to the door with her. "We'll have lunch with Mr. Lansdown and then discuss matters. I may be a while."

She suspected he would be there for the rest of the day.

Her car had been returned. She had checked in at the office and told Shelley what had happened at the Diedricks' house, then had done a little shopping for dinner, and to replace what had gone bad in her refrigerator during the past week. She had taken a long cold walk by the river.

For half an hour she had been gazing at the gaily wrapped book she had bought for Todd and had not delivered. And thinking about the lovely chess table and pieces in the trunk of her car.

She had been thinking of Darren, his magical healing hands, his magical musical voice, his warm body next to hers, their bodies in perfect harmony when they made love.

All the doubts, the uncertainties were still there. She could never be the kind of woman he should have, one who would anticipate his needs and attend to them eagerly, have nothing else in her life as important as he was. He could come to resent it, and her. She had stopped deluding herself about her practice sometime during the past week, and accepted that she would still put her work and her clients first at times, and she would still try to work within the law, but sidestep it when necessary.

She thought of Frank's final answer to her question, why do we do it? "Because we have to." She would make enemies, sometimes dangerous enemies, possibly put Darren and Todd at risk and he might decide nothing was worth risking his son. She heard Darren's words, "It's a gamble for both of us."

Finally she rose, put on her jacket, picked up the book and went out again into the frigid air.

At Darren's door she hesitated briefly, then rang the bell. Todd answered and was surprised and pleased to see her. He stepped aside for her to enter.

"I didn't get a chance to give you your present," she said, handing him the book.

"Thanks," he said. "I have something for you, too."

She saw Darren emerge from the back of the house, walking toward her. Todd glanced over his shoulder and hurried away with his gift. Darren stopped halfway to the door.

"You asked me another question," she said. "I have an answer. Yes."

From somewhere out of sight, Todd let out a whoop, and Darren closed the distance between them.

He grasped her shoulders and examined her face. When she nodded, he closed his eyes, then pulled her close, her cheek pressed against his chest, one hand on her head, the other holding her tight against him. "You're cold," he said softly, his breath warm on her head, as he nuzzled her hair.

No, she thought drawing in a long breath. *Not now.*